JAſ

Captive

Captive

The Forbidden
Side of
Nightshade

A. D. ROBERTSON

DUTTON

DUTTON
Published by the Penguin Group
Penguin Group (USA) LLC
375 Hudson Street
New York, New York 10014

USA | Canada | UK | Ireland | Australia | New Zealand | India | South Africa | China
penguin.com
A Penguin Random House Company

REGISTERED TRADEMARK—MARCA REGISTRADA

LIBRARY OF CONGRESS CATALOGING-IN-PUBLICATION DATA
Robertson, A. D., 1978–
Captive : the forbidden side of Nightshade / A. D. Robertson.
pages cm
ISBN 978-0-525-95411-8 (hardback)
I. Title.
PS3618.O316455C37   2013
813'.6—dc23   2013016257

Printed in the United States of America
1   3   5   7   9   10   8   6   4   2

Designed by Nancy Resnick
Title page photograph © dianamower—Fotolia.com

PUBLISHER'S NOTE

For Rabbit, wherever he may roam

She's beautiful, and therefore to be wooed;
She is woman, and therefore to be won.

      —Shakespeare, *Henry VI, Part I*

Prologue

From *Notes of Silas the Scribe, Tordis Archive*

WHAT HUMAN HISTORY tells of witches is but a sliver of truth. Neither agents of the devil nor figments of our imagination, those creatures, named witches for so many centuries, are in fact human beings, but exceptional human beings at that. In an age when rationality and science did not muzzle those with knowledge of the arcane and occult, a few brave souls dedicated their lives to the protection of this Earth from the dark influences of strange spirit realms. A secret branch of the Knights Templar, these warriors—collectively known as Conatus—repelled every onslaught of nether creatures. But those things that hide in the shadows are well versed in seduction, and there were those within Conatus who fell prey to the dark's allure.

A fracture developed among the Earth's sworn protectors. Led by a charismatic and rare female knight, Eira, were those who desired to harness the power of the nether realm for their own. Eira's own sister, Cian, rose to challenge these traitors to the mission of Conatus.

Thus began the Witches War, where warriors fought and fell for centuries. Eira's followers named themselves Keepers, and with the aid of a strange figure named Bosque Mar, exploited their access to the mysteries of the nether realm to overwhelm their adversaries and extend their own lives well beyond the years decreed by the natural order of the Earth.

Martyred by Eira in the first battle of the war, Cian left not only a legacy of resistance, but her dying words became a prophecy revered by her fellow knights. Cian's sacrificial death transformed her spirit into four pieces, each imbued with elemental magic born of the Earth itself for the world's defense, that when joined would become a weapon known as the Elemental Cross.

The pieces of the cross were flung to the four corners of the Earth and thus the war continued, not only in battles but also as a race to locate the resting places of the sundered weapon. The Keepers reached the sites first and, deeming them sacred, established nigh impenetrable, mystical defenses around each of the locations.

The Searchers' mission transformed accordingly, but became twofold. While their warriors attempted to infiltrate the sites and recover the pieces, their scholars searched for clues within Cian's prophecy. For their patron's words not only spoke of the weapon that would close the rift through which the nether realm gained access to the world, but also of the warrior who would wield the Elemental Cross.

Shrouded in mystery, the Searchers knew only these things: that the child would be born the first of August, the day of the ancient harvest holiday, and that this long-awaited warrior would be the child of a traitor.

1

SARAH SEARCHED THE rock face with her fingertips until she found the next hold. She placed two anchors for her team to use as they followed her up the chute. Hauling herself through the narrow crevice, Sarah was rewarded by the sound of rushing water. Had stealth not been of necessity, she would have been inclined toward a victory shout.

Sarah pulled herself up a few inches so her line of sight cleared the ledge. The impulse to holler disappeared as a profound sense of wonder stilled her soul. The rock shelf was broad, its shape carved smooth by centuries, if not millennia, by the underground river that channeled through the cavern, wearing stone away. Thick tree roots threaded in and out of the cavern's ceiling. High above, sunlight streamed through a slit in the earth. Having seen the opening from the surface, Sarah knew it was wide enough to allow her team passage. Barely enough, but barely was all she needed.

Making certain her toeholds offered the leverage she'd need, Sarah crouched against the wall. Adrenaline jolted through her veins as Sarah used the power of her calves and quads to flip herself onto the shelf. She landed on near-silent feet, her body taut and low to the ground as she surveyed the open space. She waited, watching, listening. Convinced that, as she'd suspected, their adversaries hadn't come upon this hidden chamber, Sarah called over the edge of the shelf.

"It's clear. Come on up."

From below, Sarah heard the scrabble of feet upon rough stone and the metallic clink of carabiners as her companions finished the climb. As she waited for their arrival, Sarah took off her pack and surveyed the next stage of the climb. It was only the sound of a quick release of breath that made Sarah glance over her shoulder to see a body hurtling toward her.

Sarah grunted as Jeremy's body, all muscle propelled by the force with which he'd thrown himself over the ledge, slammed into hers and sent them both tumbling along the cave floor. Jeremy ended up on top of Sarah, pinning her to the ground. Fortunately they stopped rolling before being dumped in the river.

While she waited for the air to come back into her lungs, Sarah glared up at him.

"What?" With his trademark puckish smile, Jeremy easily eroded Sarah's annoyance. "You're the only one who's allowed to do ninja moves?"

"You're supposed to look over the ledge," Sarah told him. "Not throw yourself up, sight unseen."

"I like surprises." Jeremy hadn't let her up yet. Now that she could breathe again, his weight wasn't entirely unpleasant. Adopting an irritated expression, Sarah twisted underneath him, knowing full well that her hips rocked against his provocatively.

"Hey now," Jeremy murmured, his voice suddenly rough. "That's not fair."

"You're the one who knocked me down," Sarah said with a teasing smile. "This is just getting even."

She felt his cock stiffening against her thigh. Sarah laughed and gave him a hard shove so that he rolled off her. Sarah jumped up while Jeremy climbed to his feet much more slowly.

"That was not very nice," he said.

"I wasn't trying to be nice."

"Are you two fighting again?" The third member of the Tordis strike team scrambled over the ledge.

Sarah pointed at Anika and said to Jeremy, "See how she did that? No tackling. It's a much better method."

Jeremy flashed her a wicked smile. "I think I'll stick with tackling."

"I missed a football game?" Anika asked, shooting a glance at Sarah. "That's too bad. I've always been a fan of full-contact sports."

Sarah shrugged in reply. The ever-escalating flirtation between her and Jeremy was no secret. Sarah didn't know where it was leading, or even where she wanted it to lead, but she was having fun and that was all that mattered at the moment.

Anika stretched her arms and gazed up at the light filtering into the cave from above.

"That's the next climb? Glad I'm staying down here with the Weaver." Anika nodded at Jeremy.

"I forgot to bring a deck of cards," Jeremy teased. "Hope we don't get too bored while they're gone."

"If all goes well, you won't be waiting long." The final member of their team, and the Tordis Guide, Patrice, stood at the edge of the shelf.

As she coiled up the climbing rope, Patrice asked, "Are we set for the next stage?"

"Do you need a minute?" Sarah asked their team leader.

"No," Patrice said. "Let's move on."

Sarah nodded and knelt beside her pack. She pulled out two grappling-hook guns and handed one to Patrice.

Taking aim at one of the thickest roots in the ceiling, Sarah pulled the trigger. The hooked spear sailed out, trailing braided metal cable. With a *thunk* the hook buried itself in the middle of the root, just shy of the opening that led to the surface.

Sarah gave the line a couple of tugs to test it. After clipping the mechanical pulley to her climbing harness, Sarah nodded at Patrice.

Patrice shot her gun and her hook hit a foot left of Sarah's mark.

"Very nice," Sarah said.

"Always fun when we get to pull out the Batman gear," Jeremy said. "I'm a little jealous."

Sarah threw a grin at him. "You should have been a Striker."

"I know," Jeremy said. "Tragic that the Academy decided I was too smart to go to waste on you brutes."

"Keep in mind this brute is in charge of saving your ass if this goes bad," Anika muttered.

"Of course I didn't mean *you*." Jeremy gave Anika puppy eyes.

Ignoring her charges' banter, Patrice asked Sarah, "Ready?"

Sarah nodded and flipped the switch on her grappling-hook pulley. The cable began to wind itself up, lifting Sarah into the air. When she reached the cavern ceiling, Sarah surveyed the roots that climbed out of the dim light toward the sun. It was only a couple of feet, not even a yard to get out of the cave.

"You comfortable using the roots to free climb from here?" Sarah asked Patrice, who was suspended in the air beside her.

"Yes," Patrice said, then added drily, "I'm sure Jeremy will catch me if I fall."

Sarah laughed as she took a tight grip on the closest root with her left hand, braced her feet against the curving rock wall, and unclipped the pulley from her harness with her right.

Sarah moved like a spider toward the break in the earth. The climb sent her and Patrice on a path above the cavern floor at a backward pitch of about thirty degrees. Sarah chose her hold carefully, taking her grips and placing her feet more deliberately than she would have if she'd been climbing alone. At the moment she was modeling for Patrice and wanted to make sure the Guide, a less-experienced climber, didn't choose a root that wasn't embedded deep enough in the rock to hold her.

Reaching the lip of the cavern entrance, Sarah found a snake-like root that she could follow out of the cave. She blinked against the sudden bright light as she pulled herself onto the earth's surface. Sarah immediately rolled to her feet, scanning the surrounding woods to be certain this place wasn't being watched.

Patrice emerged from the cave a minute later and took up the same defensive posture that Sarah had.

"We're good." Sarah stood up. Taking the spare climbing rope she'd attached to her harness, Sarah tucked it within the tangle of roots at the surface. They'd need the rope for the descent . . . if they made it back.

Patrice nodded and pointed at the tree-covered slope to their right. "The château is at the top of that ridge."

"And we're sure it's empty?" Sarah asked. Not that she wasn't up for a fight, but Sarah had never gotten used to relying on civilian intelligence for a mission that involved this amount of risk.

Patrice didn't answer, and Sarah silently chided herself for asking the question. Micah, the Arrow, wouldn't have sent the team on this mission if they didn't trust their informant.

"Come on." Patrice moved off and Sarah followed, feeling abashed.

It took them about fifteen minutes to reach the backside of the château. The luxurious home jutted out from the mountain slope. Trees had been cleared on all sides to afford its owners a rare view of the Alps. There was no access road, only a heliport.

"Without a doubt there's a Guardian, if not a few, on the perimeter," Patrice said quietly. "But our intelligence reported that the Keeper who owns this château doesn't permit his security detail inside."

"So we get in and out without being noticed?" Sarah gauged the distance from tree cover to back door. They could make it in a ten-second dash. But whether they would be seen all depended on the manner of the Guardian's patrol route. If their adversary kept a steady watch on the house itself, they'd find it difficult to access the château without being spotted. However, if the Guardian was actively roaming the grounds and not sitting on the house itself—that was another matter.

"We go in," Patrice said, her gaze fixed on the back door. "If a Guardian comes after us, we'll take it down."

Sarah nodded. She knew better than to argue with the Guide, and Sarah had stuck her foot in her mouth once already. She didn't want to do it again or she might end up cataloging records for the Tordis Scribes.

"On three," Patrice whispered. "One, two—"

On the third beat they burst from the trees onto the château grounds. Even as she ran, Sarah kept her eyes and ears open for sights and sounds of an imminent attack.

They reached the door and Patrice opened the panel to access the security system. Sarah turned her back on Patrice and scanned the forest line. No movement yet.

"All right," Patrice said. "We're in."

She opened the door and slipped into the house. Sarah followed, still watching the forest, but nothing seemed to be keeping an eye on the château. At least, not at the moment.

After Patrice had closed the door and waited a few minutes to be certain their entrance had gone undetected, the Guide suddenly laughed.

Sarah raised her eyebrows at Patrice.

With a wide smile Patrice said, "Our informant is one of the maids here. Apparently she came over to our side because the Keeper who lives here is so horrible to work for she wanted to see him taken down a peg. He must really be an asshole."

"Gotta love it when Keepers stay true to form." Sarah smiled.

"We're headed to the study." Patrice led the way from the humble entrance meant for the servants, replete with cubbies for their coats, hats, and boots, as well as a closet in which their uniforms hung.

They passed from the entryway into the kitchen, which was filled with immaculate stainless-steel appliances and ebony countertops polished to a mirrorlike shine.

To reach the study they crossed a great room that faced the front of the house. Floor-to-ceiling windows afforded breathtaking views of snowy mountain peaks. The study was a . . . well, *study*, in modern design.

Sarah frowned at the desk chair Patrice sat in, which looked like it had been constructed of plastic netting.

"That can't be comfortable," Sarah said.

"You'd think," Patrice replied. "But it actually is."

Patrice turned on the computer and waited until the password prompt appeared. Without missing a beat she entered the password and was rewarded with the Keeper's home desktop popping into view.

"He gave his staff his password?" Sarah frowned.

Patrice shook her head as she plugged in a USB drive and copied files onto it. "He just doesn't pay attention to them. Our informant has been in the room multiple times when he's logged onto the computer. She didn't have trouble figuring out the password. I don't think the Keeper believes his staff are capable of anything other than serving him.

"That'll do it." Patrice removed the USB drive. "We're done here. Let's go."

Sarah and the Guide exited the château as easily as they'd entered it, and when they reached the forest, Sarah was giddy with their success.

A snuffle, followed by a low grunt, was all the warning she had.

The bear, which had been hidden behind a huge fallen tree trunk, lumbered into view. Spittle flew from its muzzle as it roared its fury at the Searchers.

With a single swipe of its enormous paw, Patrice went flying. Her body slammed into a tree and she fell to the ground, horribly still.

Sarah had already drawn her throwing knives. She launched the blades at the Guardian, and the bear, still focused on Patrice, didn't have the chance to parry Sarah's attack.

The blades buried themselves in the bear's chest and it bellowed in pain, dropping to all fours.

Sarah drew two more knives, hurling them as the bear charged. The first hit home, sinking into the bear's shoulder. But the second flew wide.

The huge Guardian was coming straight at her. Sarah crouched, muscles coiling, and when the bear was a foot away Sarah leaped into the air, tumbling head over heels and landing behind the Guardian.

The bear's momentum had been too great to instantly wheel around, giving Sarah the chance to sink two more knives into its flank. The bear turned and again bellowed its rage at her.

At that moment Sarah would have given her right hand for Patrice's sword. Her knives, while they could be deadly, weren't causing enough damage to take the Guardian down.

She had only one way to really cripple it, and she knew that acrobatics wouldn't save her from the bear's attack a second time. Sarah drew her knives and waited for the bear to drop to all fours.

The second it did, and before it could charge, Sarah sucked

in a quick breath and let fly with a knife, praying that it would hit home.

The blade buried itself in the bear's left eye. The Guardian roared in agony, raising a massive paw to swat at the blade. Sarah used the distraction to throw a second knife. That blade met its mark as well, burying itself in the Guardian's right eye, blinding the beast. The bear made a sound almost like a wail and stood on its hind legs.

Sarah turned from the Guardian and ran to Patrice. When she put her hand on the Guide's shoulder, Patrice groaned and opened her eyes.

"We have to get out of here," Sarah told her. "Can you walk?"

Patrice nodded. "Nothing's broken."

Sarah helped her up. They didn't make it back to the cavern as swiftly as Sarah would have liked. Patrice was clearly concussed and Sarah had to help her down the mountain slope.

When they reached the narrow opening to the cave, Sarah attached the stashed climbing rope to Patrice's harness.

"Coming down!" Sarah called to Anika and Jeremy. "Open a door!"

After she'd lowered Patrice, Sarah used the same root to climb back into the cavern. Making her way along the web of roots to her grappling gun, Sarah clipped it to her harness and set the mechanism to reverse.

The cable spooled out smoothly and soon Sarah's feet touched the ground.

Jeremy had the portal open by the time Sarah reached the cavern floor.

The Weaver had already taken Patrice through the shimmering door.

"You first," Anika said.

Sarah didn't argue. Heart racing, she rushed through the

portal. She turned as soon as she was back in Haldis Tactical and was relieved to see Anika emerge from the light-filled door just seconds later.

As soon as Anika appeared, Jeremy closed the door.

"Good work, team," Patrice said, her smile genuine if a bit strained. "Good work."

2

NEVER WOULD SARAH have thought that simply meeting her best friend's gaze could compel her to reach for one of her daggers, but in that particular moment she found her fingers twitching toward the blade's hilt. Across the table, Anika shifted her weight against the back of her chair but didn't flinch from Sarah's glare.

Strikers lined both sides of the long, narrow table, the warriors' stares fixed on Anika and Sarah. Since Sarah had joined their ranks five years earlier, at age sixteen, she'd come to expect these monthly mission debriefings with the Arrow—the Searchers' commander-at-arms—to be raucous, bordering on irreverent. Strikers were fighters at heart, perpetually restless, and didn't take well to being cooped up in a meeting for hours at a time.

Thus, the stunned silence currently holding her peers hostage made Sarah even more furious.

At the head of the table, Micah, the current Arrow, cleared his throat.

"Thank you for your candor, Anika." Micah's gaze shifted to Patrice, the Tordis Guide and Sarah's immediate superior. "Patrice, since your team retrieved this intelligence and this will be your mission, I'll let you make the call."

Patrice was frowning. She glanced at Anika but soon found Sarah's questioning eyes.

"Despite Anika's concerns, Sarah performed exceptionally on our mission. She knows the risk and is the best Searcher for this task," Patrice said. "If she wants the mission, I say it's hers."

"Thank you, Patrice," Sarah replied. She could feel Anika's stare, but she kept her gaze on their Guide.

Murmurs ranging in tone from surprise to admiration rippled through the Striker ranks. To Sarah's relief Anika stayed silent.

Micah nodded his approval. "Report back to Haldis Tactical at sixteen hundred hours. A Weaver will be there to open a door for you."

"Thank you, sir," Sarah replied.

"That will be all," Micah said to the group. "Return to your posts."

Wood creaked and groaned as chairs were pushed back from the long table. Warriors clad in leather and wearing grim faces responded to the Arrow's command without hesitation.

As they milled toward the exit none of the other Strikers crowded Sarah. A few glanced in her direction, offering brief nods of encouragement. That she'd accepted the mission didn't merit hoots of congratulation or slaps on the back to raise her spirits. Those would come later . . . if she made it out alive. For now, her send-off would be little more than a reserved approval of her choice.

If it had been any other gathering of Strikers and their Guides—a debriefing wherein each Guide made a report of the current Keeper activities in the target zones: Haldis in Vail, Tordis in the Alps, Eydis in Mexico, and Pyralis in New Zealand—Sarah would have left the room with Anika at her side. On their way back to the Tordis division of the Roving Academy, the two women would share their own review of the meeting, speculating about the Arrow's stratagem and making bets about the Keepers' next move.

Speculation and projection were about all the Searchers had to go on of late. The war hardly deserved to be called such. Striker missions had all but ground to a halt. Barring the occasional scuffle between one of their teams and a Guardian pack near the Keepers' protected sites, a lull had overtaken the Roving Academy. The Academy's teachers still trained Searcher youth, conveying a sense of the war's urgency and the vital purpose that they all served. But outside of the classrooms an ambivalence about the war had overtaken her colleagues. The Searchers had been bleeding and dying for centuries in the hopes that somehow they would find a weak spot in the Keepers' armor of dark magic. But the years kept turning and each generation of Searchers fought and died while new warriors were trained and new scholars combed the Tordis Archives for arcane wisdom that might give the Strikers an upper hand.

The Alchemists of Pyralis painted Searcher weapons with potent enchantments that helped Strikers fight the Keepers' powerful Guardians and when the warriors returned to the Roving Academy bleeding and broken, the Elixirs of Eydis healed their wounds. With each passing year, the Searchers honed their skills, drawing on the elemental magics of their home: Earth, Air, Water, Fire—Haldis, Tordis, Eydis, and Pyralis. But no matter the innovations, no matter the fervor of their efforts, the Searchers had yet to gain any advantage over their adversary.

And that was why Sarah had volunteered for this mission. She had watched Anika breeze out of Haldis Tactical without a glance in Sarah's direction. Rising from her chair, Sarah walked at a brisk clip, quickly gaining on her friend. Sarah waited until Anika was passing an open door. Her hand snaked out and Sarah grabbed Anika by the elbow, dragged her into the empty lecture room, and slammed the door behind them.

"Don't you ever, *ever* question my abilities in front of our Guide!" Sarah gripped Anika's arm tightly. "Not to mention the

Arrow! And every Striker who is not currently out on a field assignment!"

"I wasn't questioning your abilities." Anika wrenched herself
free of Sarah's grasp. "I was merely pointing out your youth. You
should take it as a compliment."

"All of the Strikers were there," Sarah went on, shaking her fist
at Anika. "All of the teams."

"I know," Anika replied tartly. "I was there too."

"Then why the hell did you try to embarrass me?" Sarah gave
Anika a shove that ended up being a little harder than she'd
intended.

Anika teetered back but didn't stumble. And a moment later
she shoved Sarah with equal force. "I wasn't trying to embarrass
you. I'm trying to save your life."

"We don't even know what's at the castle," Sarah countered.
"It might be nothing. I'm just going to check it out."

"It doesn't have to be you."

Sarah could barely keep from scowling at her friend. "I'm the
best climber of all the Strikers. And I kicked all of your asses at
stealth infiltration. If Micah didn't know I was suited for the job,
he wouldn't have let me volunteer."

"He shouldn't have let anyone sign on for this suicide run,"
Anika snapped. "It's too big a risk with no guaranteed outcome."

"When do our missions ever have guaranteed outcomes?"
Sarah shot back.

Anika offered no rebuke other than a sullen gaze.

"The war is at a stalemate," Sarah continued. "If Micah thinks
this could be the key to turning the tide, I'm in. And you should
have my back."

"Micah and the Guides have gone loony, if you ask me," Anika
said. "A new directive from the Scribes and they're clinging to
thin air."

"The prophecy is not thin air," Sarah said, but she turned her back on Anika and paced beside the door, worried that any hint of doubt might appear on her face. "It's all we have."

"Some warrior chick from way back when sacrifices herself for the cause," Anika propped herself against the desk at the front of the room. "And her ghost—her ghost, mind you—spouts a few nonsensical lines about a traitor and a child and a miraculous weapon and we stake our lives on it?"

"What else do you think we can do?" Sarah gripped the back of one of the classroom chairs. "We can't kill wraiths, and Guardians might die, but they don't die easy. The prophecy is the only thing that points to a way to end this war."

Anika frowned, pushing herself up until she was seated on the desk. "Do you ever wonder if the prophecy was just made up?"

"Made up?"

"To keep us going," Anika replied waspishly. "To give us something to fight for so we don't just decide it's all futile and give up."

Sarah didn't know whether the cold knot in her belly was a manifestation of fury or fear. "You don't really believe that."

"Not really." Anika's shoulders slumped. "But sometimes I wonder. Sometimes it all feels like too much."

Sarah nodded, some of her hostility ebbing. "We're all under stress. Fighting so long with no sense of victory—it is too much."

Anika didn't meet Sarah's gaze, but she nodded in reply.

"And that's why I have to go," Sarah said, pushing her point. "If I can bring us anything new, anything to help us learn what the Keepers know about the prophecy, it could make all the difference. It could put us ahead of them for the first time."

"I know," Anika said softly. "I just wish it wasn't you."

Her words and defeated tone snuffed out the last embers of Sarah's anger. Crossing over to Anika, Sarah wrapped her arms around the other woman.

"Micah wouldn't send me or anyone on this mission if he thought there was no chance of its success." Sarah squeezed Anika tightly.

"Just promise me that you'll stick to the plan," Anika murmured into Sarah's shoulder. "Once you know what's at that castle, get the hell out of there. Don't get creative."

"I promise." Sarah laughed. "I can't imagine I'd have any reason to stick around some Keeper's lair."

"'Lair'?" Anika's laughter joined Sarah's. "Oooh, maybe you'll find a dragon."

"If the Keepers have added dragons to their arsenal, I think we're in trouble." Sarah pulled away from her friend but beckoned Anika to the door. "Come on. I need to hand-sharpen my daggers before I go off to live a life of danger and excitement."

"I'd take a dragon over a wraith any day," Anika remarked as they left the classroom. "A dragon might be big and fire-breathing, but at least it has flesh and bone that you can stick a sword into."

"Good point." Sarah smiled, but her chest constricted.

Whatever was locked up in Castle Tierney was important enough that the Keepers had tried to prevent their enemies from discovering both the location of the hiding place and what was hidden. Would Sarah climb the stone walls only to stumble upon a monster? Something worse?

Shrugging away the gooseflesh that crawled up her arms, Sarah stowed her trepidation. There was no sense of being afraid of what she'd find in the Keeper fortress until she actually found it.

"There you are." Jeremy smiled in relief as he ran up to meet Sarah and Anika.

"Oh, good," Anika said. "You might be able to talk her out of this."

"Just drop it, Anika." Sarah felt renewed annoyance with her friend. The issue was settled, and all Sarah wanted was for Anika to leave it alone.

"I . . . uh . . ." Jeremy's gaze shifted from Anika to Sarah. "I was hoping we could talk before you left."

"Uh-huh." Anika smirked. "You two *talk*. I'll get out of here."

Anika stalked off and Sarah offered Jeremy an apologetic smile.

"She only did it because she cares about you," Jeremy said.

"I know," Sarah told him. "But I'm still pissed."

Jeremy laughed, but then he rubbed the back of his neck, obviously on edge. "So, um, can we go somewhere? So we can talk alone?"

"Sure." Sarah felt her pulse jump up a couple of notches. "Your room? It's closest."

Jeremy nodded. He took Sarah's hand as they walked down the hall. Sarah wasn't sure she liked it—at least not when other Searchers could see them. She worried that it might make her look frightened, and she didn't want any of her fellow warriors to think she was having second thoughts about taking on the mission.

Fortunately, they made it to Jeremy's room without any awkward encounters.

Once they were inside and the door was closed, Jeremy grabbed Sarah and kissed her hard. It wasn't unpleasant, but the kiss caught Sarah off guard. Under normal circumstances, Jeremy wasn't so aggressive. This kiss wanted to devour her. Sarah responded as best she could, though her mind was reeling.

Where does he want to take this?

Jeremy broke from the kiss. "Sorry. I've been wanting to do that ever since we got back from the mission. And you've been busy."

"Yeah. The debriefing took a while." Sarah disentangled

herself from Jeremy's arms and crossed the room, unintentionally putting herself beside his bed.

Jeremy came up behind her. His arms encircled Sarah's waist and he drew her back against him.

Sarah gave a little gasp. *God, he's hard.*

"I want you." Jeremy breathed into her hair. "Sarah, before you go, I want to be with you."

Sarah turned in his arms so she could face him. Her heart was pounding. Messing around with Jeremy was one thing, but this?

She liked the Weaver . . . more than liked. He was sweet and funny and damn good with his hands.

Jeremy bent his head and kissed Sarah again, this time softly, coaxing Sarah's lips apart. His tongue slipped into her mouth and Sarah's blood began to heat her skin. Jeremy backed Sarah into the bed and she let him push her down onto the mattress.

Why not? If Anika's right and this is a suicide mission, I'll die a virgin.

Her body wanted it enough. As Jeremy pulled Sarah's shirt off and cupped her breasts, Sarah's nipples hardened and her back arched.

"Take your bra off," Jeremy said. "Show them to me."

Sarah reached behind her back and unhooked her bra, freeing her breasts. She could feel how heavy they'd grown, sensitive with desire and aching to be touched.

Sliding her bra straps off her shoulders, Sarah pushed the lacy cups aside. Jeremy moaned and lowered his head, taking one of her nipples in his mouth while his hand kneaded her other breast.

Sarah's hips arched up as desire pooled low in her body. Feeling her response, Jeremy moved his hand from her breast to cup the heat between her legs. His fingers massaged Sarah's clit through her clothing and Sarah made a small sound of pleasure as her hips bucked up against his hand.

"God, Sarah." Jeremy kissed her neck. Her cheek. "I can't wait to be inside you."

Sarah nodded. She was already tense from the meeting, from the fight with Anika, from the knowledge of how dangerous her mission would be. She needed release.

"Get your cock out."

Jeremy groaned and reached down to unzip his fly. Sarah's hand followed his. When his fly was open she slipped her hand inside his boxers and grasped his erection.

Her pulse jumped. This was it. She was going to fuck Jeremy.

His cock hardened even more in her grip and Sarah smiled. Even if it was the first time, she knew it was going to be good. From what they'd done short of sex, Sarah knew Jeremy had some serious talent.

"You have no idea how much I want you," Jeremy murmured as he began to push down her jeans. "I love you, Sarah."

Sarah went rigid. She couldn't breathe and her body numbed. *I should say something.* Sarah didn't know what she could say. *I have to say something.*

"Sarah?" Jeremy touched her cheek. It only made Sarah feel worse.

"I think we should stop." As gently as she could, Sarah pushed him away. Did she care about Jeremy? Yes. A lot. But she wasn't in love with him and she wasn't willing to lead him to believe she felt something that wasn't there.

Jeremy flinched and Sarah felt like a heavy stone was pressing on her chest.

"I'm sorry." Sarah rolled off the bed, grabbing her bra and shirt. "I'm not . . ."

She couldn't find any words that didn't sound pathetic, or worse, hurtful.

"I didn't mean to—" Jeremy sat up, trying to get his pants back on with dignity.

"It's not your fault," Sarah interrupted. "I just don't want to do this because I think I might die."

There it was. The truth, kind of. Sarah had been fully prepared to sleep with Jeremy because she thought she might die. But she hadn't been prepared for him to tell her he loved her. Because she didn't love Jeremy. Maybe she could at some point down the road, but she didn't yet, and she didn't want to sleep with him and lead him to believe her heart was somewhere it wasn't.

"Okay." Jeremy stared at the floor. "If that's how you feel."

"I'm sorry," Sarah murmured. She threw on her shirt and forced herself to walk, not run, from the room.

Her heart was pounding and her stomach churning as she retreated to her own room.

If I die a virgin, then I die a virgin. But at least I won't die a liar.

3

AS USUAL, TRISTAN found the most challenging part of the hunt to be keeping Ares from throwing him. Though one of the finest horses Tristan had ever purchased, Ares couldn't settle around the wolves. Despite the countless hunts the stallion had run alongside the Guardians, Ares was always uneasy around them—especially once they'd made their kill.

While the stallion balked and pawed at the earth, blowing hard through his flared nostrils, Tristan watched the Guardians tear the buck to bloody shreds. It wasn't a proper pack. Only five wolves served at Castle Tierney and they were veterans of the war, older but no longer deemed suitable to serve on the front lines of battle, although that was just as well. No one, including Bosque, expected the war to come to the walls of Tristan's home. His being hidden away was merely a precaution, and a frustrating one at that.

Despite the frustrations of his isolated habitat, Tristan had neither expected nor wanted to be one of Bosque's pack masters. He'd always found the war and politics that consumed the lives of a handful of his fellow Keepers to be tiresome. Particularly since it wasn't much of a war at all. The nuisance of occasional Searcher attacks near the Keepers' sacred sites was akin to summer flies that chanced to buzz around Ares's flank. The pesky creatures might irritate the stallion, but it was only a matter of time before they'd be dealt with by the swat of his tail.

"I say, man," Frederic called out. "Should we call them off and head back to the castle? Looks to me like there's nothing but blood and gristle left at this point."

They'll want the blood. Every last drop, Tristan thought, but didn't say.

Frederic waited for his reply sitting astride a Hanover gelding. Unlike Ares, Frederic's mount seemed to have misplaced its instinctual fear of predators. The horse chomped placidly on grass while the wolves sated themselves a few meters away.

Tristan half snorted in disgust. Frederic preferred the easier ride. Nary a hair of his shoulder-length, glossy brown locks had strayed from its place tied at the nape of his neck during their hunt. It seemed to Tristan that Frederic had yet to abandon the fashions and attitudes of the nineteenth century, wherein he'd come of age. He'd insisted on donning traditional riding garb for this hunt, which Tristan thought made him look like he was auditioning for a period film. Tristan preferred to ride in a T-shirt, jeans, and the black oilskin duster he favored for keeping warm and dry in the rainy weather so common to the island.

Frederic hunted for the sake of appearance; that, and the enjoyment he got out of emptying his silver flask after the wolves made their kill. Without the challenge of keeping Ares in check while they raced across the rugged island terrain, Tristan wouldn't enjoy these hunts at all.

"How many is that?" Frederic tilted his flask at the white bones poking out between the press of growling, furred bodies wrangling for the remaining scraps of venison.

"This month?" Tristan pursed his lips. "Six, I think. No. Maybe eight."

"You'll need to replenish the herd soon," Frederic told him. "I'll have some yearlings and does shipped over. They should last a bit longer. The Guardians prefer going after the bigger kills, I've noticed."

"More of a challenge." Tristan nodded. It was one way the Keepers' wolves differed from their natural counterparts. Wolves in the wild would have picked out the easiest kill. Guardians reveled in the fight.

Because it's what they were made for, Tristan thought with a grimace. Not that his Guardians got much of fighting beyond these hunts. He often wondered if these wolf warriors assigned to watch over him were as resentful of their charge as he was of being looked after.

"Seamus!" Tristan called out, and a hulking wolf with mottled brown and silver fur lifted his head. "Time to head home!"

The wolf barked gruffly at his companions and the other wolves abandoned their meal and disappeared into the brush. Though the wolves could easily beat the pair of men on horseback in a race to the castle, Tristan knew that the beasts would run beside them, just out of sight so as to keep Ares from spooking. But the wolves wouldn't stray from their charge, would never allow Tristan to wander too far from their watchful eyes. Guardians had been created to follow orders, to serve and do battle at the Keepers' bidding. The wolves did their work well. And some days it was too much for Tristan to bear.

Though he lived alone—for no Keeper would count his servants as peers—Tristan rarely claimed privacy. His movements were observed; his household carefully secured. Nothing could be amiss. No surprises or impromptu actions were permitted.

Tristan could pass each day as he liked: a ride, a hunt, reading, writing, watching films, or sleeping the hours away. But his life only bore the semblance of freedom. He couldn't leave the island, and neither could he abandon Castle Tierney to seek his fortune or wander the globe. His fate was tied to this place as deeply as if he were rooted to its soil.

Ares's hooves threw up clods of dirt as they galloped back to the castle. Its gray stone walls loomed large as the riders drew closer and Tristan's mood soured. A hard ride and a good hunt buoyed his spirit, but never for long. When the wind no longer tore at his hair and he'd left the stallion in the stables, Tristan became too aware of how confined he felt. Even when he wasn't surrounded by the fortifications of the castle, he was barricaded on all sides by a cold, turbulent sea that even the most seasoned fishermen of the mainland tended to avoid.

With reluctance, Tristan reined Ares in, letting the stallion cool down at a walk for the remaining distance. Frederic pulled the gelding up beside him.

"You're off tonight, then?" Tristan asked his companion.

"I have business in Germany," Frederic apologized. Looking pointedly at Ares, he added, "I don't suppose I could talk you into taking him with me."

Tristan's laugh carried an edge. "You come for a visit and then propose to steal my best horse?"

"Not steal, borrow." Frederic smiled, but his voice was tight. "I only meant that it's a shame to keep him here when his stud fee would be phenomenal."

"Because you're in need of funds?" Tristan asked archly. It was a snide, rhetorical question at best: there was so such thing as a Keeper with pecuniary difficulties.

Frederic shrugged off Tristan's acid tone. "There's no need to get pugilistic. You know as well as I do that withholding that stallion from stud is ridiculous. And there are plenty of other horses in your stable to take on your hunts. He'd only be away for a month or two."

When they reached the stable, Tristan swung down from the saddle. Frederic dismounted and handed the gelding's reins to a waiting groomsman.

"Have you listened to a word I've said?" Frederic asked.

Tristan offered Frederic a cursory glance. "I'll think about it."

"Do." Frederic pulled off his riding gloves. "I'll need to prepare for my journey, but I'll say my farewells before I depart."

"After I finish up here, I'll have a drink in my study," Tristan replied, flipping Ares's reins over his bowed neck. "You can find me there."

Frederic gave a curt bow and headed toward the castle while Tristan led Ares into the stable. After Tristan had tethered the stallion outside his stall, he went about unsaddling and brushing the horse. There were groomsmen to perform this task, of course, but Tristan preferred to look after his mounts himself. The only way to truly know a horse and its habits was to do more than ride the beast and then put it away.

As he brushed Ares's neck and shoulders until they were glossy, Tristan considered Frederic's suggestion. Maybe it wasn't right to keep the stallion penned up on this island. He was fine stock, from a nearly priceless bloodline that could be traced back to the Godolphin Arabian. Not sending him to stud could well be a missed opportunity, and the isle Tristan called home didn't have the space to set up a proper broodmare barn for rearing foals.

Of course, he wouldn't ship Ares off to be bred to just any mare. The bloodlines would have to be properly matched. Champion lines.

Tristan paused midstroke. A sick feeling twisted through his gut.

That's all I am at the end of the day. A stud in Bosque's stable. With the sole purpose of continuing Eira's ancestral line as he sees fit.

Tristan wondered, rather sardonically, how long it would be before Lord Mar suggested a female Keeper for Tristan to wed and father children upon. Would Bosque order some woman there to be sequestered from the world with Tristan? Perhaps he'd parade the eligible Keeper ladies through the castle until Tristan found one to his liking.

Neither scenario was appealing.

A polite cough at his back turned Tristan from the horse.

"Yes, Owen?" Tristan greeted his steward.

To describe Owen Banks as an unconventional steward was generous. His dress—a leather kilt and harness—gave him the appearance of a gladiator and revealed more skin than it covered.

Tristan knew Owen's wardrobe choice accommodated his broad, batlike wings, but Tristan half suspected that Owen selected gauche attire to mock his own role at the castle. As an incubus, Owen was accustomed to serving his master, but overseeing the mundane business of Tristan's household must have felt like a glorified babysitting post to the nether creature, far less enjoyable than the usual work of incubi and succubi: seducing and manipulating feckless humans to feed off their emotional torment.

"You're needed in the castle," Owen told Tristan. "I'll have a groomsman finish up for you."

"I'll finish myself," Tristan said, irked by Owen's presumption that he could so easily be commanded. He gave the incubus his back and continued brushing Ares.

"Lord Mar is waiting in your study."

Tristan went still. When he turned around, Owen offered a bland smile.

"But by all means," Owen continued. "Take your time grooming the horse. Perhaps you'd like to braid his tail?"

Tristan pivoted around and slammed the brush into Owen's chest. The incubus stumbled back. Where the brush had struck his bare skin, a red welt bloomed.

"You forget your place, Owen." Tristan locked Owen in a cold stare. Anger made him breathe hard. His fists clenched.

"Forgive me." Owen bowed his head in submission, but Tristan could see his smile broaden.

Dammit. Tristan knew better than to let Owen provoke him.

The incubus was always eager to stir Tristan's darker emotions and make a meal of them.

Without any further acknowledgment of Owen's apology, Tristan took long strides to swiftly exit the stable. He hurried up the stone steps of Castle Tierney's keep.

The study door was closed and Tristan heard no sounds emanating from within, but when he stepped into the room a fire crackled in the hearth and Lord Bosque Mar—who reigned over all the Keepers and was the very source of their power—leaned against the mantel. His appearance was as meticulous as ever. A well-cut, yet conservative, suit; dark hair neatly slicked back.

Bosque wasn't alone. Frederic knelt opposite Bosque's imposing figure. Frederic's head remained bowed, as if he were afraid to look directly at Lord Mar. The scene was familiar to Tristan. He was used to his fellow Keepers cowering in the presence of their overlord. Though he sometimes wondered if it was a fatal character flaw, Tristan had never understood the inherent awe that his peers showed when they encountered Bosque firsthand.

As Tristan crossed the room to greet Lord Mar his only emotion was resignation.

"Good evening, Tristan," Bosque said.

Tristan inclined his head in reply. He couldn't quite stop his derisive glance at the still-simpering Frederic. Bosque noticed Tristan's smirk and smiled.

"Rise, Frederic," Bosque said with a wry, mocking tone. "Your obeisance is duly noted."

"Th-thank you, m-my lord," Frederic stammered as he awkwardly unfolded from his kneeling position.

Bosque clasped his hands at his back. "I understand you're leaving us."

"I have business—" Frederic's eyes widened, as if he expected an admonishment.

"Of course you do." Bosque cut him off with a dismissive wave of his hand. "And I know you would never neglect matters of great import."

Tristan's brow furrowed. Something in Bosque's tone was off. His voice was smooth, but beneath the surface it seemed coiled like a snake ready to strike.

"Tell me," Bosque continued. "When did you last visit your Swiss château?"

Frederic blanched. "I'm not sure . . . a month ago, maybe two . . ."

"It is a vacation home, is it not?" Bosque's silver eyes flared with cold light. "Your visits are infrequent."

"I suppose," Frederic tittered.

"Guardians sometimes fail in their duty," Bosque said. "As lower creatures, one can only expect so much. However, in this case the failure lies with the master, not the servant."

"I'm sorry, my lord?" Frederic had gone very pale.

"What's happened?" Tristan asked. The flat, unyielding clarity of Bosque's tone set Tristan's teeth on edge. Something was about to happen, and it wasn't good.

Bosque offered Tristan an apologetic smile. "Your guest saw fit to forbid his Guardian retinue entry to his home. He also saw fit to reduce the patrol to one Guardian."

"It's just a château—" Frederic began.

"A château that Searchers broke into two days ago," Bosque told him.

"Searchers?" Frederic blurted. "But why? There's nothing—"

"Of course we don't know why," Bosque replied. "Because a single Guardian was unable to repel the attack. The Searchers escaped and we have no idea what they may have gleaned from their little excursion."

Frederic collapsed to his knees and began blubbering.

Sensing movement at the study door, Tristan half turned and saw the wolves stalking into the study.

"Lord Mar." Tristan glanced in alarm at the tall man.

"A lesson must be learned, Tristan," Bosque told him, keeping Frederic locked in his gaze. "Guardians are exceptionally skilled at their work. To forget why they serve us is a dishonor to our cause and their special place among us."

Tristan's throat constricted, knowing there was nothing he could do to help Frederic.

The Guardians silently approached Bosque; when they reached him, the wolves dropped to their bellies and licked the tips of his shoes.

"Frederic." Bosque smiled at the shaking, sobbing man. "Let me show you how proficient Guardians are in their work."

Tristan didn't even see Bosque signal the Guardians to attack, but in the space of a breath the wolves were on their feet. They wheeled around, snarling at Frederic.

Frederic only had time enough for utter horror to register on his face before the wolves were on him. Their teeth tore through his clothes, seeking flesh. Frederic screamed as the Guardians ripped chunks of skin and muscle from Frederic's arms and legs.

Despite the appalling scene, Tristan knew he wasn't permitted to leave the study until Bosque said otherwise. Tristan went to a table where several crystal decanters rested. He poured himself a scotch before he turned to face Bosque. He wasn't surprised to find the tall man's assessing gaze fixed on him. Tristan had the sudden sensation of the two of them in a space apart from the brutal execution taking place only a few feet away.

"You don't care for Frederic," Bosque said. It didn't sound like a question.

As if that matters now. Tristan shrugged. "We have different passions."

A slow smile overtook Bosque's lips. "And what are your passions, dear Tristan?"

Cursing his choice of words, Tristan quickly said, "I only meant that I prefer a brisk day and a hard ride, where Frederic would as soon watch others at sport rather than exert himself."

With a nod, Bosque turned to gaze upon the flames in the fireplace. "You speak the truth. At times I fear I've given too much to my children of Earth, let them grow idle with power so they enjoy the ripe fruits of the harvest but remember not the labor of the sowing."

"Is that how you think of us," Tristan asked, "as children?" *So you don't mind feeding your children to the wolves?*

"At times," Bosque replied. He looked directly at Tristan. The silver of Bosque's eyes made Tristan force back a shudder.

"Do you feel like a child?" Bosque asked.

Sensing he was not unlike a fly caught on a spider's web, Tristan said carefully, "You mean on this island?"

"It was an open question."

Hardly, Tristan thought, but he said, "At times it feels overly confining. But I am ever the servant of your will."

The answer seemed to please Bosque. He left the fireside and settled into a high-backed chair.

"Frederic acted a child," Bosque told Tristan. "Petulant and spoiled. And he had no grasp of the consequences such behavior might lead to. I wish I could spare you better friends, Keepers more equal to your station, but the most worthy among them are needed elsewhere. Even so, I'm sorry to take one of those I could offer as a companion away from you."

"I understand," Tristan replied stiffly.

Bosque shook his head. "Don't misunderstand me. You aren't sequestered on this isle because you lack maturity. You're not cut from the same cloth as Frederic or his ilk."

Bolstered by Bosque's praise, Tristan said, "Then let me join the others—the ones you speak of as worthy. Surely I could serve a greater purpose in the world than remaining here. Alone."

"No." Bosque breathed the hint of a sigh. "With Lumine and Efron serving near Haldis, we can't risk exposing you. You're safest in this keep. Out of the fray. The bloodline must be protected."

I'm fucking Rapunzel. Tristan knocked back his scotch. *At least the drinks are good here.*

"I don't want you to be unhappy here, Tristan." Bosque appraised Tristan for a moment, then said, "I thought perhaps Lana would be a welcome distraction. But she's suggested that you're already bored with her."

"Lana isn't the issue." Tristan poured himself another whisky. "And I understand why I'm here. It's not that I don't appreciate your concern, but the island, the castle . . . it can be a bit limiting."

"Of course," Bosque replied. "And I sympathize. You're a young man and I'm certain you feel compelled to be out in the world—what's the saying? Sowing your wild oats."

Tristan couldn't stop himself from cringing at Bosque's choice of phrase.

With a placid smile, Bosque continued. "But you are exceptional, and because of that you must make certain personal sacrifices for the good of your people."

My people. Tristan sipped his scotch. *Are the Keepers really my people? Besides Frederic, who comes to visit me? Who even knows where I am?*

And Tristan was convinced that Frederic had been, like Lana, there on Bosque's orders. Frederic to offer fraternal companionship; Lana to bed him. Frederic's motivation was obvious—having spent more than two hundred years on this Earth, he would soon face his own end. By swearing a blood oath to Bosque, Keepers accessed the dark power of the nether—the realm over which Bosque ruled—but while these magics offered Tristan and his kind preternaturally long lives, it didn't make them immortal. No Keeper lasted past 350 years, and those who lived past 250 were the exceptional players in their violent game of life. Frederic, aristocrat and playboy, could hardly be called exceptional. This current, personal favor to Bosque had probably represented Frederic's last-ditch effort to eke out another half-century. A poor wager, as it turned out.

Weariness pressed down on Tristan's shoulders. He no longer wanted to be having this conversation—he simply wanted it to be over.

"I'm grateful for the comfort and security of this castle and the island," Tristan said, trying to sound earnest. "Sometimes the isolation gets the better of me. But I understand why I'm here."

"Good." Bosque's assured smile gave Tristan the small relief of knowing that he wouldn't be harried further on this issue.

"Will you be staying long?" Tristan asked.

"No," Bosque answered. "I simply wished to look in on you and to know that you're well. And of course, Frederic had to be dealt with."

"I'm well enough," Tristan said quickly, as an afterthought adding, "and thank you for your concern."

"Of course," Bosque replied. "I'll return next month, but should you need anything, you know how to summon me."

Tristan couldn't imagine any scenario in which he'd feel compelled to summon Bosque Mar. The man's presence was nigh unbearable. And the summoning ritual . . . far too bloody for Tristan's liking.

"If you'll pardon me," Tristan said, "I'm weary from the day outdoors. I think I'll retire."

Bosque nodded in reply, but when Tristan had almost reached the study door, he heard Bosque call, "Would you like me to send a replacement for Lana?"

Tristan glanced over his shoulder.

Bosque's silver eyes were fixed on Tristan, gleaming with something Tristan thought could have been either contempt or amusement.

"Or perhaps another companion or two," Bosque continued. "To complement Lana's . . . talents."

"Ah." Tristan tugged on the collar of his shirt. "I think Lana's talents are quite sufficient. And I don't think she'd appreciate the suggestion that she needs assistants."

Bosque's teeth flashed in the firelight when he laughed. "You're a wise young man, Tristan."

Frederic's screams had become gurgles, but he still wasn't dead. The Guardians knew how to take their time in killing a man when their masters willed it so.

Bosque turned his gaze back to the macabre scene, but said to Tristan, "I understand if you prefer to go."

Without hesitation Tristan turned away from the bloody mess that had once been a man, and walked out of the study.

He found Seamus waiting for him in the hall.

"Is he dead yet?"

Tristan shook his head, continuing down the hallway. Seamus fell into step beside him.

"You're well rid of him," Seamus growled.

The wolf's comment drew a rough, sickened laugh from Tristan. "I wasn't particularly attached to Frederic, but I hardly wished such an end on him."

Seamus was the only Guardian—at least in Tristan's imagining—that would dare criticize one Keeper to another. But Tristan and Seamus had a rare bond. Seamus was something of a lone wolf. The eldest of the island pack, he played the part of their leader, but the bonds that a wolf pack would normally share were absent. Tristan didn't find that surprising, given that the wolves had been picked up from their home packs and shipped off to this remote assignment. He doubted they had any love lost for him, either—but Guardians were born and bred to be the Keepers' loyal servants. And they knew better than to so much as raise an objection, much less directly refuse an order.

Since the pack spent most of its time patrolling the island and the castle, ready to rip any trespasser to shreds, Tristan had little occasion to interact with them. Seamus, however, had become something of a steward and confidant to Tristan. Finding the wolf's dry humor and gruff sensibilities welcome, Tristan had put Seamus in charge of the castle's security.

"You should ask Bosque to send someone else," Seamus told Tristan. "There must be at least one Keeper who'd appreciate the wildness of this place."

"I don't think you actually believe there is, old wolf," Tristan answered. "I know you better than that."

Seamus grinned. "Just don't want you to despair, my boy."

They stopped in front of the door to Tristan's bedchamber.

"I hope you rest well." Seamus gave a short bow when Tristan reached for the doorknob.

"And I suppose the night's just beginning for you?" Tristan asked the wolf.

"There's a good moon in the sky," Seamus said, nodding.

Tristan managed a tired smile. "Then I hope you enjoy it to the fullest."

Entering his room, Tristan closed the door and leaned his head against the cool wood. His temples were beginning to throb and he wondered if another scotch at this point would relieve or amplify the pain.

"There you are," a husky female voice called from within the room. "I thought you'd abandoned me."

After briefly considering opening the door and walking out, Tristan turned and went to his bed.

"Good evening, Ms. Flynn."

Lana had been draped across Tristan's bed, but she crawled into a kneeling position. Her ink-dark curls fell loose over her pale shoulders. She was wearing a leather halter dress with a zipper running from its already-plunging neckline to its hem. The zipper was open to just above Lana's navel, which allowed Tristan more than a glimpse of her generous breasts.

The dress was one of Lana's favorites, and Tristan knew it well. The garment's halter style accommodated her black leathery wings, which were presently folded in mock docility. Tristan didn't buy her submissive posturing for even a moment. Succubi were never meek.

"Oh, dear." Lana's tongue wet her lower lip. Despite the fact that she wore no makeup, her lips were perpetually a deep shade of crimson, as if she'd lacquered them with fresh blood. "Whenever you get formal it means you're cross with me."

She slid her arm beneath one of the pillows and withdrew a riding crop. His riding crop. "Shall I be punished?"

"Please don't take my things," Tristan said. He was cross with her, and it was making him feel and sound much older and stodgier than his twenty-five years merited, which made him even more annoyed. "You have plenty of your own toys."

"I thought you'd like the feel of your own crop." Lana ran her hands up and down its length. "You certainly never use it on that beast of yours."

"Ares needs a firm hand, not a cruel one." Tristan replied, taking the crop from her.

"That's all well and good." Lana turned her back on him and

lowered herself to all fours. The dress was short enough to offer Tristan a fine view of her ass. Unsurprisingly, Lana hadn't bothered to wear panties.

"Not tonight," Tristan said, biting back a curse. Sending Lana away would probably mean further complaints from the succubus to Bosque, but Tristan had no desire for her company. He'd just witnessed Frederic's transformation from man to hunks of meat. Hardly an aphrodisiac.

Running her fingers up the front of her dress, Lana slowly unzipped the garment. Her breasts spilled out, revealing areolas and nipples almost as dark as the leather of her dress—a shocking contrast to her ghost-white skin.

Lana pushed the dress off and lounged back on the bed. Teasing her nipples into such hardness that they almost appeared sharp, Lana dropped her head back and moaned with pleasure.

Tristan's jaw clenched. His cock hardened with an urgency that he found difficult to ignore. As he watched, Lana spread her thighs and moved her hand from her breast to the folds of her sex. She stroked herself and in the firelight Tristan could see glistening wetness as she readied herself for him.

Tristan started toward the bed, but Lana gave a sudden cry of pleasure and Tristan heard the echoes of Frederic's screams in the sound.

"Get dressed, Lana." Tristan ignored the stiffness of his cock and the ache in his balls. He was certain it would please Bosque to no end if Tristan let Frederic's torment meld into the pleasure of sex with Lana. But Tristan never wanted to become what so many Keepers were.

Lana sat up, pouting. "But won't you be cold?"

"If I'm cold, I'll send for more blankets," Tristan answered drily. "Now get out."

He wasn't in the mood for banter with the succubus. She

smiled and licked her lips. Tristan almost groaned, but from frustration rather than desire, knowing that his irritation was giving Lana much more pleasure than his body ever could.

"You aren't supposed to feed on me," Tristan reminded her. "Get out. Or I'll be the one reporting to Bosque about *your* behavior."

The flicker of wariness in her dark eyes gave Tristan a little satisfaction. He turned his back on Lana and climbed into bed.

"And turn out the light when you go."

Tristan stared up at the frescoed ceiling of his bedroom. Even in the darkness he could make out the grotesque shapes of so many creatures familiar from myth and nightmare. To anyone else the looming beasts might have been a foil for sleep, but not for Tristan. The monsters were for others to fear, but for him to command. They lived alongside him: his protectors, his companions, his concubines. It had always been that way.

So much power lay in his grasp, Tristan thought as he closed his eyes, willing sleep. Why then did he feel like the captive of his own fate?

4

DESPITE SARAH'S ASSURANCES that it was unnecessary, Anika had insisted on accompanying her to Haldis Tactical and seeing her off.

Micah was waiting for them with Jeremy, who would be weaving Sarah a portal. When the two women entered the room, Micah gave Jeremy a brief nod. Jeremy avoided meeting Sarah's gaze, instead immediately drawing his pair of long, silver skeins through the air. Threads of light spooled out, forming an intricate pattern as the Weaver dipped and swirled in the complicated dance that created a doorway from one point on the Earth to another.

Sarah watched Jeremy's dance, utterly enrapt by his graceful movements. She'd seen it done many times before, but its extraordinary beauty never failed to amaze her.

"Careful," Anika whispered. "You might start drooling."

Sarah shot her friend a cold glance. Of course Anika would assume that she was staring at the lithe body of the young man doing the weaving rather than the powerful act of magic they were witnessing. Anika kept smirking, but Sarah lifted her chin and continued to watch Jeremy weave, refusing to give Anika any pleasure by blushing or cringing, and ignoring the annoying little whisper inside her head that insisted Anika's assumption was completely accurate.

Soon Jeremy was panting and beads of sweat had formed on

his temples, then his movements slowed and then halted altogether. The gleaming chaos of color and light suddenly revealed a clear image. A rocky shoreline and a storm-ridden sea.

"Ireland is nine hours ahead of the Roving Academy's current location," Micah told Sarah. "Our civilian contact, Ian, will be waiting for you on the other side of the portal. If all goes well, you'll be back here for a debriefing in forty-eight hours."

Sarah nodded, zipping up her leather jacket so the harness that held her silver throwing daggers would be hidden from view.

"I'm afraid the first-class cabin checked in full, darlin'," Jeremy said as she approached the portal. "You'll have to fly coach."

Jeremy flashed a teasing smile, but he couldn't hide the hurt feelings that just reached his eyes. Anika gave Sarah a sharp elbow in the ribs, which Sarah ignored. She did give Jeremy a second look, though, and had to admit he was rather drool-worthy. Sarah hadn't confessed to her friend what had happened with Jeremy. She still felt too embarrassed and guilty about it.

Sarah wondered briefly how Anika would have reacted, but it was too late for that. She probably would have told Sarah she should have just fucked him anyway, and that wasn't something Sarah needed to hear at the moment.

Sarah's thought carried a bit of chagrin but didn't make her overly morose. High risk came with their work; Strikers lived fast and hard. If she had truly wanted to sleep with Jeremy before this mission, she could have.

And she had no time for lingering regrets now.

She took another step forward, but Anika grasped her arm. Sarah was afraid to meet her friend's gaze, but Anika simply gave her a tight smile and said, "Good luck."

Sarah did her best to return Anika's smile. Not wanting this departure to last any longer, Sarah turned back to the portal and stepped into its light.

"It's about time!"

Sarah found herself face-to-face with a dark-haired, heavy-bearded man. She could barely hear him over the howling wind. At her back, the portal closed, its light vanishing like a candle flame snuffed out. The sudden darkness seemed to make the wind's screams louder and the night air much colder.

The man pointed to a small, boxy car parked on the side of the narrow lane. "Let's get going."

Somewhat bewildered, Sarah followed the man to the car and climbed into the passenger seat. When the doors were closed and the wind muffled, Sarah asked, "You're Ian?"

"And you're Sarah," Ian replied as the car's engine rumbled to life. "And you're late. Do your folk always dawdle when it comes to magical transport? Don't you think it's a bit off to just leave a door bright as the sun sitting open for five minutes? What if someone had come along?"

"That's why we only open portals in remote or well-hidden locations," Sarah answered defensively.

"Hmpf." Ian gunned the engine and then they were hurtling down the country road at an alarming speed.

Sarah first wondered when the road had last been paved, then whether it had been paved at all. She also wondered if Ian's car had any shocks.

"The fisherman who's agreed to take you across the channel won't be happy if we're late," Ian said. "And we certainly won't find another volunteer. It was hard enough to get this one to agree, and I'm sure what we're paying is more money than he'd see in a year."

"Is the crossing that dangerous?" Sarah yelped as the car hit a bump so hard that her head slammed against the roof.

Ian didn't bother to ask if she was all right. "The crossing isn't the issue. It's the island. These old villages have their superstitions. You know how it is."

Sarah really didn't know how it was, but she wasn't particularly inclined to continue the conversation. She was mostly concerned about making it to the village without a concussion.

"You have my gear?" Sarah asked, hoping the change in subject would take the edge off Ian's mood.

Ian jerked his thumb toward the backseat. Sarah craned her neck to see the ropes and holds she'd need to scale the seawall. The sight of familiar equipment eased some of Sarah's trepidation.

Since Ian was fully immersed in his mad driving, Sarah took a moment to survey the man. He was middle-aged, with thick, bushy hair and an equally thick body to match.

"How did you become one of our contacts?" Sarah asked.

Ian cast a sidelong glance at her. "They didn't tell you?"

Sarah shook her head. "I'm just told where to go and who to meet. No backstory required."

Hunching over the steering wheel, Ian went quiet and Sarah thought he'd decided not to answer her, but a moment later he said, "My wife, Adele, loved to sail. She didn't feel right on land. I used to call her my selkie."

He gripped the steering wheel tightly. "About three years ago she got it in her mind that she wanted to chart all the islands along the southwest coast in the hopes of organizing a point-to-point race around them. We lived two counties north of here. She started from our home port of Tralee and I kept pace with her on land, meeting her at each port and resupplying her boat. But when I arrived in this village, she hadn't made the port yet. So I waited. But she never appeared."

Sarah barely noticed the bumps on the road as she watched Ian's face contort with grief.

"The Coast Guard found her boat adrift in the channel three days after she was meant to meet me. They could find no damage to the boat, but Adele wasn't aboard. She'd vanished. They concluded that she'd fallen overboard and drowned, but I couldn't believe it. So I stayed in the village, believing that Adele might be found. I couldn't go home without her.

"First it was days. Then weeks," Ian said. "I left my job, our flat, and found whatever work I could in the village. Nearly four months had passed when one morning I found a letter under the door of my hotel room. It said that if I wanted to know what happened to Adele I should go the fishmonger and ask for the midnight catch."

"The 'midnight catch'?" Sarah watched as Ian's lips twisted in a self-mocking sneer.

"A code phrase, of course," he told her. "But at first I was sure it was a cruel prank. I was well known throughout the village as the obsessed, mad husband whose wife had drowned in the channel. I thought someone was having a laugh over my suffering. For a few days I ignored the message, but eventually even the risk of humiliation was outweighed by the chance that someone might have answers for me.

"Feeling half a fool, and half a nutter, I went to the fishmonger and asked for the midnight catch. The man said nothing, just pointed to a door behind his counter. I began to wonder if I wasn't just foolish, but perhaps had a death wish—though it didn't stop me from going through that door. Stairs took me into a cellar, but no one was waiting for me. There was, however, another door, which opened into a passage. It was soon clear that I was moving beneath the village, away from the fishmonger's shop. The next door I reached was locked. I knocked and a woman's voice answered: 'You lost?' 'I'm looking for the midnight catch,' I told her. The door opened."

Sarah shifted in the passenger seat; she knew where Ian's story was headed yet still found it unsettling. This was always the way civilians were recruited to the Searchers' cause—hapless souls caught in the crossfire of a war they'd never known about until it took something, or more often someone, from them.

Still swimming in his own memories, Ian spoke quietly. "The woman wasn't alone. There was a man with her. He was sitting at a small table with two empty chairs waiting."

Ian hesitated, then laughed. "I almost ran. The way they were dressed. All that dark leather and barely hidden weapons. They looked more dangerous than a pack of wolves."

"We try to be," Sarah commented drily.

"So I hear." Ian looked askance at her. "Though I'm thankful not to have seen a Guardian."

Sarah nodded, briefly wondering if she'd encounter any of the wolf warriors during her reconnaissance. It would be much better if she didn't, Sarah knew. She was there for answers, not for a fight. Even so, she reached out to run her fingers over the harness that held her throwing knives.

"You probably know the rest." Ian sighed. "They told me about your war. About witches and the nightmares they command trying to infest our world. That this all started because there's a crack between our world and theirs, and your side is trying to close it, while theirs wants to keep it open.

"And they told me that the war had killed my wife. More specifically, that their enemies, who they called Keepers, were responsible for her death."

"You believed them?" Sarah had been born into the world of Searchers and Keepers, raised with the constant drone of the Witches War humming in the background of her life. The reality of magic and monsters had always been with her. But for someone like Ian, the darkness Sarah knew could only sound like madness.

Ian grimaced as he steered the car onto the narrow streets of the dimly lit village. "I didn't want to. Over and over I told myself to turn around, get out of that hidden room, and never look back. But I couldn't."

His sudden bark of a laugh made Sarah flinch.

"Of course, it helped when they made a door out of nothing that opened halfway across the world. Seeing is believing, as they say."

"True enough," Sarah murmured.

The car slowed and Ian parked alongside the village quay. Even before she opened the passenger door, Sarah could hear waves crashing against the rough shore. As soon as the engine quieted, Sarah saw a lumpy shadow moving in the night toward the car.

"That'll be our man," Ian said, opening the door to climb out of the car. Sarah pushed hard against the wind to get her own door open and scrambled from the seat. A gale shrieked around them as Ian trudged over to meet the fisherman. Sarah opened the door to the backseat and zipped up the waterproof duffel that held her climbing gear.

When Sarah joined the two men they were already deep in conversation, but she couldn't follow their words, as the fisherman seemed to be a native Gaelic-speaker. Ian gestured to Sarah. It was too dark for Sarah to make out many of the fisherman's features, but even in the dim light she could see the lines that years of wind on the open sea had carved into his face. She opened her mouth to greet him, but when the fisherman's milky eyes met Sarah's, she flinched. He turned to Ian, speaking rapidly.

"What is it?" Sarah asked.

Ian lifted his hand, signaling her to be silent. He spoke to the fisherman again, his voice hard.

The fisherman shook his head and wagged his finger at Sarah.

Ian lowered his voice and bowed his head close to the old man's ear. The fisherman's shoulders lifted and fell with a sigh of resignation. He turned and stomped back along the quay to board his vessel.

"Come on." Ian began to follow.

"What was that about?" Sarah asked as she walked beside him.

Ian cast a sidelong glance at her. "He didn't want to take you."

"I thought arrangements had already been made for my transport." Sarah looked ahead. The old fisherman was casting off lines to prepare for their voyage. Whatever the issue had been, Ian had apparently resolved it.

"They were," Ian told her. "But when he saw that you're young—and a woman—he wanted to back out."

"I can handle myself," Sarah said, bristling. "It's just a reconnaissance mission. To find out what's on that island."

"No one comes back from the island." Ian had spoken so softly, Sarah wasn't certain she'd heard him correctly.

"Sorry?"

"The fisherman doesn't want to take you because, as he said, 'No one comes back from the island,'" Ian said, looking furtively at Sarah. "But I suppose that's why you're going. To find out why no one comes back." As if to himself, Ian added, "Why my wife never came back."

"Something like that," Sarah answered uneasily. Her mouth had gone dry. All the bravado she'd felt at the Academy was withering in the face of the rough seas, the fear in the fisherman's gaze, and the weight of responsibility transferred from Ian's sorrow.

The fact that the fisherman's boat appeared older and more worn than its owner didn't do anything to reassure her. Even docked the boat tipped precariously from side to side as it was buffeted by the rough waves. The captain was already aboard, casting lines and prepping the craft, though making no acknowledgment of Sarah as she clambered onto the boat.

"Good luck!" Ian shouted over the shrieking wind.

Sarah waved in reply and then ducked into the cabin. She

crouched in a corner of the cramped quarters, deciding it best for both the fisherman and herself to stay out of the way for the duration of the journey.

The captain stomped into the cabin. He gave Sarah a cursory grunt that was a sound of the barest tolerance rather than welcome. The boat's engine rumbled to life and then lurched away from the shoreline.

Sarah remained huddled in the corner as the boat pitched and rolled along the waves. She made herself as small as she could, not because she was seasick or frightened but because it seemed that the best chance to make it across the channel lay in the captain giving his complete attention to piloting the ship. Withdrawing into herself for the duration of the trip would also offer Sarah a chance to gather the strength and resolve she'd need to complete the mission.

About an hour had passed when the fisherman's gravelly voice drew Sarah out of her own thoughts.

"That water's cold as ice." He didn't look at her as he spoke. "You sure about the swim?"

Taking his words as the cue that they'd soon reach the drop point, Sarah unzipped the duffel and pulled out her dry suit and fins. She stuffed her jacket into the bag and then pulled the suit on over her clothes. Once she was zipped in, she slipped her arms through the duffel's straps.

The boat slowed until the engine was idling. The fisherman didn't turn around or tell Sarah that they'd arrived. His white-knuckled grip on the wheel told Sarah she was exactly where she needed to be.

"Thanks," Sarah said.

The captain flinched. "Tomorrow. Midnight. I'll be back to pick you up. Same place."

"I'll be here."

Sarah stepped out of the cabin onto the lurching deck. She grasped the boat rail as she donned the fins. Checking one last time that the straps of the duffel were snug, Sarah hopped over the rail and into the turbulent sea.

The dry suit protected Sarah's body, but the waves punched the bare skin of her face like a frozen fist. Sputtering through the frigid saltwater, Sarah churned toward the shore with powerful strokes. It wasn't easy going, but she was thankful to see that despite his misgivings, the fisherman had dropped her as close to the island as he could without running afoul of the sharp rocks banking its shores.

After ten minutes of struggling through the choppy waters, Sarah reached the island. Though the waves grabbed at her, wanting to tow her back out to sea, Sarah hauled herself onto the slippery rocks coated in seafoam. She traded her fins for climbing shoes from her pack and kept her body flat against the rough surface as she slowly crawled toward the cliff face that composed the south wall of Castle Tierney.

The medieval structure used the island's natural features for its own defense. Carved into the very rock wall that enclosed three-quarters of the island's circumference, Castle Tierney offered only two approaches. The first required an overland path from the one sheltered harbor on the western shore, and that route required several miles of travel through both dense forest and open moors. If something truly important was hidden within the stone keep, that territory would undoubtedly be overrun with Guardians or worse. Thus, the Searchers had elected to pursue the second approach: scaling the one hundred-plus-foot rock wall to reach a long-unused cistern that would give access to the castle's interior.

When Sarah reached the wall, she stripped out of her dry suit, stashing it in a crevice below the cliff. She slipped into a climbing harness and gathered the ropes and cams she'd need for the ascent. It would be a slow, arduous climb. Not only was the surface slick with rain and sea spray, but she also couldn't risk drawing the attention of anything that might be watching from above. Given how imposing and impenetrable the cliff appeared, Sarah hoped that it would be unguarded, but she couldn't take any chances.

Slipping the duffel back over her shoulders, Sarah found her first holds. Years of battering from the wind and sea had left the rock wall pitted and grooved—one of the few things working to Sarah's advantage. Forcing herself to take calm, steady breaths, and careful never to look down, Sarah made her way up the cliffside. She placed cams as she needed them but was careful to keep them tucked into the rock face.

By the time she reached the round hollow of the cistern, Sarah was drenched with moisture—a mixture of saltwater, rain, and her own sweat. Her muscles were shrieking from the exertion. She rolled into the dark tunnel and coiled up her rope. After she'd shimmied out of the climbing harness, Sarah put her equipment into the duffel, retrieving a headlamp before she stowed the bag.

The wind beat mercilessly at the entrance to the cistern, heavy and rhythmic like the beating wings of an immense bird. The climb had been tricky, but her next moves would be trickier still: she had to navigate the crumbling, uncharted labyrinth of tunnels that would lead her into the castle. Sarah switched on the headlamp and turned away from the sea. She didn't see the shadow swoop past the hollow in the rock. Neither did she sense the creeping presence at her back until it was too late.

5

TRISTAN DIDN'T KNOW how long he'd been staring at the frescoed ceiling of his bedroom, but he was fairly certain the sleep he hoped for would continue to elude him. He rolled out of bed, not minding the cold of the floor on his feet. Neither did he bother with a robe before he left his room.

Seamus caught up with him halfway down the hall. Though currently in his human form, Seamus still moved with the cautious grace of the predator whose shape he preferred.

Does the old wolf never sleep?

"Restless night, eh?" Seamus asked with genuine concern.

Tristan shrugged. He hadn't taken the time to check a clock before he left his bedroom, but the wolf's presence informed Tristan that he'd been tossing and turning for at least a few hours—long enough for Seamus to have enjoyed and returned from his nightly run across the island.

"Where are you headed now?" Seamus asked.

"I thought a bath might help," Tristan replied.

Seamus nodded and slowed as Tristan's destination made it clear he was in the mood neither for company nor conversation.

When he reached the stairs, Tristan glanced over his shoulder. "Get some rest, you mangy beast," he said, offering Seamus an apologetic smile.

Seamus laughed and the sound deepened Tristan's melancholy.

The wolf was as close as Tristan had to a friend, but Seamus was a servant—here on orders like all the others. Tristan didn't doubt Seamus's loyalty; he even believed the Guardian held some affection for him. But their respective stations threw up an obstacle to true comradeship.

His sour mood worsening, Tristan made his way from the uppermost floor of the castle to the subterranean space that was home to the baths. A hot bath was actually Tristan's second objective. His first was to tire the hell out of himself with a long swim.

The castle's pool was narrow, but long and deep—ideal for laps. The natatorium itself wasn't particularly to Tristan's liking. Clad in ebony, the chamber featured sleek columns around which twisted giant tentacles that were far too lifelike. He'd learned to ignore the creeping sense that a great slumbering beast rested beneath the turquoise and jade mosaic of the pool floor.

Tristan pulled off his cotton pajama bottoms and dove into the pool. The cold water snatched his breath, but he welcomed the shock. It was the most alive he'd felt all day and it was the reason he ordered that the pool be maintained at such a low temperature.

He swam hard, stopping only when the burning in his shoulders, chest, and legs was unbearable. Hauling himself out of the pool, Tristan dripped water as he left the natatorium and went into the adjoining chamber.

Steam from the baths swirled around him, so thick Tristan could barely see. While the pool had been laid in severe, sharp lines, the baths were designed for soaking. Tristan waded into one of the sunken bowls, following its sloping floor until he was waist deep in the hot water. Then he slid onto the submerged shelf that ringed half of the bath. He let his head tip back and his eyes close as the heat sapped tension from his spent limbs.

When exhaustion had sufficiently cleared Tristan's mind to the point where he thought sleep inevitable, he lazily climbed out of the bath. He toweled himself off and slipped his pajama bottoms on. As he slowly made his way back to his bedroom, Tristan was pleased to find himself genuinely drowsy. Perhaps he'd even pass the night without troubling dreams.

At that late hour Castle Tierney was quiet, but Tristan knew better than to believe he moved through its halls without notice. There was never a time when all the creatures within the castle walls slept. It was a place of wariness and watching.

Tristan stepped into his room and welcomed the long yawn that signaled how soon he'd be asleep. He was halfway across the room when he froze. His bed wasn't empty.

The woman was on her stomach. She wasn't wearing a stitch of clothing, but a single black calla lily rested on the small of her back.

Chains at her wrists and ankles bound her spread-eagle to the bedposts. The sound of Tristan's footsteps caused her to lift her head from the pillow, and Tristan saw that she'd been gagged. Her dark hair spilled across the pale skin of her shoulders. Her eyes widened when she saw him, but she didn't make a sound.

Who was she?

That she was tied down and gagged made it clear that the woman wasn't there by choice.

Tristan pivoted on his heel and went right back out of the room. He found Seamus on the other side of his bedroom door. And the bloody wolf was grinning.

"Seamus," Tristan said, keeping his voice level, "there is a woman tied to my bed."

"Yes, sir." Seamus had the decency to tamp down his grin and nod solemnly.

"She's naked."

"I assumed so, sir," Seamus replied. "Given her being tied to the bed and all."

Tristan let that pass. "Do you happen to know how she got there?"

"It was Lana's idea." Seamus's mouth turned downward enough for Tristan to know the old wolf disapproved.

The woman on his bed had been chained facedown. The black calla lily lay upon her like some dark offering. Of course Lana was the architect of this scheme.

"Where is she?" Tristan asked Seamus.

Seamus lifted his grizzled face and sniffed the air. "She headed toward your study."

As Tristan turned away, Seamus asked, "What do you want me to do about this one?"

"For the moment, nothing," Tristan answered. "Just guard the room. No one goes in. I'll be back soon enough."

However ready for sleep Tristan had felt a few minutes earlier, he was now wide-awake. And furious.

When he slammed through the study door, Tristan found Lana curled up on a sofa with a snifter of brandy.

"Hello, Tristan."

"What the fuck, Lana?" Tristan glared at her. "What did you do?"

"I left you a gift," Lana purred. "I hope you don't mind that I unwrapped it for you."

"Hardly necessary," Tristan replied curtly. "And by that I mean both the gift and its unwrapping. Who is she?"

"Isn't it obvious?" Lana rose so she was kneeling on the sofa and spread her wings in a way that was almost menacing. "She's a Searcher. Most likely an assassin. Owen caught her climbing the seawall. Nimble little thing."

"Assassin?" Tristan rested his elbows on the back of the divan. "You think the Searchers sent someone to kill me? I thought no one knew I was here."

"Perhaps someone found out," Lana replied, folding her wings once more as she settled back onto the cushions. "And perhaps you should be asking *her* these questions. That *is* why I left her for you."

"You captured a Searcher and you want me to interrogate her while she's naked on my bed?"

"That was the idea."

"I thought that's what we had wraiths for."

"This way is a bit more creative." Lana smiled. "And of course more hands-on for you. And more delicious for all the loyal servants of your household."

Tristan grimaced. "How very thoughtful." He didn't want to consider how delighted the succubi and incubi of the castle would be at the prospect of gobbling up the captive's distress and torment. No doubt Lana had made quite a meal out of stripping and binding the Searcher.

Degradation was something Lana craved, but Tristan had no taste for violation. He desired only a woman in his bed who wanted to be there, who was as hungry for his touch as he was to caress her skin. Explaining that to Lana would be pointless, of course, so Tristan simply said, "I'll deal with the Searcher." He reached out his hand. "Give me the key."

"Shall I inform Lord Mar that she's here?" Lana twirled one of her glossy curls around a long red fingernail before dipping her hand into her bodice and drawing out a large iron key.

Tristan hesitated. If he said no, Lana was sure to run straight to Bosque and tell him that Tristan was trying to hide the woman's capture. If he said yes . . . Tristan wasn't sure he wanted to deal with Bosque until he'd decided how to handle the prisoner himself.

"Whatever pleases you, Lana." Tristan smiled, taking the key, and then leaned in to kiss the succubus on the cheek before he left the room.

That would confuse the hell out of her. And it would likely buy Tristan some time.

Tristan returned to the hall outside his bedroom and found Seamus standing watch.

"Do you know where her clothes are?" Tristan asked.

Seamus shrugged. "I can track them down."

"Do that quickly," Tristan told him. "Then come back here. I'll wait for you."

"Shall I summon any other Guardians?" Seamus lifted a bushy eyebrow.

It was a prudent question, but Tristan wished it wasn't. He had no idea what he would do with his captive, but he did know he wanted to handle it himself, and quietly.

Reluctantly, Tristan nodded. "Just make sure it's someone who can hold his tongue."

"Understood." A moment later, a wolf trotted down the hall and Tristan was alone.

He looked at the door, half tempted to enter.

He couldn't, though, not until Seamus returned. Prisoner or not, Tristan had no desire to humiliate this woman. He wouldn't ogle her while she was chained up. It wasn't as though the sight of her hadn't been seared onto his mind's eye.

Even the brief glimpse of the Searcher had been arresting. Whoever she was, she was beautiful. It was too easy to recall the slope of her back and the lovely curves of her bare ass. The sight had been far too sudden and startling to be forgotten. If he'd been another sort of man—the sort Lana wanted him to be—he might have been grateful to come upon that scene.

As it was, however, Tristan was uneasy that the memory of the naked Searcher made his cock twitch with lust. A life that granted his every wish had made Tristan wary of sinking into hedonism. He acknowledged the fact that Bosque would encourage such a lifestyle was likely the reason he resisted it—but the truth remained that he did resist it.

Turning a prisoner of war—if that was who this Searcher was: a soldier from the enemy lines—into a sex slave was neither a fantasy of his nor did he want it to become a reality. If she belonged in Tristan's dungeon, so be it. But she had no place in his bed.

Tristan paced in front of his bedroom door. His choices left him unsettled. As much as Lana had gotten under his skin that night, Tristan couldn't help but wonder if summoning Bosque was the best course of action. After all, a Searcher had breached the castle, his hiding place. If nothing else, that fact alone signaled that Tristan's enemies had somehow learned of his whereabouts. What if this woman was only the first of an impending attack?

That's why I'll have to interrogate her.

Though he knew he had no way around it, Tristan didn't savor the idea of torturing the woman to uncover her intentions.

But there was no other way, was there?

The sound of toenails clacking on the stone floor drew Tristan's attention. Seamus's brown and gray was accompanied by a younger, russet-hued member of the pack.

Tristan addressed the red wolf. "Good evening, Joseph."

The wolves shifted into their human forms, and Tristan took the folded clothes Seamus offered while Joseph dipped into a bow.

"This is what she was wearing," Seamus told Tristan. "Owen also recovered a pack full of climbing gear and a dry suit. She swam here."

Tristan raised an eyebrow when he noted the leather harness lined with gleaming silver knives.

Definitely an assassin. Maybe I'm a fool to even consider keeping her alive.

Tristan grimaced, accepting that he'd kill the woman if he had to, but he wouldn't do so before he knew who she was and how she'd found him.

"Be as wolves and stay close to me," Tristan ordered. "Don't attack unless she makes the first move."

Joseph cast a nervous glance at Seamus, but the older wolf nodded. Without further prompting the Guardians shifted forms.

Still not entirely certain of what he was about to do, Tristan gritted his teeth and opened the bedroom door.

6

SARAH TWISTED ON the bed. The manacles cut into her wrists and ankles, and the cloth gagging her was bound so tightly it was hard not to choke whenever she drew breath.

She was close to succumbing to panic. A man had been in the room, staring at her. He had to be a Keeper. No one else had incubi and succubi serving as sentinels in their home.

The memory of the way the incubus had snatched her from the mouth of the cistern made Sarah shudder. The creature's taloned fingers had sunk into her shoulders, yanking her backward. Then she'd been dangling high above the frothy sea as the incubus's wings beat, taking her higher and higher until they flew over the castle wall and into one of its towers.

The incubus took care to remain aloft when he dropped Sarah, hovering at a height that made her hit the stone floor of the tower with a jolt that jarred her bones. Despite the shock and pain, Sarah had rolled over, ready to fight. And if it had been that single creature to defeat, Sarah believed she could have done it. He wasn't armed, though his ability to fly and his clawlike nails were weapons enough. Once she'd taken out this cliff-watcher, she'd be in the perfect position to continue her mission—inside the castle.

But the incubus hadn't been alone.

Just as Sarah had moved to draw a throwing knife, she'd been seized from behind again. A husky female voice said, "What have you brought me, Owen?"

Alighting on the floor, Owen replied, "A trespasser. She made it all the way to the cistern."

The female sniffed her hair. "She's a Searcher." Then she shoved Sarah into Owen's grasp.

"I know that, Lana," Owen said; then he glared at Sarah. "You don't belong here, precious."

He whipped Sarah around, pinning her arms behind her back so she faced his companion.

Unsurprisingly, Lana was a succubus. Her body was voluptuous to the point of excess, its sensuality only emphasized by the tight leather dress she wore. Familiar as Sarah was with the reputation of this sort of nether creature, the clothes were just too much and Sarah had to swallow a derisive laugh. Given that the incubus was bare-chested and clad only in a leather kilt, Sarah was tempted to apologize for interrupting their staging of *The Rocky Horror Picture Show,* but decided against it. Pissing off her captors could too easily prove fatal. As long as Sarah stayed alive, she had a chance of getting out of the castle.

Determined to remain calm, Sarah didn't struggle against Owen. The only strategy that might work required that she conserve her energy until the right opportunity presented itself. She also hoped that if the nether beasts thought her fearful and submissive, they might do the work of revealing the castle's secrets for her.

"I'll take her to the dungeon," Owen said to Lana. "You should inform Lord Tristan we've captured a Searcher."

Lana shook her head. She came close, stroking a long red fingernail from the base of Sarah's throat to her chin. "I have a better idea."

Sarah let herself shudder at the woman's tone, which dripped with hunger and lust. The more intimidated she seemed, the more likely they'd keep talking like she wasn't there. She'd already learned the name of their master: Tristan. He would be the one who held the secrets of this place.

The succubus licked her lips and sighed with pleasure as her nails dug into Sarah's jawline. "Follow me."

Lana led the way to the tower stairs while Sarah—stumbling due to the awkwardness of having her arms pinned—clumsily followed at Owen's urging. They took her down a spiraling stone staircase, but much to Sarah's disappointment, their conversation ceased for the duration of the descent.

When they emerged from the tower into a broad hallway of the castle keep, a low growl slithered out of the shadows. A moment later a large brown and gray wolf followed the path of the sound.

Sarah tensed and reflexively jerked against Owen's restraining arms. Every instinct was telling her to defend herself.

Lana faced the wolf, sniffing with disdain. "Yes, Seamus?"

Where a wolf had been bristling suddenly stood a man, his face worn with age and his cold eyes revealing that there was little love lost between Guardian and succubus.

"You want to tell me what's going on here?" Seamus snarled despite his human visage.

"Not really." Lana smiled.

"Lana." He barked her name.

The succubus fluttered her batlike wings irritably. "If you must know, Owen discovered a Searcher climbing the south wall."

"I've always said wolves are of little use on an island," Owen sneered. "We'd be better off with albatross Guardians. Or maybe sea turtles."

Seamus spared him a spiteful glance, then said to Lana, "You're putting her in a cell, then?"

"Dear Seamus," Lana cooed. "Why be boring when captivity offers so much sport?"

Sarah gritted her teeth. She wouldn't let herself imagine the kind of sport Lana had in mind. She just wanted them to keep talking.

"You should be waiting for orders from Tristan about what to do with her." Seamus frowned.

"Tristan will tell me, tell all of us, what to do with the prisoner soon enough," Lana replied. "I'm just going to offer a suggestion in the meantime. Don't go spoiling my fun. Is Tristan in his room?"

"He's in the baths."

The tips of Lana's wings curled with delight. "Even better."

"He won't like it if she comes to harm before he's had a chance to question her," Seamus said with a warning growl.

"We're not going to hurt her," Owen said, but he added to Lana, "Are we?"

"Of course not." Lana's laugh made Sarah's gut curdle. "Not without orders."

Lana pursed her lips at Seamus. "So do we have your permission to continue, pack leader?"

Seamus winced at her address and he turned away, shaking his head. A moment later a wolf slipped back into the shadows from whence it came.

"What a bore," Lana muttered before leading them farther along the hall.

"Guardians like rules," Owen replied. "They're bred that way."

"I know." Lana sighed. "It's tiresome."

When Lana stopped in front of a tall, carved wooden door, Owen asked, "We're not taking her to Tristan?"

"We are taking her to Tristan." Lana opened the door. "Just not to the baths."

Owen pushed Sarah into the room.

Lana closed the door, then took her time looking Sarah up and down. "I don't think she's properly attired to meet our master, do you?"

That was when they'd stripped Sarah and chained her to the bed. A bed that obviously belonged to this Tristan the nether creatures spoke of.

All thoughts of gleaning information from her captors evaporated in the face of her rapidly changing circumstances. Sarah didn't want fear to overrun her reason, but she hadn't considered this scenario. Torture: yes. Being drained slowly by a wraith: of course. Too many Strikers went that way.

But being violated by some Keeper playboy sadist? That filled Sarah with a dread she didn't know how to face.

She lay there, on the bed, with cold air blanketing her bare skin and even colder terror sluicing through her veins.

When the door opened again, Sarah wanted to scream but forced herself to remain silent.

The man—whom Sarah presumed to be Tristan—was dressed only in dark cotton pajama bottoms. And seeing her tied to his bed was an obvious shock. He'd stared at her for only a minute or so, but to Sarah it felt like an eternity.

But just as suddenly as he appeared, Tristan turned and left the room. He hadn't said anything.

He left her there, bound and naked. Alone.

Sarah's mind turned against her, questioning her every move, from volunteering for the mission to submitting to her captors. Why hadn't she fought back? She couldn't help but fear that what awaited her would be more horrible than death.

She squeezed her eyes shut, trying to force away the racking grief and fear that threatened to wring desperate sobs from her.

Sarah was shaking from the effort to control her emotions when the door opened again. She dared to open her eyes.

Tristan was back, and he had two Guardians flanking him. He

approached her slowly. Though her bindings made the possibility of a fight unlikely, Sarah quickly assessed her foe. Strength would be Tristan's advantage for certain. Tall and broad-shouldered, the Keeper was more than fit. His bare chest and abdomen featured lean, chiseled muscle, and he moved with a grace that bespoke the kind of balance and dexterity that would prove deadly in close combat. Sarah didn't doubt that she could offer him a serious challenge in a fight, but she wouldn't be able to over-power him.

Sarah frowned when she saw that he had her clothes in his hands.

Panic took over when he was within a foot of the bed. Sarah thrashed against her bonds. The chains clanged against the broad headboard, and Tristan scowled at her.

"That wood is older than your great-grandparents would be today. Stop struggling, or you'll damage it."

I'm chained up and he's lecturing me on how to treat his heirloom fur-niture? Sadist and *pretentious asshole.*

But those characteristics were par for the course with Keepers, so it was hardly surprising. Had she not been gagged, Sarah would have cussed at him until she ran out of breath. He watched until she stopped struggling. Then, setting the folded clothing on a bedside table—though without her dagger harness—Tristan opened his hand to show Sarah an iron key.

"I'm going to get you out of these chains," Tristan said. His voice was low and steady, but not menacing, even when he added, "If you move, the wolves will kill you."

Whether this was some sort of trick, Sarah was compelled to obey. She had no doubt that the Guardians would tear into her if she threatened their master. Unarmed, she didn't stand a chance against the wolves.

Tristan went to each of the four bedposts and unlocked the

manacles. Sarah remained perfectly still, even after she'd been freed of the chains. It took a lot of her effort not to shrink away when he bent down to remove the cloth that gagged her. Now that his face was close to hers, Sarah noticed that the arrogance she'd expected was absent from Tristan's features. His expression wasn't harsh or haughty, and she was surprised to find an anxious flicker in his gold-flecked eyes and that his mouth turned slightly down in a frown borne of worry, not irritation.

"Get dressed." Tristan stepped back from the bed. "I'll return in a moment."

He retreated into an alcove across the room. Sarah rolled over, drawing her knees up to her chest. She couldn't stop shaking.

The wolves remained at the bedside, watching her closely. Sarah wanted to reach for her clothes, but she was frozen in a huddled ball against the pillows. The larger of the two wolves gave a low whine and then shifted.

Sarah recognized Seamus from his encounter with Lana and Owen in the hallway. Seamus picked up the folded clothes from the bedside table and set them next to Sarah on the bed. Without a word, he shifted back into his wolf form and returned to his watch beside the second wolf.

Managing to disentangle her arms from the way they'd locked around her knees, Sarah dressed as quickly as she could. She didn't look at the wolves. She didn't glance at the alcove into which Tristan had vanished.

It was much easier to breathe now that she had clothes on.

Tristan's voice called, "Seamus?"

The big wolf barked in reply, and Tristan reappeared. Sarah wasn't the only one who'd gotten dressed. Tristan had swapped his pajama bottoms for jeans and a white T-shirt. He still had her dagger harness; it hung loosely in the crook of his arm.

The Keeper crossed the room to stand between the two wolves.

"I apologize for the state you were in when I first came upon you," Tristan said.

Sarah gazed at him warily, not feeling particularly compelled to respond.

"This island is private property," Tristan continued. "Would you care to tell me who you are and what you're doing in my home?"

Sarah remained silent. The smaller of the two wolves bristled and bared its teeth at Sarah. Tristan lifted his hand and the beast quieted.

His hand still aloft, Tristan's fingers danced through the air, leaving a flaming symbol in their wake. The fiery image trembled and shadows boiled out of it. Dark tendrils appeared in the air, building until a turbulent mass of smoke hovered beside Tristan, waiting.

A wraith.

Sarah shrank back against the headboard. She'd learned about the shadow creatures, knew they were impervious to harm. Stories of wraiths and the rare survival of an encounter with one usually involved unbearable pain and watery bowels. Facing the writhing mass of shadow, Sarah wondered how long she had to live—and longer didn't mean better. Death delivered by a wraith wasn't swift; it would be a slow, nightmarish ordeal.

"I see you're familiar with our usual means for dealing with your kind." Tristan glanced at the wraith as if it were a bothersome, rather than terrifying, creature.

Mustering what courage she could, Sarah straightened up and gave a brief nod.

"We could go through the motions with my wraith," Tristan said. "But I was thinking we might try something different."

He waved his hand and the wraith vanished. "Something more sporting."

"Sport" was the same word the succubus had used. Sarah stared at the Keeper. He was as twisted as the creatures that served him. That was the only explanation for this behavior. She was the prisoner of a complete nutter on a power trip.

Tempted as Sarah was to point out just how crazy he obviously was, the wraith was gone and she didn't want it to come back. For the moment she could only play along with whatever lunatic notion had caught the Keeper's fancy.

"What did you have in mind?"

Sarah noticed the slight furrow of Tristan's brow, as if he hadn't anticipated her question. Could it be that he hadn't thought this through? Did he think she wouldn't call his bluff?

"A series of contests," Tristan said after a moment. "Challenges, if you will."

"What sort of challenges?"

"The sort I deem entertaining."

And here comes the crazy. Sarah fought back a welling despair. *He just wants to torment me himself rather than let the wraith do it.*

"If you fail to meet the challenge," Tristan continued, "you will answer the questions I ask."

"And if I don't fail?" Sarah shot back.

"I won't kill you. Nor will I allow any of my charges in this castle to cause you harm."

Sarah tried hard not to snicker. "And will any of these challenges allow me to win my freedom?"

"Freedom isn't on the table." Tristan settled into an armchair. "I'll remind you that you are the trespasser here. You entered my home with ill intentions, while I've done nothing to merit your hostility."

"You're a Keeper." Sarah glared at him.

Tristan smiled blandly in return. "Racist."

"What if I don't like your questions?" Sarah asked.

"You'll like the wraith even less." His voice was dead calm. A smile ghosted across his mouth. "Though I'll need my room back, if you don't mind."

Down to the dungeon with me, then.

"Seamus." Tristan beckoned to the wolf, who immediately shifted forms. "Take our guest to more appropriate quarters. I think Fand will serve."

Seamus hesitated but then said, "As you wish, my lord."

Returning his attention to Sarah, Tristan said, "Since you'll be under my roof, I hope you'll tell me your name."

Sarah balked. She wasn't inclined to tell the Keeper anything.

"Or," Tristan offered when she didn't speak, "I could come up with my own name for you."

"My name is Sarah." She didn't trust the oddly playful gleam in his eye.

"Welcome to Castle Tierney, Sarah," he said quietly. "I'm Tristan."

7

TRISTAN WAS STILL awake and still dressed when Seamus returned an hour later. It hadn't been his intention to stay up. At first he'd tried to return to his copy of Marcus Aurelius's *Meditations,* but was far too restless to read. Instead, Tristan ended up pouring himself a scotch and mulling over his actions.

When he'd entered the bedroom with the wolves at his side, Tristan hadn't known how the scene would play out. He wanted to return the captive woman's clothes and give her back some of the dignity Lana had stolen. He hadn't anticipated the visceral effect seeing her stripped and chained to his bed would have on him.

With the initial shock of finding the woman gone, it had been too easy to let his gaze roam over the slopes and planes of her form. Her body was strong but beautifully curved—pressed into the bed, her full breasts had spilled out from beneath the weight of her body. Tristan had had to pull his gaze away because his gut had clenched and his cock had begun to stiffen at the sight of her.

Once he'd freed her from the chains and gag, Tristan had sought refuge in the alcove that served as a walk-in closet. He needed to clear his head and get a better hold of the situation. The vague notions that had formed in Tristan's mind were that he would interrogate the Searcher, but would attempt to appeal to her survival instincts to extract information rather than immediately resort to the wraiths.

But when he'd seen her again, Tristan suddenly abhorred the notion of stowing her away in the bowels of the castle. He wanted her close. He wanted to question her himself, but not under threat of torment.

His impromptu plan had formed as he grabbed jeans and a T-shirt. He didn't think he'd be able to make his proposal and be taken seriously while shirtless.

When Seamus had escorted Sarah from his room, Tristan began to grope for justifications for his actions. He wasn't trying to deny the primal attraction that drew him to Sarah. But Tristan believed he was in control of his baser instincts—simple lust wasn't enough to explain his impulse to keep his prisoner close.

What Tristan finally settled on was the need for purpose. For the first time since he'd been sequestered in Castle Tierney, Tristan had the opportunity to participate in the war that shaped his world but that he'd been forced to remain aloof from. The enemy had scaled his walls, gained entry to his home. Tristan could turn the Searcher over to Bosque, or he could take matters into his own hands. The former held little appeal, while the latter . . . well, the latter was more than interesting.

Convincing Bosque that he'd made the right decision would likely be Tristan's greatest challenge—but he thought he knew how to persuade the Keeper overlord. While his minions preferred to inflict suffering upon humans in a direct manner, Bosque had always been a master of subtlety. Given that Lord Mar constantly reminded Tristan that he was one of the few Keepers who could trace a direct line to their founding mother, Eira, and Bosque himself, Tristan believed that Bosque would be intrigued by Tristan's handling of the Searcher.

This game would be one of wit and will. Well played, it would earn Tristan Bosque Mar's admiration and alleviate the apathy with which Tristan had regarded his life of late. He pushed away a nagging thought that the subcreatures' tactics with prisoners might be more honorable. Honor had never been a priority among the Keepers; their aim was and had always been power.

Seamus had knocked and then waited politely for Tristan to call him into the room. Tristan sensed immediately that the Guardian was on edge. He poured a second scotch and handed it to Seamus.

"How is our guest settling in?" Tristan asked the wolf.

Seamus gave a slow shake of his head. "She's confused and . . . so am I. My lord, forgive me for asking, but what the hell has gotten into you?"

Tristan looked at Seamus with a rueful smile. "It probably won't reassure you to hear me say I'm not sure."

When Seamus frowned, Tristan continued. "I have every intention of finding out who she is and why she's here and how she came to know that 'here' exists, but I'm going to be rather unorthodox in the way I go about it."

"Unorthodox, eh?" Seamus chortled before taking a sip of the whisky. "Is that a fancy way of saying you're going to trick her into shagging you?"

Tristan choked a little on his drink. He shouldn't have been surprised that Seamus read him so easily, but the bluntness of the wolf's words were still startling.

"That's not how I'd put it," Tristan replied.

"No, you prefer to call it unorthodox, but the truth is you had a lovely thing laying bare-ass on your bed. A man's blood won't soon forget such a sight." Seamus tipped his glass toward Tristan. "Be careful, lad. I won't deny that the Searcher's a fine-looking woman, and I'd be as wary about bedding Lana as you've become, but this stranger is still your enemy and your prisoner."

"Don't worry. I haven't forgotten." Tristan sighed and looked directly into Seamus's war-weary face. "You think I should just give her to a wraith?"

Seamus's lip curled back and Tristan saw the wolf's canines sharpen. "That's not what I said. Just keep your eyes open."

Tristan nodded, and Seamus swirled the amber liquid in his glass.

"How do you expect Lana to take it?" Seamus asked.

"Yes." Lana stood in the doorway. "How do you expect me to take it? You certainly know how I like it, which is why I'm quite puzzled with what I've been hearing about the treatment of our prisoner."

Setting his glass aside, Tristan glanced at Seamus. "Give us a minute."

The Guardian took the time to bare his canines at Lana as he passed her, but otherwise left without objection.

When Seamus had closed the door, Lana shot up in the air. She circled the room twice, buffeting Tristan with gusts of wind from the punctuated flaps of her leathery wings.

Tristan knew it was meant to be a show of power, to remind him that the succubus wasn't to be trifled with. But the spectacle failed to impress Tristan. Lana could access powerful magics, but Tristan was still her master. She posed no real threat to him. She could, however, be a terrible nuisance and that was what Tristan aimed to avoid.

When Lana finally landed face-to-face with Tristan, she splayed her fingers across his chest, letting her long fingernails dig into his shirt.

"Well?"

"I've decided to take a different tack with the Searcher," Tristan told her calmly.

"That much is obvious." Lana sniffed with disdain. "What I want to know is, why? Are you really so emasculated that you can't take what's yours by right of conquest?"

Tristan didn't bother to reply, knowing her rampage wasn't finished.

Lana's mouth hooked into a taunting smile. "Or perhaps you were too chilled after your midnight swim to perform? Did you need me to warm you up first?"

Her hand darted out and grasped Tristan's balls. He drew a hissing breath as his fingers clamped around her wrist, shoving her arm away.

"Take care, Lana," Tristan murmured, determined not to lose his temper.

"You gave her a room instead of a cell," Lana snarled. She tried to wrench her arm free of Tristan's grasp, but he was stronger and didn't relent.

"I know."

"Why?" Lana's fury turned to a whimper and Tristan let her go, convinced she wouldn't physically assault him again.

"Machiavelli, Sun Tzu." Tristan picked up his scotch and took a leisurely swallow.

Lana smirked at him. "Dead writers?"

"Philosophers and tacticians," Tristan answered. "Men who understood that wars are fought in the mind as much, if not more, than on the battlefield."

"You're at war with that woman?" Lana scoffed.

"She's a Searcher," Tristan replied coolly. "Of course I'm at war with her. But being that she's here and disarmed, it offers a fine opportunity for a more nuanced attack."

"How so?" Lana tried to sound bored, but Tristan knew he'd piqued her interest.

"By bringing her around to our way of thinking," Tristan said.

Derision filled Lana's gaze. "You think you'll convince Bosque to elevate a Searcher? You're a fool."

Tristan answered her with a harsh laugh. "Of course not.

I only propose to persuade our captive to join us, so that she'll give us what we want. And when we have that, hard truths will be hers to deal with."

Lana stalked up to Tristan. He stayed perfectly still as she cupped his face and kissed him.

"That is delicious," she said breathlessly.

Tristan waited until she'd backed off, then said, "I expected you'd appreciate the benefits of such an approach."

Lana nodded eagerly. "So will Owen. Her misery . . . just thinking about it makes me—"

She stopped abruptly, glaring at him. "*You'll* have to pull it off though."

"You don't think I can?" Tristan peered at her over the rim of his glass.

Lana eyed him for a minute. "Perhaps. I guess we'll have to see."

"I guess we will." Tristan returned her assessing gaze. "If you'd like to tip the odds in our favor, I could use your assistance."

"What do you need?" Lana asked.

"Supplies," Tristan answered with a smile. "Supplies of a very particular nature."

8

SARAH STARED OUT the narrow slit of a window, wondering if she should make every possible effort to escape. The window, obviously a notch in the wall designed for archers, was not an option. She could have hidden behind the door, knocking out the next person—or creature—who opened it, and run like hell. Since Sarah already knew the castle was secured by Guardians and nether fiends, it seemed unlikely that an escape on foot would be successful.

Irrational as it seemed, escaping wasn't the first thing on Sarah's mind. Her thoughts continually returned to the bizarre scene that had played out with her captor—the Keeper named Tristan. Relieved as she'd been that Tristan had not assaulted her, nor suggested that he at any point intended to, Sarah had no idea what to make of him.

Sarah's bewilderment only increased when the Guardian Seamus had taken her not to a dank cell carved out of the stone beneath the castle but had instead deposited her in a spacious bedchamber appointed with Tudor furnishings. Massive tapestries upon which entire bestiaries frolicked covered the stone walls.

There was also a large fireplace, and Sarah considered whether scaling the chimney was a viable means of escape. It had potential, but Sarah suspected that escape wasn't her best course of action. At least, not yet.

She was in the castle and she was about to have access to the master of this secret isle. She could think of no better way to continue and fulfill her mission. The chimney would still be there after she learned more about this place. The drawback to her plan remained that she wouldn't return to the fisherman's boat the following night, and Ian would report to Sarah's fellow Searchers that she'd been lost. Sarah hated to think of how distraught Anika would be, but she wasn't worried that Micah would send a rescue team after her. This wasn't the sort of mission one could be rescued from. Sarah had known that when she volunteered for it.

If Sarah played this game of Tristan's, and could avoid harm while gleaning knowledge from the Keeper, she could return to the Roving Academy having accomplished the mission. It meant that her friends would suffer for the time being, but Sarah decided that the end goal trumped that point. She'd also have to find another way off the island—but Sarah knew that food and other sundries had to arrive at Castle Tierney by some means of transportation. If she could locate a boat, she could devise a way to commandeer it for her own escape or possibly stow away on one of its trips to the mainland.

A knock at the door turned Sarah from the window—yet another strange moment in this most bizarre of days: who knocked on a prisoner's door?

Another knock and Sarah fumbled for a reply, settling on "Yes?"

"May I come in, miss?" The voice was young and female, and more than a little nervous.

More curious than anything, Sarah called, "Yes. Come in."

The door opened and a girl who Sarah guessed could be no more than sixteen meekly edged into the room. The girl made a quick curtsy. She was dressed in a gray smock and apron. Bright copper curls peeked out from beneath her starched white cap.

Looking at the girl, Sarah had the sensation of being transported back in time at least a century.

"My name is Moira, miss," the girl told Sarah, keeping her eyes downcast when she spoke. "I'm to attend you while you're a guest of Master Tristan."

"Attend me?" Sarah frowned.

"Yes, miss," Moira replied, dipping into another curtsy. "As your lady's maid."

Sarah gave a snort of disbelief and Moira looked at her with wide eyes.

"Have I offended Your Ladyship?"

"Dear lord." Sarah shook her head. "First of all, you cannot call me Your Ladyship."

"But—" Moira wrung her hands, glancing at the open door behind her as if she wanted to run. "What am I to call you?"

"Sarah is fine."

Moira appeared even more distressed. "But . . . miss . . . I'm just a servant. To use your Christian name would be a sign of great disrespect. Master Tristan would be cross with me."

Frustrated, Sarah considered the girl. She certainly didn't want to force Moira to behave in such a way that could land her in trouble.

"Is 'miss' okay?" Sarah asked.

Moira nodded.

"Let's go with that, then," Sarah told the girl. "Just no Lady or Ladyships."

"Yes, miss." Moira curtsied again, and Sarah had to stop herself from telling the girl to knock off the curtsying, but she didn't want to get into another discussion about propriety.

An awkward silence filled the space between them. Sarah had no idea what to do with Moira, and Moira was obviously waiting for instruction.

At last Moira offered, "Would you like me to escort you to the baths before you retire for the night?"

"Excuse me?"

Moira's freckled cheeks bloomed with a blush. "The baths are located in the lowest part of the castle."

"I don't think I need a bath tonight." That wasn't quite true. The climb, her capture, and fear had left her sweat-covered and grimy. Even so, Sarah wasn't ready to embrace this role that Tristan seemed to have molded for her. Lady of the manor? Was that how he intended to play things?

Unwelcome thoughts of dollhouses and serial killers sprang into Sarah's mind.

"Would you like me to help you prepare for bed then, miss?" Moira tried again.

"Uh"—Sarah glanced at the bed—"what exactly does that entail?"

Moira covered her mouth to stifle a giggle, and then cast a horrified glance at Sarah. Sarah quickly offered her a reassuring smile—she was glad that the girl seemed to be less frightened than when she'd first appeared.

Casting Sarah a shy smile in return, Moira said, "I will lay out your nightgown and turn down the bed. Then if you like, I will brush your hair so it isn't tangled when you go to sleep."

"Does Master Tristan have his hair brushed every night before bed?" Sarah asked.

Moira gasped, then clapped her hand over her mouth again, though she couldn't completely muffle her giggling.

With a conspiratorial grin, Sarah said, "I'm happy to have your company, Moira, but I don't have a nightgown or a brush. You're welcome to turn down the bed."

"I've been told that clothing is being brought up for you, miss,"

Moira replied brightly. "That's part of the reason I thought you could go to the baths. I'm sure your things will arrive in the meantime."

While getting cleaned up had appeal, Sarah wasn't keen to be naked and exposed in this strange place just yet. The memory of being stripped and tied down was still too fresh.

"Maybe some hot water and a washcloth for now," Sarah told Moira.

The girl curtsied yet again and scurried from the room, leaving Sarah alone once more. Her gaze strayed to the fireplace. The chimney wasn't going anywhere.

As she waited for Moira to return, Sarah went about inspecting the non-escape-related features of her quarters. The bed was carved of dark wood, clothed and canopied in burgundy velvet. And it was enormous; Sarah thought she was just as likely to drown in it than sleep. In addition to the tapestries, stout wooden chests and tall armoires—all carved as intricately as the bed— huddled against the walls. Sarah opened a few of the chests and found spare bed linens and towels, but when she checked the armoires she discovered they were completely empty.

Continuing her exploration, Sarah was pleased to find that a windowed alcove in the room had been retrofitted with a thick wooden door to offer privacy for a quarter bath.

Medieval castle, yes, but not without modern amenities. Though apparently no showers in the en-suite bathrooms.

"Miss?"

Sarah exited the bathroom at Moira's call. "I'm here, Moira."

Steam rose from a ceramic pitcher in Moira's grasp and she also held a matching bowl. The ridiculousness of the scene made Sarah curse under her breath. Moira could have pointed out that there was a sink with hot and cold running water in the small bathroom, but apparently the young girl had been trained to do exactly what her master or mistress asked, not offer more pragmatic alternatives.

Moira smiled at Sarah. "Where would you like these, miss?"

Sarah couldn't help herself. "Ummm, probably in the bathroom is best."

"Yes, miss." Moira breezed past Sarah into the alcove, oblivious to Sarah's sarcasm.

Someone coughed politely at the still-open door to the room. Sarah was startled to see four women, dressed in servants' uniforms similar to Moira's, carrying armloads of boxes.

"May we put your things away, Your Ladyship?" the woman at the front of the group asked.

Sarah started to object to the unwanted title, but gave up and shrugged. The women trotted into the room with their boxes and began to unpack them with remarkable efficiency.

Moira reappeared from the alcove and clasped her hands in delight. "Oh, good, they've arrived."

Turning to Sarah, Moira said, "Miss, if you want to wash yourself now, I can have your nightclothes laid out for when you've finished."

"*Tsk,* Moira!" One of the other servants narrowed her eyes at the serving girl. "You're to address her as Your Ladyship."

Moira cupped her hands over her mouth and loudly whispered, "She doesn't like it."

"She's right here!" Sarah exclaimed, deciding that this whole charade was likely some new form of interrogation by befuddlement. "And what is all this?"

She pointed to the clothes, some of which were carefully folded and placed inside the once-empty drawers while others were hung in the armoires.

"Master Tristan arranged for you to have proper attire while you're a guest in the castle," Moira told her.

Inching forward to peer at what sort of clothing constituted "proper attire" to her captor, Sarah had to stifle a gasp when she saw the wardrobe that was being put away. The items being hung were gowns. Not dresses, but gowns of silk brocade, chiffon, taffeta, and velvet. Sarah had never worn anything resembling such dresses. Nor was she certain she wanted to. Her eyes moved to the fireplace as she considered the logistics of scaling the chimney in couture.

While her surprise upon seeing the gowns was substantial, the swirl of confusion turned to dread when the servants opened new boxes from which sprung lingerie of the most sensual variety.

Why would I want or need lace and silk bras and panties? And how the hell did they get the right size?

"Does the selection please you?" an unpleasantly familiar voice purred from doorway.

Sarah had to swallow bile at the sight of Lana. The succubus smiled and flapped her wings, making Sarah work hard to tamp down her violent emotions. She knew any distress she felt was akin to spoon-feeding the nether creature.

Straightening her spine, Sarah said to Lana, "This is your work?"

"I was tasked with providing you an appropriate wardrobe," Lana answered, crossing the room to pick through one of the boxes. She lifted a bra of creamy silk and sheer paneling for inspection. "It's all a bit tame, if you ask me, but you struck me as a little meek."

Sarah's chest tightened. "You don't know me very well, then."

"I suppose I don't," Lana replied, dropping the bra into the box. "Would you like me to find some more daring items to add to this collection?"

"I'm sure all of this is fine," Sarah replied. "No. Forget that. It's unnecessary. What is this circus you're subjecting me to?"

Lana's eyebrows shot up. "I'm not subjecting you to anything, lovely. I simply do as my master orders." Her ruby lips curved. "As you will as well . . . soon enough."

That made Sarah shudder, and Lana licked her lips.

"Get out of here." Sarah turned away from the succubus.

"Your pleasure is my command," Lana replied. "Enjoy your new things."

A wave of relief poured over Sarah when Lana was gone, but not only because of that. Sarah felt a bit more at ease knowing that this wardrobe had been put together by the succubus and not specifically requisitioned by Tristan. The lingerie, the gowns—all of it was calculated to exacerbate Sarah's distress for Lana's enjoyment. But that was to be expected from a creature such as Lana, and Sarah could cope with Lana's petty provocations.

Tristan, on the other hand, Sarah needed to handle with cool confidence, to interact with him as normally as possible in order to surmise who he was and what was so important about this castle.

"Are you all right, miss?" Moira was peering at Sarah. The girl's face was noticeably paler.

Sarah nodded, then glanced from Moira to the other women. "But you're all human," Sarah blurted.

Moira glanced around uncomfortably, and seemingly not knowing what else to do, dropped into a teetering curtsy. "Yes, miss."

Trying to recover from her outburst, Sarah stammered, "I just meant, um, what I'm trying to say is, how do you accept the strange creatures who live and work beside you?"

She thrust her finger in the direction in which Lana had just departed. "You did see that she had wings, right? What the hell are you doing here? Any of you?"

"We don't speak of it, miss." Moira's voice dropped low, and she twisted her fingers together anxiously. She cast a quick, worried glance at the other servant women.

Biting back further questions, Sarah nodded and said, "I think I'll wash up now."

"Very good, miss." Moira brightened. "I'll get you a towel and dressing gown."

"Thank you."

Sarah managed to keep herself collected until she closed the bathroom door. Then she pivoted, gripped the basin, and bent her head, trying to sort through her cluttered thoughts. That humans worked as servants in a Keeper household shouldn't have come as a surprise, but Sarah still found it unnerving. It also explained why Castle Tierney operated as if it were still the nineteenth century. The Keepers held human beings in contempt, and while they were happy to manipulate anyone for their benefit, the one thing Keepers would not suffer was the treatment of humans as equals.

Why were Moira and the others here? Had they somehow been persuaded to accept employment at the castle, or had they been coerced into service? Could some of the servants be those men and women, like Ian's wife, who'd gone missing?

The Keepers controlled those who served them through fear and lies, as well as bribes and power plays. If she could figure out how the humans on this island had been co-opted into Keeper service, Sarah might be able to use that to her advantage—possibly even to the point of turning them against their master. It had been done in the past; fear begat submission but not loyalty.

So Castle Tierney was home to humans, Guardians, nether creatures, and a Keeper. But was Tristan the only Keeper who resided within these walls, wondered Sarah, or was he simply the man in charge? In order to find a way out of her prison, Sarah would need to know as much about the castle and its inhabitants as possible. And she'd have to uncover that information while keeping herself alive. At the moment, Tristan wasn't interested in killing her.

Sarah still didn't understand why that was the case, but it was clear that she'd have to make sure the Keeper didn't change his mind.

9

TRISTAN RARELY WENT to the castle's massive kitchens, but he was on his third visit of the day. He could tell it was putting the cook and her staff on edge. They couldn't help stealing nervous glances at one another, as though they expected to receive the bad news that they would soon be reassigned, or worse.

In an attempt to reassure his servants, Tristan kept a pleasant smile on his face as he surveyed the evolving meal for that evening: fresh vegetables being prepped for roasting; fragrant herbs piled into a mortar and pestle; gleaming copper kettles and saucepans arranged on stovetops, waiting to be filled with ingredients.

"Duck, then?" Tristan asked the cook. He'd asked this question twice before.

"Is Your Lordship wanting to change the menu?" The cook frowned. "Does he perhaps prefer venison? Or pheasant?"

"No," Tristan replied with a shake of his head. "Duck is fine. Just stopping by to see how it's all coming together."

"Very well, my lord." With a brusque nod, the cook shooed her staff back to their respective tasks.

Tristan watched them settle into their familiar roles and then retreated from the kitchen, swearing to himself that he wouldn't return. He found his sudden interest in the evening meal's preparation odd. He'd never had complaints about the food at Castle

Tierney. The cook was skilled, and Tristan could request any dish he craved. However, having whatever he pleased, whenever he pleased, had encouraged a sort of apathy to develop within him. He approached the fine cuisine set before him, meals that he often took alone, as yet another duty.

But Tristan wouldn't be dining alone that night. He had a guest.

A prisoner. He corrected his thought, though he did consider Sarah to be something of a guest, despite her captivity. This was all part of the game. Each piece had to be set up and played perfectly, and that included the time Tristan and Sarah would spend sharing meals.

So Tristan had been compelled to descend to the ground floor of the castle and ensure that dinner would be both delicious and impressive. From the exasperation on the kitchen staff's faces, however, Tristan had to admit that his continued presence would hinder, rather than help, the culinary efforts of the day.

Bidding the cook farewell and trying not to notice the relieved sighs he heard at his back, Tristan trudged back up the stairs, wondering what to do with himself. He was restless. Most of his days passed without incident. He read. He rode Ares around the island. Sometimes he climbed the castle towers to gaze at the frothing sea. The hours turned and Tristan simply was.

Now that Sarah was present in the castle, however, Tristan was filled with the compulsion to *do* something. He'd planned for his first encounter with the Searcher to take place over dinner, and he'd given instructions to the castle's servants to let Sarah relax in her room until the evening meal. He'd meant it to be an act of kindness, as he imagined the woman must be exhausted from her ordeal the previous night.

What Tristan hadn't anticipated was how much he'd want to see her. Thoughts of Sarah, speculation about how she'd passed the night and how she'd fared thus far through the day occupied him to the point of distraction.

Given the bent of his thoughts, it probably shouldn't have surprised Tristan as much as it did to find himself standing in front of Fand—the quarters he'd designated as Sarah's. His intention had been to retreat to his study and pass the time with a book, but his feet had led him to Fand instead.

Tristan gazed at the tall oak door for a moment, then knocked. Was he not the master of his own house? If his desire was to see his prisoner, then he would do so at will.

The door opened and Tristan was greeted by a slight serving girl whose eyes went very wide at the sight of him. She curtsied so quickly that she almost fell forward into Tristan's arms.

"How may I serve, my lord?" The girl remained crouched in the lowest part of her curtsy. It looked very uncomfortable.

Tristan searched his mind for the girl's name but couldn't come up with it. He didn't usually interact with the general staff of the castle; his orders were passed along by Owen, Lana, or Seamus.

"Good afternoon . . ." Tristan paused, hoping that somehow the girl's name would miraculously spring into his mind.

"Moira," a voice within the room answered drily. "Her name is Moira."

Moira snapped to attention, her face going chalk white.

Sarah appeared at Moira's shoulder. "Good afternoon, Tristan."

A night of rest and a bath had transformed the Searcher. Not that Tristan hadn't found Sarah striking from the moment he first came upon her—how could he not, given the way she'd been bared and splayed on his bed; now her presence emanated strength and resolve. The frenetic, coiled energy of a captured wild animal that had pervaded her limbs the previous night was gone. She'd plaited her dark hair and was dressed in suede riding breeches and a cashmere sweater of dove gray.

"Stand up, Moira," Sarah murmured to the girl. Moira's eyes flicked nervously from Sarah to Tristan, but when Tristan gave a small nod Moira popped up and backed away to stand alongside Sarah.

Tristan met Sarah's gaze and found her pale green eyes unflinching, ready for a challenge. The sheer grit in her demeanor made Tristan question the wisdom of his desire to give her so much freedom even as she remained his captive. But his curiosity about the Searcher was unrelenting.

It's not as if she won't be watched whenever she moves about the castle, Tristan reassured himself.

Guardians would skulk in the shadows wherever Sarah went, ensuring that any attempt at escape or attack would be instantly quelled. Even knowing that, Tristan was unsettled by the cool determination in the Searcher's expression, but he was equally determined not to reveal his discomfiture.

"You don't bother to learn the names of the people who live here?" Sarah asked.

Tristan ignored her question, looking at Moira instead. "My apologies, Moira. Your name slipped my mind."

Moira looked startled and curtsied again. Sarah let out an exasperated breath.

Returning his attention to the Searcher, Tristan said, "I thought you might like a tour of the castle."

"With you?" Sarah eyed him for a moment, calculating.

"It is my home." Tristan smiled coolly.

"Just you?"

The question startled Tristan, as did the slightly suggestive tone with which she asked it. It only took a moment of staring at her in puzzlement for Tristan to realize she'd been trying to provoke him . . . no, not provoke, test. She was already gauging his words, his reactions, in order to situate herself and take advantage.

This discovery pleased Tristan more than it worried him. If she'd been sullen, he would have doubted the viability of his plans. However, if Sarah approached his challenges as a true competitor, things could prove more than interesting.

"Yes," Tristan answered her. "Just me, more or less. I'm never without Guardians, of course."

Sarah nodded. "Okay. Let's have a tour."

Tristan offered his arm and Sarah balked. He smiled at the sudden break in her confidence.

Recovering, Sarah said tartly, "I can walk without assistance, thank you."

"As you wish." Tristan shrugged.

"Would you like tea when you return, miss?" Moira piped up.

Sarah stiffened a little.

She's not comfortable with this sort of attention, Tristan noticed with a small smile. That was good. He needed to keep her off balance for things to go as he hoped.

"I suppose that would be nice," Sarah answered Moira. "Thank you."

Moira beamed, clearly relieved to have something to do.

"Shall we?" Tristan gestured toward the hall.

Sarah stepped out of the room, and Moira closed the door.

The castle keep was a stout block, constructed with the purpose of repelling enemies. Its walls were thick and its windows were small. Tristan had done his best to imbue the cold stone with some warmth, covering the walls with exquisitely woven tapestries and keeping the halls well lit.

"The castle keep has four levels, including the sublevel where the baths are," Tristan told Sarah as they walked to the middle of the hall. "I spend most of my time here. My quarters are there."

"Yes," Sarah said with a bitter edge. "I'm aware of that."

He offered her an apologetic smile. "All the bedrooms in the castle are named for major figures in Celtic mythology. My rooms are called Cú Chulainn. You're staying in Fand. The two rooms that I combined in a renovation to become a library and study is Ogma."

"Is your heritage Irish?" Sarah asked.

"The castle is Irish," Tristan answered. His ancestry wasn't a topic he felt inclined to discuss. "Would you like to see the study?"

When Sarah nodded, Tristan quickly moved down the hall to the study. He opened the door and stepped back to let Sarah enter first. Only a few steps in she stopped and gasped.

Tristan came to stand alongside her, stealing a glance at her face. What he found in her slightly parted lips and wide eyes was wonder. Tristan felt a sudden tightness in his chest. Though he'd lived in the castle for years, the same fascination and reverence took hold of him anytime he was alone in this room—his favorite of the castle.

Rather than taking down the entire wall that had separated two bedrooms, Tristan had instructed that three archways be cut into the existing stone. The resulting effect gave the larger space a cloisterlike atmosphere. Bookshelves had been built into the walls of the room, stretching from floor to ceiling, with tall ladders on casters giving access to the highest shelves. The only wall spaces not covered with books were the two stone fireplaces, left in their original places in the onetime bedchambers.

"I spend most of my time here," Tristan said quietly as Sarah gazed at the thousands of books Tristan had carefully collected over the years. He'd stocked the library with content in mind to complement his reading preferences—the volumes ranged from seminal works of philosophy to all of Ray Bradbury's works. There were, of course, the other books too. The kind of books that find a home in the library of someone whose life dovetails with the arcane and occult.

Sarah started at the sound of his voice. "I— It's . . . it's lovely." She winced at the insufficient word, but Tristan smiled.

"I'm glad you approve."

Regaining some of her wryness, Sarah said, "I hope you're a reader and this isn't just for show. Not that it isn't a good show."

"I'm a reader." Tristan laughed. "And if you are as well, please feel free to make use of this study whenever you like."

"Okay," Sarah replied with hesitation, but under her breath she said, "I don't know where I'd even begin."

With a slow smile, Tristan said, "Let me help you with that."

Clearly having meant her last words only for herself, Sarah gave Tristan a startled look.

"Your first challenge," Tristan continued, trying not to show his mirth. The idea had been spontaneous. When Tristan had proposed this unusual set of terms for Sarah's captivity, he hadn't fleshed out what his challenges would be, nor did he know how they would play out. But the notion that jumped into his mind while standing with Sarah in his study seemed like the perfect starting move for this game. Gesturing toward the rows upon rows of books, Tristan said, "Find my favorite book."

Sarah scanned the library, then returned her gaze to Tristan, frowning. "One book out of all these? I take it my tasks are modeled after the labors of Hercules."

"I do have stables you could clean," Tristan replied. "I told you these are challenges. The word itself reflects their difficulty."

Her shoulders bunched up with frustration. "How long do I have?"

"I'll give you two days," Tristan said. "Use that time as you see fit to aid you in the task."

"Just to clarify"—Sarah's eyes narrowed—"these challenges in no way offer me freedom?"

"That's correct."

"How many challenges will there be?" Sarah asked. "Ten? Fifty?"

Tristan folded his hands behind his back. "I don't have a specific number in mind."

"Oh, come on. Even Scheherazade got a reprieve after one thousand and one nights," Sarah said lightly, but then frowned. "God, how long is that . . . ?"

"A little under three years," Tristan answered. When Sarah gave him a skeptical glance, he added, "I looked it up once."

"Three years . . ." She gave a little shudder. "Maybe she's not the best example."

"There are only a few ways this can end," Tristan said with a smile. The moment had arrived to show his winning hand.

"Really?" Sarah cast a suspicious glance at him.

"Only three ways, if I'm being truthful," Tristan replied. "The first: you try to kill me, fail, and my Guardians kill you."

"How lovely," Sarah murmured.

"The second," Tristan continued, "you try to escape, fail, and I give you to a wraith."

"And the third?" Sarah asked.

"You grow to like it here," Tristan replied without missing a beat, "and decide to stay."

Sarah's skin took on a chalky pallor. "Excuse me?"

"I'd say it's your best option," Tristan said, offering no reaction to her increasingly anxious expression. "You get to survive."

Backing toward the door, Sarah couldn't hide her panic. "I think I'll pass on the rest of the tour."

"Feel free to explore on your own," Tristan told her. "Everyone in the castle knows you have leave to move about the grounds without harassment—provided you aren't trying to escape."

Sarah nodded mutely, then fled.

When she was out of sight, Tristan wondered if he'd gone too far. He needed Sarah curious, not frightened. At the same time, he also wanted her to understand the gravity of her situation. This castle was his domain, and as such Sarah was subject to his rule. He could be a kind master, or cruel. The choice was hers.

What an adventure this will be. Full of a deep satisfaction he'd never experienced before that moment, Tristan pulled a random volume from one of the shelves. Flipping to the title page, he discovered that fate chanced to give him an 1885 edition of *The Book of a Thousand Nights and a Night*.

Laughing quietly to himself, Tristan settled into a chair and began to read.

10

THE TEA MOIRA prepared proved much more comforting than Sarah had imagined it would be. Steam curled from the porcelain cup as Moira hovered nearby.

"Can I get you anything else, miss? Biscuits. A scone?"

"This is fine, Moira," Sarah replied. "I've been told I'm expected for dinner."

"Yes, miss." Moira went to one of the armoires. "Do you know which gown you'd like to wear?"

Sarah glanced down at the sweater and leggings she was wearing. "What's wrong with this?"

"Nothing, miss." Moira tittered, opening the armoire. "But you'll be expected to dress for dinner."

"And will Tristan be wearing a gown as well?" Sarah asked bitterly.

Moira giggled, and Sarah gave her a pointed look.

"Master Tristan will likely wear a suit to dinner," Moira explained. "That's his custom when he entertains guests."

"I am not a guest!" Sarah set her teacup down with a bit too much force, and its saucer clattered on the silver tray. "I'm a prisoner. Doesn't anyone in this castle understand how different those two things are?"

Inching away from the hanging gowns, Moira ducked her head. "I'm sorry, miss. I didn't mean to upset you."

"Don't apologize, Moira." Sarah rubbed her temples. "I shouldn't have shouted at you. None of this is your fault."

"I'm instructed to give you anything that will make you more comfortable," Moira offered meekly. "You're meant to enjoy your time here, miss."

Sarah had to grit her teeth to keep from snapping at the girl again. Her brief interaction with Tristan had left her deeply unsettled. She wasn't simply a prisoner in this castle; she worried she might be at the mercy of a psychopath.

You grow to like it here and decide to stay.

The mere suggestion of such an outcome was preposterous, but more disturbing had been the smooth confidence with which Tristan had spoken, as if what he'd said was perfectly reasonable.

I'd say it's your best option. You get to survive.

Had he meant it as a threat? Or was it just a twisted joke, a way of telling her that she wouldn't leave the island alive?

Who the hell is he? Why would he ever want me to stay?

"Are you unwell, miss?" Moira asked.

Sarah didn't answer. She had to pull herself together. If Tristan intended a slow, cruel unraveling of her sanity, she couldn't succumb to fear. That he could make her quail even a little infuriated Sarah.

Seizing upon that flare of outrage, Sarah stood up and went to the armoire. She would beat the Keeper at his own game. And then some.

"I'm fine, Moira. Help me find a dress."

⚬⚬

When a knock sounded at the door several hours later, Moira was close to swooning from giddiness.

"Oh, miss, oh, miss. You're so lovely!"

Sarah gave Moira an indulgent smile. For the girl, Sarah's

gown represented a beautiful dream of romance and luxury, but Sarah knew she was about to do battle of a different kind. Silk would simply be her armor this evening.

Moira skipped across the room to answer the door. Sarah couldn't help but wonder if there were any other girls or boys near Moira's age in the castle. The girl had shown such enthusiasm when helping to pick a gown for the evening, Sarah suspected that Moira was starved for female companionship.

"Oh!" Moira's cry yanked Sarah out of her musing and brought her attention to the figure at her bedroom door.

Though she didn't voice her surprise, Sarah had expected Tristan to appear. Instead the Guardian Seamus stepped into the room. He nodded politely at Sarah.

"I'll escort you to dinner now."

Sarah noted that Seamus hadn't made a request, but she offered him a smile. "Of course."

Moira curtsied when Sarah swept past her. "I'll lay your nightgown out and turn the bed down, miss."

"Thank you, Moira."

Seamus walked stiffly and remained silent as they passed through the castle halls, so Sarah took the opportunity to make up for the tour she'd ended so abruptly.

From what she could surmise, only one additional room occupied the castle's uppermost floor beyond those she'd already seen.

They descended a narrow stone staircase until they reached Castle Tierney's ground floor. Sarah hadn't given much thought to how hungry she was until rich scents wafted through the air and made her mouth water.

"The kitchens," Seamus jerked his head toward a door to their right. "The dining hall is this way."

He turned to the left toward a set of double doors. Seamus

pulled one open and gestured for Sarah to enter. She stepped into the dining hall and heard the door shut at her back. The room stretched, long and narrow, the full length of the castle's ground floor.

The dining hall's central feature was a table nearly as long as the hall itself, large enough to seat two dozen people for a feast. This evening, however, only two places had been set: one at the head of the table, the other to the right of the first. The table linens and fine china were the only signs that the room expected guests that evening.

Sarah was alone.

She walked the length of the table, trailing her finger along the mahogany surface, which had been polished to a mirror shine. Flames licked across kindling and logs that had been carefully laid in the fireplace set into the outer wall, casting a warm glow throughout the room.

Sarah heard the door open and turned. Tristan strode into the room but halted abruptly when he saw her standing alongside the table. He'd changed from jeans and a button-down shirt into a dark, slim-cut, three-piece suit. Sarah might have found the look pretentious, but Tristan had neglected to wear a tie, instead leaving his shirt collar open.

While he stood very still, watching her, two thoughts jumped to the fore of Sarah's mind. The first: that she'd picked the perfect dress for her intentions that evening. The silk charmeuse gown draped beautifully over her figure, its bias cut clinging to her curves. The midnight blue of the fabric highlighted the contrast of her dark hair and pale skin.

And Tristan couldn't take his eyes off her.

The second thought battling for her attention was that, once again, Sarah had become captivated by how strikingly beautiful

Tristan was. Lean and tall, he exuded a strength that was graceful rather than brutish. The firelight emphasized the golden undertones of his skin and the honeyed shade of his light-brown hair. His gaze was riveted on Sarah, and she observed the clench of his jaw, the tension in his lips.

Rather than greet him, Sarah turned away and was rewarded by the sound of his sharp intake of breath when he met with the sight of bare skin revealed by her backless gown. Sarah preferred to wage war with her daggers, but in this place her blades weren't an option and her adversary had elected to meet her on a different field of engagement. She'd never used seduction as means to an end, but with little else to draw upon Sarah had determined it was her best path to freedom. Tristan was a Keeper, but at the end of the day he was also still a man.

As Sarah moved toward the high-backed chair she presumed was intended for her, she heard Tristan approaching. He breezed past her, pulling out the chair so she could sit. When she'd settled at her place, Tristan took his own seat at the head of the long table.

Sarah sat quietly, her eyes fixed on the bob and weave of the flames, but she felt Tristan's gaze resting upon her.

After a long minute, he said, "You look lovely."

She turned to him, offering a hard-edged smile. "You should thank your succubus for that. I understand she procured my entire wardrobe."

Tristan cleared his throat, shifting uneasily in his chair. "I should have already offered you an apology for Lana's poor choices regarding your treatment. It was appalling."

"So you don't like to find women tied up on your bed?" Sarah asked archly. "What a relief. I'm completely reassured that you're the consummate gentleman."

"I—"

Sarah cut him off. "You seem intent on keeping me to your-self." She gestured to the two lonely place settings at the long ta-ble. "Will I ever be introduced to the rest of your household? Or do you have a 'finders keepers' rule when it comes to prisoners?"

"The rest of my household?" Tristan frowned at her. "You want to meet the Guardians?"

"Not your servants," Sarah replied. "The other Keepers who live here."

"The other—" Tristan blanched, obviously taken aback. "There are no others."

Sarah stared at him, searching for clues in his expression that he was lying. She could find none.

"But this castle . . ." She might not have finished her tour, but there was no denying that Castle Tierney was far too large to be one man's home, not to mention too heavily guarded if truly only one Keeper resided there.

She was denied Tristan's reply when a bevy of servants entered the room. One poured wine while the others placed the first course in front of Sarah and Tristan. Troubled by the short ex-change, Sarah dropped her gaze so she could sort through her thoughts. She felt a twinge of pity for him that she quickly shrugged away. Sarah needed to regard Tristan with nothing but wariness and disdain. She also couldn't forget the way he'd looked at her when he first entered the dining hall. She'd thought his expression had been appreciative and lustful, but now that she considered it, she realized there had been a shadowed quality to his gaze, one that bespoke loneliness.

Loneliness that Sarah could use to her advantage.

When the servants left them to the first course, Sarah raised her wineglass. "To the game."

With a half smile, Tristan lifted his own glass. "To the game."

The wine was exquisite, and when Sarah sampled the steaming

bowl of fish chowder in front of her, she found its delicate seasoning utterly scrumptious.

"You have a talented chef," Sarah said, taking another sip of wine. She didn't add, *It's a shame he or she cooks only for one.*

"Very," Tristan replied, his eyes brightening in relief at the change in subject.

"About this challenge," Sarah began.

Tristan smiled. "Yes?"

"Am I expected to blindly seek your favorite book?" she asked. "Or may I ask you questions to help me with the task?"

"You can ask questions," Tristan replied. "Just not about books."

With a quiet laugh, Sarah said, "Fair enough."

They ate in silence for a few minutes, then Sarah set her spoon aside. "How long have you lived here?"

Tristan hesitated, but then answered, "Since I was eighteen."

"Why eighteen?"

"That was when my parents died." Tristan looked away from her and into the flames of the fireplace.

Tensing, Sarah ventured quietly, "Were they killed in the war?"

"No." A thin smile crossed Tristan's mouth, but he didn't look at Sarah. "They simply reached the end of their time."

Sarah traced the base of her wineglass with her finger. Tristan had just touched on a subject of which Searchers were aware, but understood little. Keepers lived far beyond a normal human life expectancy—courtesy of their overlord, Bosque Mar—but why and at what point that extension of life was cut off remained largely a mystery.

"How old are you now?" Sarah asked. Her gaze lingered on his unlined face, but Tristan's youthful looks meant nothing. He could be more than a century old and still look like this if his master willed it.

Tristan swirled the wine in his glass. "I'm twenty-five."

"Are you really twenty-five?" Sarah pressed. "Or do you just *look* twenty-five?"

"You think I'm lying about my age?" Tristan asked, his tone playful.

Sarah tried to ignore how amiable he seemed whenever his mood lightened. "I think you easily could, and I'd have no way of knowing."

"That's true." Tristan nodded. "But I'm not. I was born twenty-five years ago."

"So you've been in this castle for seven years," Sarah mused. "Always alone?"

Tristan winced and took another swallow of wine. "Not alone, exactly. But the only Keeper, yes."

When he caught Sarah's eye, he added, "I have visitors."

"I'm sure," Sarah replied. "And you have captives."

"No," Tristan said. "You are the first captive of this castle. At least since I've been in residence."

Servants reappeared to clear away the first course, refill their wineglasses, and serve up the second course.

"I hope you like duck," Tristan said, toying with his fork as the plates were set before them.

Sarah frowned at him, surprised by the nervous edge in his words. Did he actually care what she thought of the meal?

Meeting Tristan's anxious glance, Sarah realized that he did. That knowledge should have made her gloat, since it signaled another means by which she'd be able to exploit her captor's emotions. But her new awareness of Tristan's vacillating moods made Sarah uneasy rather than smug. However he attempted to exert control over her and convey his dominion over this place, Sarah could see that he was also vulnerable.

Watching the flurry of thoughts register on Sarah's face, Tristan sighed. "You don't like duck."

"No," Sarah blurted. "I mean, yes. I mean—duck is fine. I'm not a fussy eater."

When Tristan still looked uncertain, Sarah quickly cut herself a small bite of the sliced duck breast. Genuinely pleased by the meat's rich flavor, Sarah smiled at Tristan. "It's delicious."

The stiffness eased from Tristan's shoulders. "I'm glad."

They fell into a quiet enjoyment of their meal, though Sarah remained distracted by the contradictions presented by both this castle and her captor. If no other Keepers resided here, and yet a pack of Guardians as well as nether creatures had been deemed necessary defenses on the island, then the intelligence that sent Sarah on this mission had proven accurate. Something about this place was of great value to Bosque Mar and the Keepers.

But what was it?

Sarah was also distracted by the dissonance of giving a Keeper as young as Tristan charge of a castle that held something of such import. Most of the Searchers' skirmishes with Guardians took place near the four sacred sites within which pieces of the Elemental Cross rested. The Keepers who secured those sites around the globe were always among the eldest of their kind. Not only was Castle Tierney nowhere near any of those sites, but Tristan was also close to a century younger than his counterparts in similarly authoritative roles.

It didn't add up.

"How old are you?" Tristan's question broke the silence of the room so abruptly that Sarah dropped her knife.

"I'm sorry?"

"You asked me my age," Tristan replied. "I'm simply returning the favor."

"I'm twenty-one," Sarah answered.

"Isn't that a bit young to be scaling castle walls without backup?" Tristan asked.

Sarah stirred in her chair, uncomfortable that his line of thinking so closely mirrored her own.

"I believe our agreement was that I don't have to answer your questions unless I lose a challenge," she dodged.

"That's true." Tristan nodded, though his eyes were disappointed.

Not willing to give ground, Sarah added, "And I have two days to name your favorite book."

Tristan smiled. "Care to venture any guesses yet?"

"How about 'The Pit and the Pendulum'?" Sarah answered, but regretted provoking Tristan when he flinched.

Tristan's voice was flat when he said, "That's actually a short story."

"That actually was a joke," Sarah replied.

"I don't want to hurt you, Sarah," Tristan said quickly and very quietly. "I don't want you to be afraid of me."

Those words, so unexpected, made Sarah grip the edge of the table. He sounded so sincere, but he couldn't possibly be. How could she not fear him?

Having no clue how to respond, Sarah focused on finishing her meal despite the uncomfortable weight of silence in the room. Even after plates from their main course had been cleared and a dessert of fresh fruit and artisanal cheeses was offered, neither Tristan nor Sarah had ventured another word.

Without warning, Tristan pushed his chair back and rose. "If you'll excuse me, I have some business to attend to. Good night."

Sarah had no time to respond as Tristan swiftly crossed to the door and was gone, leaving Sarah to sit alone, utterly perplexed. By all appearances, she'd achieved her aim for the evening—to throw Tristan off balance and thereby gain an advantage. But Sarah didn't feel triumphant, only confused.

Castle Tierney and its master remained a puzzle to be solved, but Sarah had a nagging suspicion that the solving could prove treacherous in ways she'd never expected.

11

TRISTAN DIDN'T KNOW he was heading for the stables until he reached them. All he'd known was that he needed to get out of that room and away from Sarah and that any delay would mean disaster. He went to the tack room and grabbed Ares's bridle, then headed for the horse's stall.

Scenting his master, Ares bellowed and knocked at the stall door with his iron-clad hoof.

"Easy, lad," Tristan said. "You'll be out of there soon enough."

Tristan slipped into the stall and bridled the stallion. He shed his jacket and vest, tossing them onto the stall floor without a second thought.

Once he'd led Ares through the stable and into the castle courtyard, he swung up onto the stallion's back. Gripping Ares's mane in his fist, Tristan lightly touched his heels to the stallion's flank. For a moment the great horse's muscles bunched up and then he exploded forward.

Though he knew it was risky, Tristan didn't bother to check Ares's stride, instead letting the stallion have his head as they plunged into the night.

At least there's a bit of moonlight to guide us, Tristan thought. Galloping at this breakneck pace after dark was foolhardy for both the horse and his rider, but Tristan needed to burn away the turmoil that felt like poison in his veins.

I don't want to hurt you, Sarah. I don't want you to be afraid of me.

The wind carried away Tristan's string of curses.

Why in the bloody hell had he said those things to her?

In truth, the problem wasn't that he'd said them. The problem was that he'd meant them.

When Tristan arrived at the dining hall, he'd felt he had the situation well in hand. Sarah had fled the library earlier that day confused and wary—exactly the way he wanted her. But the sight of her at dinner, the way the firelight played on her porcelain skin when she turned to reveal the open back of her gown, had made his entire body tighten.

Their conversation had only made things worse. All signs of Sarah's discomfiture had vanished, while Tristan found himself fumbling for confidence. It wasn't simply her beauty that stole his wits. Her very presence radiated something Tristan hadn't known he'd been longing for until he was face-to-face with it.

Companionship.

Sarah was the only person he'd spoken with in seven years who hadn't been sent to "befriend" him on Bosque Mar's orders.

She's not here because she likes you, you idiot, Tristan reminded himself. *She's a prisoner. She's* your *prisoner.*

But anytime Sarah had raised that point over dinner, Tristan felt as if she'd plunged a blade into his belly and was slowly twisting it.

That was when he realized he wanted her to be there voluntarily. He wanted Sarah to choose to be with him. What he'd described to Lana as a means of trickery—a cruel ploy intended to make Sarah divulge the information Tristan needed—had in the space of hours become something he desperately hoped for. The madness of that desire nearly undid him.

So he'd fled, not knowing what else to do in that moment of panic.

Tristan leaned into Ares's neck, letting the stallion take them where the horse willed. Closing his eyes, Tristan lost himself in the rhythm of Ares's hoof strikes on the moors, the scream of the wind around them. He straightened only when Ares slowed to a trot and then a walk. The shrieking wind died, replaced by the crash of surf.

Ares had run the length of the island; now his hooves sunk into the sand of the only shoreline not made treacherous by rocks. Steam rose from the stallion's coat, his neck bowed with exhaustion. Tristan sucked in deep breaths of the salt air, letting its cool yet pungent flavor still his rioting spirit.

Tristan had to suddenly grasp Ares's mane and grip the stallion's sides with his thighs when the horse tossed his head and shied. Ares gave a sharp whistle of alarm and began to prance along the shore. Familiar enough with the stallion's behavior to know the cause of Ares's fear Tristan called out, "Change forms and get over here!"

From within the shadows of a copse of trees a wolf slunk into the moonlight.

Ares snorted and pawed the sand, even after the wolf was gone and a man walked toward them. Guardians could change their shape, but they still smelled enough like wolves to frighten some of the horses.

Tristan jumped down from Ares's back and flipped the reins over the stallion's head. If he gave the horse a few feet of space from the approaching wolf, Ares wouldn't bolt. Probably.

"Seamus," Tristan greeted the pack leader.

Seamus nodded, scratching at the rough whiskers on his chin. "You know I don't like it when you disappear."

"I don't think I could ever really disappear on your watch," Tristan replied. "Don't try to tell me you weren't keeping an eye on things all night."

"It's my job." Seamus shrugged. "Even so, you could have broken your horse's leg or your own neck riding like a *dullahan* in this dark."

"There's a moon," Tristan argued.

"Barely." Seamus glanced at the dimly lit sky. "Can I ask what happened? If something's wrong, you know I can deal with it."

Tristan rolled his shoulders, uneasy at the thought of any Guardians "dealing" with Sarah.

"It's not that kind of problem."

Seamus fell silent, then coughed uneasily. "Might you tell me what kind of problem it is?"

Tristan regarded Seamus. Could he confess his troubles to the wolf?

Of all his servants, Seamus was the one he most trusted and was the closest to offering a real friendship despite their respective stations.

"I'm unsure what to do with the girl," Tristan said haltingly. "My sense of who she is has become . . . complicated."

Seamus nodded thoughtfully. "Because you want to fuck her."

"That's not—" Tristan gripped the reins tighter.

"You don't want to fuck her, then?" Seamus cut him off.

The moonlight was just bright enough for Tristan to catch the curve of the wolf's lips. The damnable Guardian was goading him into a confession. And it was working.

Looking out at the waves, Tristan let himself admit, "Yes. But it's more than that."

"It's more than that because you could fuck her now, but she'd hate you for it," Seamus continued for Tristan. "And rightly so, if you'll pardon me. But you don't want her to hate you."

"You should be a fox, not a wolf," Tristan said. "How did you manage to put all that together? I haven't been able to get there myself."

"That's because your head's too full of what you think you should be doing to see clearly what you want," Seamus answered. "And Guardians serve, but we also watch. I've been watching for a long, long time now. Things are clear to me faster than for most. Particularly in the case of pups like you."

"Did you just call me a pup?" Tristan gave Seamus a sharp look.

The grin Seamus answered him with was so wolfish, Tristan gave a little shudder.

Feeling the urge to defend himself, Tristan said, "I may not be as old as my fellows, but I'm still the master of this castle."

"I never said you weren't," Seamus replied. "And that makes it all the more true that you have the power to do as you wish. But first you have to know what your wishes are. Lana and Owen will try to make those decisions for you. Stop letting them."

"I didn't let Lana persuade me into violating Sarah," Tristan objected.

Seamus nodded. "And that was a good first step. But it was only one."

Tristan suddenly felt exhausted. His shoulders slumped and he looked at Seamus, not knowing what he hoped the wolf would say. Tristan was taken aback by the genuine concern in the Guardian's eyes.

"You've always been too hard on yourself." Seamus looked away and kicked at the sand. "Just because others will try to make choices for you, it doesn't mean you can't ever make your own."

"Except when it comes to Bosque," Tristan said quietly. "If he gives me orders about Sarah . . ."

"Don't borrow trouble before it's on your doorstep," Seamus told him. "If you want the girl, then win her. If she's come around to your way of thinking by the time Lord Mar returns, you'll have a good bargaining chip to use."

Tristan nodded slowly. "Yes. Yes, that's true."

"Wolves don't lie." Seamus growled, but it was a playful sound. "If you don't mind, I'd be grateful for your return to the castle. Though there's no need to run that beast of yours into the ground this time."

"I'll keep it to a canter." Tristan smiled ruefully. "Ares and I are both exhausted from the run out here."

"And I'll try to keep enough distance so your horse doesn't spook," Seamus said. He walked off the beach, not shifting forms until he was half hidden by darkness.

Tristan's mind still churned with ideas, their source no longer fear but possibility, as he gently tugged on the reins and beckoned Ares to approach. Ares remained a bit skittish after Seamus's departure, but stopped prancing long enough for Tristan to mount. He turned the stallion away from the shore and set off at an easy, rolling gait toward Castle Tierney. Toward a different sort of challenge from the one he'd first set out to overcome.

12

SARAH DISMISSED THE idea of sleep as she climbed the staircase to the upper floor of the castle. Her body remained taut even though it had been nearly an hour since Tristan's abrupt departure. She hadn't waited for anyone to collect her from the dining room.

When she reached the top floor, Sarah paused, weighing her options. She could return to her room. Given that dinner had ended so suddenly, Sarah wouldn't have been at all surprised to find Moira still awake. Perhaps Sarah could share a cup of tea with the girl and learn more about how she came to serve at Castle Tierney.

Sarah quickly abandoned that idea. As much as such a conversation would be useful, Sarah knew she was far too distracted to pursue it. Instead, she went to the library—for within the book-filled rooms lay the most likely salve for her mind's current ailment: the solution to Tristan's first challenge.

She stood at the door for a moment, letting the tips of her fingers rest against the carved wood. Tristan would likely be inside. Since he'd told Sarah that the study was his favorite place in the castle, it only made sense that he'd seek refuge there.

Does that make me cruel for not giving him respite? He obviously wanted to get away from me.

Sarah quickly curbed that thought, reminding herself that

Tristan's feelings were no concern of hers. She also ignored the nagging unhappiness that he seemed so desperate to part ways. Resolved, she opened the door, ignoring the sudden uptick of her pulse and hating the twinge of disappointment she felt upon finding she had the spacious rooms to herself.

After she'd taken a leisurely turn through both rooms, Sarah paused to gaze at the floor-to-ceiling shelves. Tristan had designed the task to either be impossible or to nudge her a bit closer to the edge of insanity. Thinking about how ridiculous the challenge was could only work against her, so Sarah decided to bury any thoughts of the end goal. Instead she tried to start by browsing the shelves, hoping she would at least glean a bit of enjoyment from exploring the library.

The books at least appeared to be shelved according to subject, then alphabetized by author, giving Sarah the chance to do a quick survey of the whole library to gain a sense of the types of books Tristan had collected. She quickly noted a predominance of philosophy, with a particular strength in the works of medieval and early modern scholars. Perusing the volumes further, Sarah discovered a large section of the library dedicated to cartography. She found atlases from the ancient world and nautical charts from the Age of Exploration. Near the cartographic collection were volumes on art history, then a variety of books focused on natural history—including an original edition of John James Audubon's *The Birds of America*.

Next came history, and Tristan's interest in the subject appeared wide-ranging. Texts from the nineteenth century appeared, as well as the latest publications from renowned university presses. The books covered every era and every corner of the globe. Though Sarah could appreciate the depth and breadth of the collection, she had a hard time imagining anyone's favorite book being a history text.

When she came upon her first shelf of fiction, Sarah felt a surge of anticipation. Surely Tristan's favorite book would be a novel—though she noted several shelves filled with poetry, particularly the works of Irish poets, that gave her pause. Given that the castle's chambers were named after figures from Irish mythology, perhaps Tristan had an affinity for the literature of his homeland.

Once she had a vague sense of the library's holdings, Sarah puzzled over her next step. Should she narrow options by title, making her best guess about what Tristan would be drawn to in a narrative?

She scanned some of the possibilities: a political thriller à la John le Carré, an Agatha Christie murder mystery, a saga like *Beowulf*, or perhaps a classic of Irish literature—something from James Joyce's oeuvre.

Sarah ground her teeth in frustration. Guessing which of these books was Tristan's favorite made her feel like she was groping around helplessly in a pitch-black room. She peered more closely at some of the book spines. Maybe she could discern what books had the most wear, and thus had likely been read the most times.

It didn't take long for Sarah to dismiss that strategy. The age of the books varied too widely, making it nearly impossible to differentiate between books that had been taken from the shelves and read frequently and those that were simply, well, old. Her head began to ache.

Though Sarah told herself she hadn't given up yet, she decided to take a break. Returning to the part of the library that Tristan used as a study, Sarah dropped into a leather club chair. Exhaustion spread through her limbs, but her mind remained far too frazzled for Sarah to believe she'd be able to sleep. Her gaze wandered to the polished wooden bar near the fireplace.

Maybe a nightcap would help.

Sarah poured herself a brandy from one of several crystal de-canters on the bar. She settled against the soft leather of the chair and sipped her drink. After a few swallows, Sarah roused herself for another stab at finding Tristan's favorite book. She set the glass on the accent table beside the chair . . . and noticed the book that had been left there.

Like so many of the other volumes in Tristan's collection, this book was old and likely of great value. Sarah flipped the pages until she reached the title page: *The Book of a Thousand Nights and a Night,* published in 1885.

Sarah spent several minutes gazing at the title. It couldn't be that simple, could it? She recalled one of her favorite short stories by Edgar Allan Poe, "The Purloined Letter," in which the detective solved the crime by pointing out to his more hapless peers that the best means for hiding something was to leave it in plain sight.

Had Tristan pulled this book from the shelves, leaving it in the open for Sarah to find? Was this yet another means for him to toy with her?

Her gut told her this wasn't the right book; its presence was too precious for serendipity. But finding it nudged her thoughts in a new direction.

Why would Tristan shelve his most-loved book alongside all the others? A favorite book was one returned to again and again. It belonged near the reader, not hidden within the library stacks.

Sarah pushed herself up from the chair and strode out of the library. When she reached Tristan's bedroom door, she paused. Steeling herself, Sarah lifted her hand and rapped sharply on the door.

No answer.

She knocked again and was met with silence once more. Ten-tatively, she reached for the doorknob and was surprised to find it unlocked.

He rules this castle and lives here alone, Sarah reminded herself. *Why would he need to lock his door?* Her arrival obviously hadn't rattled his sense of security one bit.

Tristan's bedroom had been turned down in anticipation of his arrival. The chamber was softly illuminated by a bedside lamp and well-banked fire. Ignoring her sudden urge to snoop through Tristan's things, Sarah crossed quickly to the bedside table.

She'd opened its single drawer only a crack when the sound of the door opening turned her around.

"What are you doing here?"

Tristan stood in the doorway, his tall figure framed by the brighter light of the hallway. His crumpled coat and vest hung from the crook of his arm. Tossing both aside, he crossed the room in a few long strides and grabbed Sarah's wrists.

Sarah lifted her chin, defiant. "Solving your riddle."

He didn't fight her when she pulled her right arm free. Reaching for the drawer, she opened it and drew out the book that rested within, just as she'd hoped—though she was surprised at how small and light the book was; she'd been expecting a much stouter novel.

Tristan didn't let Sarah go; instead, he drew her closer. "Well played."

Sarah's nose crinkled up. He smelled of sweat and hay—not an unpleasant scent, but also not one she'd expected.

"I went for a ride." Tristan laughed softly at her scrunched face.

"Do you often go riding in the middle of the night?" Sarah asked. Tristan's grip on her wrist loosened, but Sarah didn't pull away. She didn't want to.

"I try not to make a habit of it," Tristan answered. "I apologize for leaving dinner so abruptly."

"No worries." Sarah smiled. "It gave me a chance to visit the library, and while it's a lovely collection, no one keeps their favorite book so far out of reach."

Tristan returned her smile. His fingers moved along the inside of her wrist. It was a whisper of a caress, but Sarah had to fight off a thrilling shiver from that light touch.

What the hell? She quickly raised the book between them to distract herself.

"So what is the winning book?" She glanced at the cover. "Seriously?"

"What's wrong with my book?" Tristan asked, sounding rather injured.

"Nothing," Sarah told him, still eyeing the book with disbelief. "It's just . . . unexpected. *The Tale of Peter Rabbit*?"

"That was a gift on my fourth birthday—it was the first book I read on my own," Tristan said, still defensive. "And if you look again, you'll find there's another book in the drawer."

With her free hand Sarah reached into the drawer and drew out a much thicker book. "*The Count of Monte Cristo*. Why these two?"

Tristan released her arm and took a step back. "You found the book—or rather, books. Congratulations. You don't have to answer any of my questions tonight, but this challenge is done."

"Hang on." Sarah frowned. "I won this round. Answer *my* question."

"No." Tristan squared his shoulders.

Sarah knew he was attempting to intimidate her, but she refused to back down. "You want me to keep playing this game of yours, then you need to give me an incentive. You've made it clear that my freedom isn't in play."

"I've promised not to resort to less pleasant modes of interrogation," Tristan countered, though she noted the way his gaze shifted away from her, uneasy.

"Am I going to stay here, then, in your castle, and be subjected constantly to one-sided conversations?" Sarah glared at him. "You asked me to find your favorite book. I did. Now you won't tell me how it is that Beatrix Potter and Alexandre Dumas won that honor?"

Tristan's jaw clenched, but Sarah's gaze was unrelenting. "Why are they your favorites?"

"Because they both manage to escape." When Sarah didn't say anything, Tristan added, "I mean Peter and Edmond."

"I know who you mean," Sarah said quietly.

They both manage to escape.

Tristan had uttered the words as if they were a terrible confession. Sarah considered his uneasy stance, the way he no longer could meet her eyes.

"Thank you," Sarah murmured. "Since I'm the intruder here, I should bid you good night."

Tristan nodded but kept his gaze averted. Sarah sidled past him and moved quietly toward the door.

"Sarah."

She half-turned, looking at Tristan.

"Tell me what your favorite book is."

"I will," Sarah answered. "When you win."

13

SARAH CRAWLED INTO bed and tried to recall how much she'd enjoyed Jeremy's touch. His skilled hands had never failed to make her crave more of him. His soft, teasing kisses had always left her restless with desire.

And the night before she'd come on this crazy mission, Sarah had fully intended to fuck the hell out of Jeremy. She hadn't stopped him because she'd changed her mind about wanting to sleep with him, knowing it would not only be their first time, but Sarah's first time altogether.

I love you, Sarah.

Even now, the memory of Jeremy whispering those words tossed an icy bucket of water on any embers of lust that Sarah had managed to keep smoldering.

What the fuck is wrong with me?

Jeremy's words had to be exactly what a person should want to hear from a lover, particularly when giving up one's virginity to the person who's said it.

But not when you don't love them back.

She'd been in bed less than five minutes, but Sarah threw back the covers and jumped up. She was much too restless to sleep. Restless and frustrated.

After weeks of messing around with Jeremy, feeling comfortable with the idea that their casual relationship would eventually develop into something more, Sarah had utterly freaked when Jeremy tried to make that happen.

But that wasn't the worst of it. She'd barely begun her stay at Castle Tierney and . . .

No, not "stay." Sarah interrupted her own line of thought to correct herself. *I'm a prisoner here.*

And yet she couldn't get Tristan out of her mind. He'd barely touched her, and she was ready to tackle him in the hall and tear his clothes off. Sarah didn't think she'd care that much if the Guardians, Lana, and Owen all saw her do it. Hell, maybe she'd even get off on that.

Again, Sarah mentally smacked herself. *What the* fuck *is wrong with me?*

Leaving her silk chemise in a crumpled heap beside the bed, Sarah dressed and quietly left her room. If Jeremy couldn't force Tristan out of her mind, maybe the mission could. It was the only reason she was still there, after all.

Yeah. Keep telling yourself that.

Sarah batted away the thought and moved quietly down the hall, intent on searching the castle until she found something that would reveal why its secrecy remained so important to the Keepers.

She passed by the study, dismissing it as a potential target of her hunt. After winning the first challenge, Sarah felt confident that whatever was hidden behind these stone walls wasn't in the study.

Knowing she wouldn't be able to finish the search in a single night, Sarah settled on a divide-and-conquer approach. She crept down the stairs until she reached the bowels of the castle. It seemed unlikely that the baths would be the hiding place of any great secrets, but Sarah thought it just as unlikely that a stone fortress would relegate its deepest recesses to bathing facilities alone.

Sarah passed by the doors to the pristine swimming pool and steaming baths, sparing only a cursory glance at the whimsical yet disturbing depiction of sea life that ranged from sea horses to mermaids to the monstrous kraken. Walking the length of the wall that sealed the baths off from the open space at the bottom of the stairs, Sarah soon ran into a dead end. She frowned and turned in a slow circle to survey the seemingly empty chamber that served as an entryway to the baths.

At first glance it looked as though the plain stone walls had been deemed serviceable enough and left in their original state, while all decorative art and design had been allocated to the baths. Sarah slowly followed the perimeter of the room, eyeing the walls as she walked. After one pass, she still saw nothing out of order.

Despite a spike of irritation at coming up empty-handed, Sarah forced herself to make a second survey of the blank walls. Without tapestries or paintings to cover them, the stone walls struck her as bleak. She shivered, thinking of how oppressive the structure would be if none of the castle bore colorful coverings to hide its true nature.

It's all a disguise, isn't it? Sarah ran her fingers along the rough stones. *Opulence designed to hide the brutish reality of this place.*

Sarah had nearly completed her second turn around the chamber when her fingers slipped into a crevice between two stones. Startled, she snatched her fingers back as if something in the small space might have bitten them off had she not moved quickly enough.

The dark pocket in the wall was barely noticeable, particularly where it was—at shoulder height rather than in a direct line of sight, and half-hidden in the shadow of the rising staircase that was built into that particular wall. Though her stomach clenched, Sarah forced herself to reach back into the crevice. She flinched when her fingers met something cold. Once she'd overpowered the instinct to recoil, Sarah felt around the object.

It was metal. A lever?

The pocket in the stone was so small, Sarah could only twist her hand to curl one finger around it. But one finger was enough; she pulled the lever.

The grinding of stones against the floor made Sarah jump back. The wall had retreated beneath the staircase, revealing a shadowed opening just large enough for a person to fit through. Sarah's pulse drummed in her veins, too fast and loud for her liking, but she ducked into the gap.

The hole opened into a narrow passageway lit by dim, oily light that was a horrible yellow shade, far too similar to bile, which was also the awful scent that filled the cramped space. Sarah examined one of the lamps, held in the wall by iron sconces that appeared at regular intervals in the corridor. The glass globes contained a viscous substance, the surface of which was alight with flame. Whatever the stuff was, it seemed to be the source of the foul odor.

Sarah had to stop and steady her breathing. The noxious scent of the burning ooze tried to force the contents of her stomach up her esophagus.

Hold it together.

She put her hand against the wall and waited for the wave of nausea to pass. When it did, Sarah opened her eyes and continued down the hall. The passageway sloped downward, taking her deeper beneath what she'd been told was the lowest level of the castle.

When the floor leveled out, Sarah found herself standing in front of a door. Unlike most of the doors she'd seen in Castle Tierney, which were ornately carved and polished until gleaming, this door was built of heavy wood planks and banded with iron.

Sarah reached for the iron handle, and found it so cold she almost thought it would burn her skin.

The door was locked.

Shit.

Picking a lock would have been no problem for Sarah, but those tools had been taken from her, along with her weapons.

"You shouldn't be down here."

Sarah's training kicked in and prevented her from screaming, but her heart still tried to punch through her breastbone. Seamus stood a few feet behind her.

Damn wolves and their silent paws.

The old Guardian's expression wasn't menacing; instead he looked oddly sad and disappointed.

"I'll take you back upstairs."

Sarah couldn't fight Seamus, but she had a strange suspicion that she might be able to negotiate with him.

"I'm going through this door," she said.

Seamus's grunt sounded a bit like laughter. "You have a key?"

"No," Sarah answered. "But you do." She met Seamus's steady gaze without flinching.

"You won't like what you see in there," he said.

"I don't usually like what there is to be seen in a dungeon," Sarah told him. "But since I'm going in with low expectations, I don't think I'll be that disappointed."

Seamus shrugged and pushed past her. A little charge of confidence passed through Sarah. She hadn't been certain that the locked door led to a dungeon. It could have been a storage room, hiding dangerous or valuable possessions, or a secret passage out of the castle. But Seamus's response confirmed that Sarah's first guess had been correct.

What Sarah still wasn't sure of was why Seamus was opening the door for her, and neither could she pinpoint why she'd had a hunch that he would. Something about this wolf was different from most Guardians. He carried a weariness with him that bespoke sorrow, and he treated Sarah with respect that most prison guards wouldn't afford their wards.

Seamus pushed the door open, and its weight groaned as it swung forward. A rush of fetid air filled the passage, and Sarah dropped to her knees, retching.

The cold of the hall mingled with an awful heat that had been trapped behind the heavy door. And along with that heat came unbearable odors. Rot, sweat, urine, feces—all of it mixing together in a cloud of fear and despair.

When Sarah's choking had become dry heaves, Seamus said, "I can close the door again."

She was tempted to nod. To nod and then run. But Sarah forced herself to stand.

Wiping her mouth, she shook her head and walked past the Guardian into the dungeon.

This dungeon hadn't been designed as a place to hold prisoners. It was clearly a den of torment. The room's walls curved in a broad circle and featured a vaulted ceiling that could have been beautiful if not for the macabre array of devices dangling from its stone arches and lining its circumference.

With each blink Sarah saw something she wished she could unsee. A crow's cage that was home to a pile of bones. A chain that ended in manacles from which a rotting corpse still hung. Another chain that ended in a silver meat hook. An iron maiden that was closed and that Sarah hoped to God she would never see opened. A cauldron large enough to hold three men.

A wheel. And oh God. The wheel held a body that wasn't rotting.

Though her body wanted to collapse into a shivering heap, Sarah forced herself to cross the room to the still figure.

The woman's face was covered by her long, thick hair. Sarah reached down and took the woman's wrist between her fingers.

No pulse.

Sarah hated herself a little for being relieved.

"She died last night."

Sarah snapped up but didn't turn around. It hadn't been Seamus who spoke.

"It's a shame." Lana's voice was closer now. "I was hoping she would last."

Slowly pivoting to face the succubus, Sarah asked, "Who were these people?"

"Lost little lambs." Lana's wings curled around her body like a dark cloak.

With a soft growl, Seamus came forward to stand beside Lana, but he spoke to Sarah. "The waters around this island are treacherous. Ships run aground. Fishermen. Sailors."

Sarah glanced at the dead woman. *That could be Ian's wife.* She didn't look at the skeleton or the rotting cadaver, knowing they could be Ian's wife too.

"Anyone who comes ashore without permission cannot be allowed to leave." Seamus sounded apologetic. "Bosque Mar ordered it so."

With a laugh that tinkled like breaking glass, Lana said to him, "Don't be silly, old dog. We could send them away with a pretty story and a warning."

Turning to Sarah with a smile that was wide and wet, Lana continued. "But we have to eat."

Lana might as well have shoved her hand in Sarah's gut, twisting her intestines, for the sudden pain and sickness she felt. She wobbled from the dizziness and reached out to steady herself but ended up grasping the dead woman's arm. This time, Sarah couldn't stop herself from screaming.

"Lana!" Seamus gave a warning snarl.

"It's just a little snack," Lana purred at him. "It won't hurt her. Besides, this one needs a lesson."

Lana came close to Sarah, grabbing her upper arms to hold her steady.

"Whatever compelled you to wander into the belly of the beast?" Lana's breath was sweet as roses and rain, but with a cloying edge. "They say that curiosity killed the cat, but if you think we treat kittens differently, I'll show you how wrong you are."

The succubus tilted her head, her gaze sweeping over Sarah, assessing. "How deeply does your sympathy run, Searcher? Would you like a taste of what these doomed souls had?"

Leaning closer, Lana whispered, "You might surprise yourself. Toward the end, some begin to like it. You'd be amazed at how addicting pain can be."

Sarah gasped when Lana nipped her earlobe. A trickle of warmth on her neck told Sarah that the succubus had broken her skin. Sarah felt a spiral of horror at the sudden mix of heat and desire that coursed through her limbs.

It's not you. It's her. This is her magic.

Summoning what strength she had, Sarah jerked out of Lana's grasp. The succubus hissed at Sarah, reaching for her again, but Seamus was there—a wolf snapping at Lana and barring her path to the Searcher.

Lana glared at Seamus. With a flick of her wrist a whip snaked out from her hand, its length composed of shadow rather than leather.

"You're a fool to challenge me, dog."

Seamus barked his rebuke.

"Lana!" Owen stood at the open door to the dungeon. His wings were spread wide, threatening. Bare-chested and wearing his usual leather kilt, he looked like a demonic gladiator entering the arena. "What the fuck are you doing?"

"Dealing with trespassers," Lana answered, chin jutting out in defiance.

Owen looked from Lana to the still-bristling Seamus and then to Sarah.

Returning his gaze to the Guardian, Owen pointed at Sarah. "Get her out of here."

"But—" Lana began.

"Hold your tongue," Owen cut her off. "You know Tristan's wishes, and you're not above his authority, as much as you like to think so."

Lana glared at the incubus. Seamus, still in wolf form, nudged Sarah's hand with his muzzle. Still dazed, she managed to cross the room and pass into the corridor. With Seamus nipping at her heels any time she faltered, Sarah clambered up the passageway and finally stumbled into the chamber that adjoined the bath. Gulping air free of hellish scents, Sarah couldn't stay on her feet. She dropped to her hands and knees, taking deep breaths and making no attempt to hide her tears.

"You'll be all right." Seamus stood over her.

He waited several minutes while Sarah cried, wanting desperately for her tears to wash away the images that had been etched in her mind. At some point, Seamus decided that she'd cried enough. He grabbed Sarah under the arms and hoisted her to her feet.

"I'm sorry you had to see that," Seamus said. "Don't ever speak of it."

Sarah's brow knit together as she peered at the wolf. Her eyes burned and her vision was still blurred, but she could see that beyond warning her, the Guardian was also afraid.

"He doesn't know," Seamus told her.

"Who doesn't know?" Sarah's voice was globby with mucus. It made her feel sick again.

"Tristan." Seamus glanced at the staircase behind him. "He doesn't know about the dungeon. Not this one. There are other cells in the castle. This place is hidden, even from my master."

"How could he not know about that?" *Seamus has to be lying.*

"As much as I can't stand her, Lana's right," Seamus answered. "She and Owen have to feed, and they feed less often if they can draw out the torment of their victims. If they didn't take prisoners, they'd go hunting on the mainland every night. It would draw too much suspicion."

"But Tristan must know what they feed on," Sarah said. "Where does he think their food supply comes from?"

"From Bosque," Seamus told her. "When he brought Tristan to the island and sent his nether minions here as sentries, Bosque told Tristan he'd keep them fed with prisoners from the war and that Tristan never need worry about his human staff. But Bosque would never waste Searchers on the likes of Lana and Owen. Searchers have too much mettle to make good meals for incubi. Bosque saves warriors like you for his wraiths."

When Sarah didn't reply, Seamus lunged forward and scooped Sarah up. Too shocked to do anything other than go rigid in the Guardian's arms, Sarah didn't speak. Seamus vaulted up the steps and barreled through the castle at an alarming speed until he finally deposited Sarah in front of her bedroom door.

Still reeling from the shock of the dungeon and her unexpected transport from the bottom of the castle to its top floor, Sarah reached for the doorknob. She wouldn't be able to sleep, but she could bury herself under pillows and blankets and hide from the world for a few hours.

The wolf took a step toward Sarah, baring sharp teeth. "Don't say a word to him."

Sarah nodded, remaining mute. It was a promise she could keep for now. Her thoughts hadn't moved beyond chaos, and it would be some time before she'd be able to sort through them with any detachment. But Sarah knew that what she'd just witnessed, and what Seamus had just told her, might prove vital as she tried to solve the puzzle of this place. She wouldn't tell Tristan about the horrors beneath him. At least, not yet.

14

I WILL NOT lose again.

When Tristan had gone in search of Sarah that morning, he'd been greeted by a flustered Moira, who, after a few minutes of blushing and stammering, managed to tell Tristan that Sarah had gone to the study.

Upon entering the study, Tristan found Sarah curled up in the leather club chair, a steaming cup of tea beside her and a book open in her lap.

Looking up at Tristan, Sarah flinched at his approach. He hesitated, watching as fear slipped over her features. Sarah closed her eyes and gave a quick shake of her head, and just as quickly the expression vanished. Sarah lifted the book to show him the edition of *The Book of a Thousand Nights and a Night* he'd pulled off the shelf two days earlier.

"I'm hoping Scheherazade has some good survival tips for me," Sarah told him, a sly curve on her lips and eyes alight with mischief.

Infuriatingly, the expression filled Tristan with the desire to grasp Sarah's shoulders and kiss her breathless. He'd battled that same instinct the night before, when he'd found Sarah hunting through his room. Her face had been so close to his. Her skin so warm as he'd held her. Leaning down to press his mouth against hers would have been so easy. But the moment for that had not yet arrived, and Tristan reminded himself to be patient.

He folded his arms at his back and cleared his throat.

"You've had breakfast?" he asked her.

Sarah snapped the book shut. "Well, good morning to you, too."

Tristan ignored the reprimand implicit in her tone.

"Yes," she answered with a withering glance. "Moira brought it to my room."

"Good," Tristan said. "If you'll come with me, we'll get on with the next challenge."

"No rest for the wicked, I see." Sarah stood, but when Tristan stepped back to look her up and down, she put her hands on her hips. "What?"

"I just wanted to be certain your attire would serve for this task," he answered.

Sarah glanced down at her leggings, long-sleeved tunic, and suede vest. "There's something wrong with what I'm wearing?"

"No, it should be fine," Tristan told her. "Follow me."

He walked out of the study, not looking back to be sure she was following. A moment later he smiled, hearing the rush of her footfalls as she hurried to catch him.

"Where are we going?" Sarah asked.

"It's a rare, fine day." Tristan cast a pleasant smile in her direction. "I thought some fresh air might be nice."

"You mean you didn't get your fill of it on your midnight ride?" Sarah teased him.

He grimaced in return. "If you knew how often it rains here, you'd also know that only a fool lets a sunny day go to waste."

They exited the castle and were rewarded by a near-blindingly bright day. The sky boasted a rare turquoise hue broken by only a few tufts of cotton-white clouds.

Tristan led Sarah past the stables to a flat, grassy space in the courtyard, where Seamus and Owen awaited them. Tristan turned when he heard Sarah draw a hissing breath. She'd stopped walking, her eyes fixed on the incubus.

"Are you all right?" Tristan asked in a low voice, returning to her side. Some of the color had bled from her cheeks.

"Why is he here?" Sarah asked without removing her gaze from Owen.

"Owen and Seamus are here to assist with the challenge," Tristan answered carefully, though inwardly he cursed himself for not considering how Owen's appearance might affect Sarah. After all, the incubus had snatched her from the cliffside and made her prisoner within the castle, not to mention assisting Lana with stripping her and tying her to Tristan's bed.

Tristan laid his hand on Sarah's shoulder, giving a gentle squeeze. "Neither of them will harm you. You have my word."

As if suddenly aware of how much raw emotion she'd given away, Sarah shook her head and pulled back. "I'm fine."

Without waiting for Tristan, she continued toward the incubus and the Guardian, though her movements were forced and stiff. Tristan smiled grimly. Her discomfort would give him an advantage in the challenge, and while he didn't take pleasure in her uneasiness, he intended to win this round.

Sarah's steps slowed when she noticed that Seamus held two sabers. When she glanced back at Tristan for reassurance, his pulse ratcheted up.

"How are you at swordplay?" Tristan lengthened his strides to catch Sarah.

"Fair."

"Only fair?" Tristan lifted his hand and Seamus tossed him a blade, which he easily caught by the grip beneath the bell guard. "We Keepers are schooled from birth in the notion that Searchers do nothing but weapons drills—that even at night you continue to fight in your dreams, living only for thoughts of killing us."

"That's a bit overdramatic," Sarah said, a smile reappearing on her mouth. "We do get Sundays off."

"Seamus." Tristan nodded toward Sarah. The wolf sauntered over and offered Sarah the other sabre.

Tristan watched as she tested the weight of the sword and took a few practice swings.

"So, we're dueling?" Sarah asked.

"Within specific parameters," Tristan replied. "These are fencing sabers, which means the tips are blunted but the blades can still do damage. The challenge isn't to draw blood—the winner is the first person to disarm his opponent three times."

"Or her," Sarah said.

"Excuse me?"

"You said 'his' opponent," Sarah told him. "I'm merely pointing out that you must have meant his *or her* opponent. Or have you already forgotten that I won the first challenge?"

"Forgive me, gracious lady." Tristan offered a sweeping bow. "His or her opponent."

"Thank you, good sir," said Sarah, returning his bow.

"Ready?" Tristan lifted his sword.

Sarah nodded.

They began to circle each other. Sarah never took her eyes off Tristan, and while he'd planned to let her strike the first blow, it became clear that she was waiting for him to do the same.

If that's how she wants it. Tristan smiled and lunged. The suddenness of his movement caught Sarah off guard. She stumbled back but managed to parry his thrust. Tristan backed off, inviting Sarah to attack. He hoped she'd be angered enough after having allowed him to surprise her that she'd strike recklessly.

She did.

Sarah rushed at Tristan, cutting the blade at his flank. Tristan blocked her attack and captured the blade against his own. He jerked his arm and Sarah lost her grip on the sabre.

"Dammit!" Sarah swore when the sword hit the ground.

"That's one."

Owen began to laugh, but Tristan silenced the incubus with a look.

Sarah picked up her sabre. "That's only one."

Tristan nodded, raising his sword once more.

Their blades danced through the air, steel singing out in clear, bright tones each time the swords met. Tristan was pleased to note that Sarah was a quick study. She didn't make the same mistakes in their second bout, forcing Tristan to bring fresh tactics to the duel.

Tristan's admiring thoughts got him into trouble when he failed to note Sarah's shallow feint followed by a cutting blow that came down with enough force to jar Tristan's sabre from his hand.

Seamus gave a low whistle of approval. "One for her."

"Nice work," Tristan said, shaking his arm, which was still vibrating from the impact of Sarah's blow.

"I'd hate to disappoint you," Sarah answered, lifting her sword. "Whenever you've recovered."

Tristan laughed, picking up his sabre. He took a couple swings to loosen his arm and then nodded at Sarah.

This time they both moved with caution. Tristan attacked first, but warily, paying closer attention to the style and pace of Sarah's strikes and parries. When Sarah struck another forceful, cutting blow, Tristan feigned a stumble, drawing her into an attempt at disarming him once more. When she threw her weight into the blow, Tristan abruptly dodged and brought the flat of his blade down hard on the hilt of her sword.

"Ow!" Sarah cried out as she dropped the sword.

"Two." Seamus called from the side of the field. Sarah shot a murderous glance at the wolf.

Tristan frowned at Sarah while she rubbed her sword hand. "Are you hurt?"

"I'm fine." Sarah said, picking up her sabre. "But I don't think I like this challenge."

"Why not?" Tristan asked, unable to stop his grin. "You're doing very well."

"Don't patronize me." Sarah glared at him. "And if at any point you tell me that you're not actually left-handed, I *will* find a way to stab you."

"I'm sorry?" Tristan's brow crinkled.

Sarah laughed, brandishing her sword. "Not a fan of *The Princess Bride*, eh? Maybe if I can channel Inigo Montoya, I'll manage to beat you."

"I have no idea what you're talking about." Tristan's sabre sliced through the air and Sarah stopped his attack with a deft counterblow.

"That's your loss."

"Well, I am left-handed," Tristan told her. "So whatever was worrying you, you can put it aside."

"I'll do that."

Their blades rang as the speed of their duel became faster and faster. Sarah was catching on quickly, though Tristan could tell she had chosen to focus on blocking his attacks and was reluctant to attempt to disarm him.

"Stop smiling." Sarah thrust with her sabre and Tristan easily parried her attack. "It's just rude."

"I'm enjoying this," Tristan replied as their blades rasped against each other once more. "Aren't you?"

"Shut up." Whether because of frustration or anger, Sarah

gave up her defensive approach to the fight and lunged at Tristan. Her attack came so quickly that Tristan stumbled back, caught off guard by her sudden furious strokes.

It only took a few moments for Tristan to recover his balance, parrying her thrusts and cuts and slowly driving her into a retreat. Sarah balked, giving Tristan an opening. He turned his wrist and, with a swirling strike, pulled Sarah's sabre from her grasp. Her sword went flying.

Sarah glared accusingly at her sabre where it lay in the grass.

"That's three," Tristan said. "I win."

He tossed his sword to Owen. The incubus caught the sabre and immediately set about polishing its blade.

Sarah nodded at Tristan, her expression sullen. It made her look much younger than she was, like a child who'd lost a favorite game, and Tristan had to bite back laughter.

"Walk with me." He strolled away from the practice field, wanting to put distance between Sarah and Owen before he asked any questions of her.

Sarah fell into step beside him, though she kicked at any stones that happened to be in her path. "If we were throwing at a target, I would have kicked your ass."

"I wouldn't be surprised if you did." Tristan smiled at her. "You were in possession of not a few knives when you were captured."

"I don't suppose I could have those back?" Her lips curved teasingly.

"No." Tristan laughed. "But you can tell me why you ended up in my castle wearing all those knives."

Sarah's smile faded.

"I won the challenge," Tristan reminded her. "Answer my question."

"Reconnaissance," she told him.

"Did you come alone?" Tristan watched her face for any signs of deceit.

Sarah glanced at him in surprise. "Yes."

Tristan's jaw clenched before he asked, "Will others be coming for you?"

She went silent.

"This is something I must know," Tristan said in a quiet, slightly dangerous voice.

"If I don't return, they will assume I'm dead," Sarah replied, her voice flat. "No one is coming for me."

Her answer should have been a relief, but Tristan found it both surprising and unsettling. Did Searchers abandon their own so easily?

He found himself asking, "Why won't they come for you?"

"This mission was designated high-risk," Sarah said wearily. "There aren't enough of us to keep hurling ourselves at walls deemed impenetrable."

"So I'm an impenetrable wall." Tristan grimaced. "How interesting."

"I don't know what you are." Sarah stopped, turning to face him. "I meant the island is the impenetrable wall."

Tristan almost said, "I'm the only thing that matters about this island," but stopped himself. Sarah might be his prisoner, but she was also still his enemy.

"You handled yourself well in our match," Tristan told her. "You may not have won, but you were a worthy opponent."

"Are we done with questions?" Sarah asked, surprised by his sudden change in tone.

"For now. Enjoy your day, Sarah." Tristan lifted her hand and pressed it to his mouth. Then he pulled her close and kissed her temple. "I look forward to seeing you at dinner."

When he released her hand, Sarah's expression was stunned, and Tristan watched a blush wash over her pale cheeks.

Tristan headed toward the stable, intending to spend the afternoon riding about the island. He wore a smile that refused to leave his face, for he knew without a doubt that he'd won more than just the challenge.

15

SARAH RUMMAGED THROUGH her mind, seeking a thought that would distract her in some way. She needed a distraction because she didn't want to think about how strange it was to be both looking forward to and dreading dinner with Tristan. She knew she absolutely should not be looking forward to dinner with her captor, but every time she thought about the approaching time when she'd be near him again, her pulse took off like a racehorse out of the gate. But Sarah also couldn't rid her mind of the corpses beneath the castle, the freshly dead bodies equally as horrifying as the long-decayed victims. She meant to keep her word to Seamus and not tell Tristan about what she'd seen, but the awful sights had been etched in her mind and continued to haunt her.

Frustrated, Sarah let out a long sigh.

"Are you not happy with this dress?"

Sarah caught Moira's beaming face in the reflection as the girl finished buttoning up the gown. Moira met Sarah's gaze and blushed.

"You look so lovely, miss," she murmured.

"Thank you, Moira," Sarah replied, running her palms over the forest-green silk taffeta. She'd selected a strapless sheath for that evening. "I think that this color would be even better on you, though. It would make that gorgeous auburn hair of yours absolutely gleam."

Moira flushed from her neck to the tips of her ears. "Oh, no, miss. I could never wear anything so fine."

"Of course you could." Sarah turned around to face her. Moira ducked her head and tried to scoot back, but Sarah took the girl's hands in her own. "In fact, I think you should try a dress on right now."

Moira's eyes widened. She covered her mouth in horror and shook her head furiously.

"Yes," Sarah pronounced. "This is what we're doing. Pick a gown, Moira."

It took a few more minutes of Sarah standing with her hands on her hips and Moira offering protests before the girl finally relented and timidly began to search through the dresses.

"Might I try this one, miss?" With the utmost care, Moira pulled a gown from the armoire.

"Good choice." Sarah smiled and took the cap-sleeved dress of amethyst brocade out of Moira's hands. The gown was beautiful, but its full skirt and princess-seamed bodice were too traditional for Sarah's taste. It was perfect for Moira, though—the type of dress a young girl dreamed about.

Moira smiled, but then bit her lip and looked at Sarah with uncertainty.

"Go on," Sarah said. "Take off your uniform, and we'll put this on. If you want privacy, go to the alcove to change."

Curtsying as a reflex, Moira giggled and hurried into the alcove. A few minutes later she emerged still wearing her maid's cap but dressed only in a plain white slip.

Sarah helped Moira into the gown. It was lucky that Moira had chosen a dress with a lace-up bodice. The gown wanted a curvier figure, which Moira needed a few years yet to grow into. Though it wasn't a perfect fit, Moira's smile was full of wonder when Sarah turned her to face the mirror.

"See how beautiful you are." Sarah squeezed the girl's shoulders.

Moira blushed, but didn't reject the compliment out of hand, which Sarah took as a marked improvement.

"Now, what's next?" Sarah tapped her finger on her cheek. "I know. Jewelry."

The frightened look reappeared on Moira's face, but Sarah shook her head to deter any objections. Sarah could understand the girl's reservation. The previous night Sarah had rejected Moira's attempts to bedeck her with jewels.

But if they were playing dress-up, Sarah saw no reason to hold back. Though she'd been a little horrified by its excess when she'd been presented with the armoire that held jewelry, this time Sarah went to it without hesitation.

She pulled open a velvet-lined drawer that held several necklaces. Moira crept up beside her.

Not able to hold back her sigh as she gazed down at the glittering array of gemstones, Sarah said, "I suppose these are all real?"

Moira stared at Sarah as if she didn't understand the question.

"That's what I thought," Sarah said. "Hmmm. I think with that purple shade you should wear onyx."

She drew out a teardrop pendant framed by diamonds, as well as matching earrings. "Put these on."

Though Moira's hands shook the whole time, she managed to fasten the necklace and earrings without dropping any of them.

"Yes." Sarah nodded her approval. "Those are perfect. Now, you pick mine."

Grinning suddenly, Moira opened nearly all the drawers before she selected a platinum and tiger's eye choker and matching studs for her ears.

"I believe you've an eye for this, Moira," Sarah commented as she finished putting on the earrings. "Let's see how we've done."

Sarah took Moira's hand and led her to the full-length mirror. The moment Moira caught sight of her reflection, she squealed and began to jump up and down.

"Oh! Oh!"

"Ha!" Sarah clapped in delight. "Now, give us a twirl."

Moira spun around, her skirt blooming out. Sarah continued to clap, and Moira giggled as she turned faster and faster. Suddenly Moira's laughter became a shriek. She stopped twirling, and Sarah had to catch Moira around the waist to keep the girl from tipping over.

"What's wrong?" Sarah asked, but she followed Moira's frightened gaze and found her answer.

Tristan was standing in the doorway with a bemused expression on his face.

Moira was shaking in Sarah's arms. "Sir, I'm so sorry. Please, I'm so sorry."

"Hush, Moira," Sarah whispered. "You've done nothing wrong."

Moira began to cry.

Sarah threw a pleading look at Tristan.

Awkwardly he came into the room, returning Sarah's beseeching gaze with a frown.

"Tristan," Sarah said firmly, "please reassure Moira that you aren't cross with her."

Moira sniffled and attempted to curtsy, but since Sarah was still holding the girl, she almost took them both to the floor.

"I didn't mean to act beyond my station, Lord Tristan."

"I— Uh," Tristan said. "Well, of course you didn't."

"Please don't tell Mrs. Cranston," Moira begged. "She'll take the cane to me."

"Someone beats you?" Sarah exclaimed, then glared at Tristan. *"With a cane?"*

"I didn't know," he said quickly. "I'll take care of it."

After a moment's hesitation, Tristan added, "I'm only here to ask if you're planning to join me for dinner."

Sarah frowned. "What time is it?"

"I've been waiting for you for half an hour."

Moira wailed, and Tristan held up his hands in alarm. "I'm not angry about it. Please don't cry."

Looking at Moira and Tristan, Sarah realized that the girl was on the verge of hysterics while the man frozen in the doorway was beginning to panic.

Sarah leaned down and whispered, "Moira, calm down and take your time to change and go about your tasks for the evening. I'm going to dinner with Tristan. I promise that nothing bad will come of this."

Moira whimpered, but she nodded.

"All right, then." Sarah released the girl and grabbed Tristan's elbow to draw him out of the room. She stopped to close the door, to be sure Moira had a quiet space in which to recover.

"Dinner, then?" Sarah said stiffly, and moved toward the stairs.

Tristan followed her, remaining silent until they reached the dining hall. The first course was already laid out.

Sarah took her place before Tristan could pull out the chair for her. She stared at the mixed greens on her plate, realizing she hadn't a smidge of appetite.

"You look lovely," Tristan said quietly.

Shaking her head, Sarah murmured, "Don't."

"Don't give you compliments?" Tristan frowned.

"Don't talk," Sarah replied. "I'm not ready to talk to you yet."

"Are you angry with me?" The furrow in his brow deepened.

Sarah shifted her angry gaze from her plate to Tristan. "Of course I'm angry. You allow your servants to be beaten?"

Tristan reached for his wineglass. "I told you I didn't know about that, and I'll put a stop to it. You have my word."

"How could you not know?" Sarah replied, unwilling to drop the issue. "These people live with you."

With a sigh, Tristan said, "The servants don't interact with me in that way. We rarely speak."

"Ah, yes, I forgot," Sarah said. "You often don't know their names."

"No." Tristan's voice had taken on an edge. "I don't befriend my servants, but neither do I condone their ill treatment."

"You don't bother to know how they're treated," Sarah countered. "You take them for granted. For God's sake, they're people, Tristan."

"What's gotten into you?" Tristan asked. "Why this sudden interest in the servants? Or is it about the servants at all? Is this just about Moira?"

Sarah opened and closed her mouth, wanting to protest but not finding the words.

Tristan pressed on. "And why was she wearing one of your dresses?"

"Because she's a young woman who has never had the pleasure of a pretty dress, or a necklace." Sarah was horrified to hear her voice quaver. "I don't think she knows how to dream of better things. All she knows is this place. Does she even go to school?"

"The servants' children have tutors," Tristan said, clearly uncomfortable.

"But they don't leave the island for their education?" Sarah felt a bit ill. "Do they have friends?"

"They have each other," Tristan replied. "You must understand, the positions at Castle Tierney have been held within families for generations. This place is their way of life."

"*You* have to understand how wrong that is," Sarah argued. "It's their way of life because they've never been offered anything else. Didn't you see how terrified Moira was that you'd be angry? Do you want your servants to feel that way about you? Do you realize that it's utterly ludicrous that you have servants at all?"

Sarah felt the corners of her eyes burn and she quickly turned her face away, mortified that she'd let her emotions overwhelm her.

"Sarah, I don't—" Tristan's voice was soft but hesitant. He was silent for several minutes while she tried her best not to let more than a few tears slip from beneath her eyelids.

"I don't live here by choice." Tristan spoke so quietly, Sarah barely heard him. "The rules the servants follow are rules I follow as well. Things are a certain way here. The way they've been for many generations. It's not the sort of place that changes along with the outside world. It is a place apart."

Taking a moment to be sure she had her turbulent emotions in check, Sarah stole a glance at Tristan. His expression was troubled, verging on wan.

"You don't want to live here?" Sarah asked carefully.

Tristan grabbed his wineglass and downed half its contents. "Would you want to live here?"

Sarah shook her head. Despite all its luxuries, Castle Tierney was a bleak place, and Sarah would have thought the same even if she wasn't a prisoner within its stone walls.

"Then why are you here?" Sarah took a sip of her wine, keeping her eyes on Tristan all the while.

"For protection."

"From whom?"

He gave her a rueful smile.

"I didn't come here to hurt you," Sarah protested. "I only came to find out what was here."

Tristan's smile twitched, and Sarah cursed her loose tongue. She'd offered more information than she'd intended.

As though he sensed her regret, Tristan offered, "Do you really want to know why I'm here?"

His question wasn't coy, but almost shy. Sarah met his eyes and was startled by the fragility she found there. He wanted her to know his story. She wondered how long he'd been wishing for someone to tell it to.

"Of course I do," Sarah said.

Tristan drew a ragged breath and broke his gaze from hers. For a moment, Sarah thought he'd decided against revealing more of himself to her.

"Do you know who Bosque Mar is?"

Sarah went rigid in her chair. "Yes," she whispered. "The Harbinger."

"Then you know he rules over every Keeper," Tristan said. "And I'm no exception. I live at Castle Tierney because Bosque ordered it."

Sarah's mind was racing. Her knowledge of Bosque Mar was limited. She knew he was the source of the Keepers' power and that he was not of this world. That was all.

She groped for the right question. "Does he tell all Keepers where to live?" It struck her as a rather mundane interest for a creature as powerful as the Harbinger.

"No."

"Then why are you the exception?" Sarah's heart was drumming beneath her ribs. She was on the cusp of discovering something vital—that was apparent.

The dining-hall door swung open, and servants appeared with the second course. Sarah eyed the women among them, wondering if any were the horrid Mrs. Cranston. When they'd gone, leaving a savory beef stew in front of Tristan and Sarah, she looked to him for an answer to her question but found his vulnerable demeanor had vanished.

"I hope you enjoy your dinner," Tristan said curtly, and Sarah knew her questions were no longer welcome.

They passed the rest of the meal mostly in silence, with Tristan or Sarah occasionally offering a brief comment about the food. Given that Tristan didn't abandon her in the middle of dinner, Sarah considered it a significant improvement from their first meal.

After dessert had been cleared away, Tristan stood up and offered Sarah his hand. She accepted it as she rose from her chair, but then pulled her fingers away, alarmed by how warm her skin had grown from that simple touch.

Sarah walked beside Tristan up the stairs until they reached the upper floor and stood in the hallway where their bedrooms faced opposite each other.

"I suppose this is where we say good night." Sarah toyed with the choker around her throat. She found she didn't want to leave Tristan yet, though she was loath to admit that she craved more of his company.

"You can come in for a nightcap if you like," Tristan said, surprising her, and walked into his room.

16

SARAH HOVERED JUST outside his door. She didn't want to stop talking with Tristan, but she questioned the wisdom of so willingly accepting an invitation into his bedroom. She stood there, looking at the open door.

It's just a room. A room where there happens to be a bed. No need to read anything more into the situation. God, I'm terrible at lying to myself, Sarah thought as she went through the door. No matter how much she tried to convince herself otherwise, she was well aware of the thrill she felt at being invited into Tristan's bedroom and how much she wanted to be there.

Once inside, however, she found herself alone but for the jumping flames in the fireplace.

"Tristan?"

"I'll be out in a second," his call came from the alcove.

An image of Tristan emerging from the closet shirtless, as he had been the first time Sarah saw him, snuck into Sarah's mind and made her fists clench.

But when Tristan did appear, he'd only shed his jacket and vest, and hadn't divested himself of his shirt.

Why would he? Seduction by way of presenting himself as some kind of beefcake didn't strike Sarah as Tristan's M.O., and she was a little disturbed when her imagination began to suggest more plausible scenarios in which she might come upon Tristan shirtless.

"So, I've been thinking about your next challenge," Tristan said, then frowned at her. "Is something wrong?"

Sarah realized she'd been undressing him with her eyes, and quickly looked away. "Fine. The next challenge—what about it?"

"I know we've set a pattern of one challenge per day," Tristan said, "but I wonder if you might be open to some improvisation."

"This is your game." Sarah shrugged, tamping down her rising curiosity.

Tristan went to a curved cabinet of polished wood and withdrew a bottle of single malt and two glasses. "True, but I don't want you to accuse me of unfairly changing the rules."

"There are rules?" Sarah teased.

Tristan answered her with a wry smile.

"More than one challenge in a day is fine, as long as it's not too taxing for your poor mind to devise them," Sarah told him. "What torture have you concocted for me now?"

He ignored both her barbs, answering, "Tell me a story."

Sarah frowned at him. "I don't think I follow."

"We keep coming back to Scheherazade," Tristan said, pouring Sarah a scotch. "I think it's an avenue worth pursuing further."

"I don't know that I'm much of a storyteller," Sarah replied, taking the glass he offered.

Tristan poured a glass for himself. "We won't know until you try."

He walked past Sarah. She tensed when he settled on his bed, stretching his legs out and propping himself up against the headboard with pillows.

"A bedtime story, then," Sarah said, taking a quick nip of whisky to steady her nerves.

"If you put me to sleep, I'm going to go ahead and say it wasn't a very good story."

"So I'm not only to come up with a tale"—Sarah walked to the bedside—"I'm also supposed to keep you riveted?"

"Riveted would be excellent." Tristan rested an arm behind his head. "But mildly interested is acceptable."

"As long as you don't fall asleep?" Sarah sat cross-legged at the foot of the bed, facing him.

"Too difficult?"

Sarah offered him a half smile. "Let's find out." She took a gulp of whisky so large it made her shudder.

"Easy there." Tristan laughed. "Or this will surely become a bawdy tale."

She blamed her warming cheeks on the whisky. After making a show of straightening her shoulders and clearing her throat, Sarah began in a lofty tone: "Once upon a time—"

"Ugh." Tristan waved a dismissive hand at her. "Don't you know you're not supposed to begin a story that way?"

"It's my story," Sarah objected.

Tristan shook his head. "I'm trying to help you out. 'Once upon a time' is no way to begin a story. And don't try 'It was a dark and stormy night,' either."

"Are you going to let me tell this story or not?"

"Go ahead," Tristan told her. "But if you don't start off well, the tale is ruined from the first sentence."

Sarah gave him a withering glance. She sipped her whisky, thinking.

"Have you conceded?" Tristan grinned at her.

"No," Sarah replied. "I'm just composing the perfect opening line."

"Oh, good." Tristan eased back against the headboard.

Sarah knew the shape she wanted this story to take. It was a challenge that could aid her immensely—but the tactic was a risky one to be sure. She looked at Tristan. His eyes were closed.

"Hey!" Sarah knocked his foot with the back of her hand.

"What?" he asked lazily.

"Are you listening?" She glared at him. "I'm about to begin."

"Then begin." His smile told Sarah he'd only closed his eyes to provoke her.

"The island was getting smaller," Sarah said.

Tristan sat up. "That's your beginning?"

She held up her hand to shush him. "Or at least that was how the prince felt about his home. He'd ruled over his tiny kingdom for many years, but the green grass of his lands had lost their jade luster, and the shadows of the forests grew longer at the end of each day."

Tristan's jaw twitched from tension, but Sarah continued. "The prince knew it was his duty to keep peace on his island and care for his subjects, but the strength of his castle couldn't stop the weakening of his soul."

Sarah watched Tristan's face pale. Her voice dropped to a whisper. "He worried his home had become a prison instead of a refuge and that soon he would rule because of his dedication to his subjects, but that he would do so with an empty heart."

A tiny sound slipped from between Tristan's lips, a sigh that had barely escaped. Sarah swallowed the sudden hard lump in her throat.

"Then, one day, without invitation or announcement, a stranger appeared at his castle gates. A woman who traveled alone."

"Is this a love story?" Tristan's question startled Sarah, snatching her out of the story's cadence.

"Would you like to hear a love story?" Sarah countered,

hoping the room was dim enough to cloak the rush of blood into her cheeks.

"It's a matter of plot development." Tristan shrugged. "There's a prince in a castle, and a strange woman has just arrived. That seems like the setup for a romance."

"She might be a monster disguised as a woman," Sarah said, wagging her index finger at him. "You don't know who she is."

"Intriguing." Tristan laughed softly. "Please go on."

"Despite the mystery of the woman's sudden arrival, the prince welcomed her into his home," Sarah told him. "For the island was isolated and too much time had passed since the prince had received a visitor. He offered her the hospitalities of the castle, a room of her own, and dined with her each night."

"Is she beautiful?" Tristan asked.

"I don't . . ." Sarah looked away, wrapping her fingers tightly around her glass. "Does it matter?"

"It seems that the prince would be more likely to let her into his home if she's beautiful," Tristan said. "After all, you said he hadn't had visitors for a long time, but even so he'd probably be wary of strangers—except if she was too beautiful for him to resist. Perhaps he had no will to turn her away."

"Perhaps." Sarah dared to look at him. "I suppose she might be beautiful."

Tristan held her gaze. "She is."

He pushed himself away from the headboard and knelt beside her. Sarah couldn't take her eyes off him, nor could she move when he lifted his hand and lightly cupped her face. His thumb traced the shape of her jaw and her lips.

"What are you doing?" Sarah whispered. She knew it was a silly question, but those were the only words she could muster.

I shouldn't let this happen. God, I want this to happen.

Tristan bent his head to hers. "Suggesting a plot twist."

Sarah felt the light brush of his lips on her cheek. She let her eyes close. Her instincts wanted her to lean into him, to turn her mouth toward his.

"But what if her beauty is an illusion?" Sarah murmured. "What if it's a spell to help her entrap the prince and then kill him?"

Tristan stilled, and Sarah's eyes fluttered open. He was still close, watching her. She searched his face for signs of alarm or anger but didn't find them, only curiosity.

"That would also offer a surprising turn in the narrative," Tristan said. He slowly pulled away to sit beside her, though he kept his hand curved along her neck, his palm pressed against the pulse at her throat. "What would you prefer: sex or violence?"

"Are those the only two options?" Sarah asked with a nervous laugh.

"In the story you've set up, it seems so."

Sarah placed her hand over Tristan's. Touching him was much too easy, too natural. She turned her face and lightly kissed his fingertips. She hoped he hadn't seen how her hands were trembling. Then she stood up.

"Good night, Tristan."

"You aren't going to finish the story?" Tristan stayed on the bed, watching her.

She smiled, hoping to hide the frantic beating of her heart. "Don't you remember? Scheherazade never finishes a story. It's the only way she can save her own life."

Sarah got up and crossed the room quickly, hoping that Tristan wouldn't call out to her, because if he did—if he so much as whispered her name—she didn't think she'd have the will to leave. She made it out of Tristan's room and crossed the hall, ignoring the pinch of disappointment that he hadn't tried to stop her.

The subtle glow of a banked fire greeted Sarah when she

entered her bedroom. Its warmth should have been soothing, but Sarah's skin remained too sensitive, uncomfortably heated. She kicked off her shoes, then stripped down to her bra and panties.

Sarah went to her bed and stretched out on top of the covers. She laid her palm flat on her stomach. The heat of her skin made it silken to her touch. Her fingertips slid down her abdomen and her back began to arch even before her hand slipped beneath her panties.

Enough of an ache had been building in Sarah's core that she knew she'd be wet. Even so, a little moan escaped her lips when her fingers stroked over the soft folds of her sex.

Closing her eyes, Sarah let her mind take her back into Tristan's bedroom, where, instead of fleeing from him, she kissed him the way she'd wanted to, pressing him down into the bed. When Sarah imagined straddling Tristan's hips, her fingers moved to her clit and her other hand slid beneath her bra to cup her breast.

Sarah's hips rose and fell with the rhythm of her stroking fingers. Her breath came fast as her mind conjured images she'd worked so hard to keep in check: her hands fisted in Tristan's hair, her lips rimming his cock, her sex hot and wet as she rode him until she, until she . . .

A cry of pleasure broke from Sarah's throat as she came, ripples of pleasure moving through her limbs. She rolled onto her side, listening to her labored breath and the rapid beating of her heart.

Fuck. How can I want him this much?

Twisted as it appeared to her, the desire was real, and Sarah didn't know if she was strong enough to keep it at bay. She'd never wanted someone this way; Jeremy had the skill to coax her into craving his touch, but her body seemed to *need* Tristan. Unlike anything she'd experienced before, the pull of her new lust was both intriguing and frightening. She didn't know what it would be like to have him inside her, but she was terribly aware of how desperately she *wanted* to know.

Her breath had finally begun to slow, and Sarah thought she'd be able to let the echoes of her climax carry her into a pleasant slumber, when a knock at the door sent her bolt upright.

"Just a minute," Sarah called, cursing the sound of her voice, which was still husky with her recent pleasure.

Sarah hurried to an armoire and grabbed a long satin dressing gown. She quickly tied the robe, hoping her appearance wasn't in too much disarray as she went to the door.

If Tristan was at the door with the aim of bringing Sarah back to his bed, or joining Sarah in hers, she hoped that having indulged her pleasure just prior to his arrival would give her the willpower to send him away—though she was doubtful of her resolve. Her mind was already prodding her with flashes of Tristan's mouth and hands on her body.

But when Sarah opened the door, the rising warmth of her blood was swept away by a sudden cold. She could barely tolerate Lana's presence, given that the nether creature had stripped her down and tied her to Tristan's bed, and Sarah's discovery that the succubus, in league with Owen, tormented hapless victims in the bowels of the castle, taking pleasure and sustenance from the prolonged anguish of their prisoners. Finding Lana at her door was enough to make Sarah instantly queasy.

"I thought I'd see how you're settling in," Lana said.

The succubus was dressed in a leather catsuit, though given the freedom of Lana's wings, Sarah presumed the back of the suit had been cut out. Those wings were spread wide now, either to impress or intimidate.

Lana sniffed the air and licked her lips. Her eyes raked over

Sarah's body. "I'm sure Tristan would be interested to know what you've been up to in here."

Disgusted, Sarah drew a sharp breath. "What do you want?"

"How rude." Lana flapped her wings in chastisement. "I'm simply here to make sure you have everything you need, sweet thing. After all, I'm the one who provided all these lovely adornments for you."

Lana reached out and touched the sleeve of Sarah's robe. Sarah jerked her arm back.

"*Tsk.*" Lana shook her head but smiled. "You have nothing to fear from me, Searcher."

"I'm not afraid," Sarah snapped. "I do, however, find you appalling."

"So quick to judge," Lana said with a throaty laugh. "Don't forget that I know what you truly desire. You reek of it."

Sarah wrapped her arms around herself, hating how exposed she felt. "You said you wanted to know if I have everything I need. I do. Please leave."

"You're lying, my lovely." Lana's gaze flickered across the hall to Tristan's bedroom door. "What you need is over there."

"Shut up."

Lana laughed again. "How precious it is when a kitten tries to show her claws."

The succubus gazed at Sarah for a long moment, then her lips curved into a cruel smile. "Ah. I didn't see it before."

Sarah edged back from the doorway. "What are you talking about?"

"You must be a bit frightened," Lana continued, "to want something that you know so little about. I won't lie to you. There will be pain when he takes you—that's the burden of your delicate human flesh—but afterward you won't care because the pleasure is more than you can imagine."

Sarah didn't want to react but couldn't fight off her body's sudden visceral response. The wrench of sickness and pain was overwhelming to the point that Sarah faltered and had to steady herself in the doorframe.

How could she know?

"I'm sure Tristan will forgive your inexperience," Lana said, her eyes bright with pleasure. "If you'd like some coaching, though, don't hesitate to ask. Though I should tell you, when it comes to teaching, I take a very hands-on approach."

"Go to hell." Sarah stumbled back into her room and slammed the door in Lana's face.

17

TRISTAN DIDN'T WANT to add up the number of times he'd risen from bed and gone to his door over the course of the night. From the moment Sarah had left after he'd almost kissed her, Tristan couldn't shake her from his mind: her scent, the softness of her skin, the press of her lips against his hand. It would have been a simple thing to go to her room and pursue the matter further. Had Sarah remained on the bed beside him for a few more minutes, Tristan was certain she would have yielded up the kiss he'd wanted. Their attraction was palpable, and Tristan had no doubts about its power. But he did think Sarah likely to be skittish in their interactions. She was wary of him, and rightly so—no matter how drawn to the Searcher Tristan might feel, neither of them could forget that she was his prisoner.

Tristan had his own reservations about the way in which things were progressing with Sarah as well. Seducing her in order to coax information from her seemed to be going as he'd hoped. But he was troubled by the allure Sarah held for him. Try as he might to justify his actions as solely the means to an end, in truth he wanted to know Sarah, to be close to her regardless of what he might learn of his enemies by her captivity.

Despite his restless night, Tristan had fought off the impulse to go after Sarah, instead biding his time and planning a challenge that would keep them together for the better part of a day.

He made himself wait until midmorning before he went to knock on her door.

"Good," Tristan said when Sarah greeted him. She was dressed in jeans and a simple cotton button-down. "That outfit will work. Though you may need a jacket. It's a cool day."

Sarah arched a brow at him. "I take it you've concocted another challenge?"

"I have," Tristan answered.

Sarah went to the wardrobe and returned wearing a shearling-lined leather coat. Tristan offered Sarah his arm, and after a moment's hesitation, she took it.

The light touch silenced both of them, and neither Tristan nor Sarah spoke as Tristan led them through the castle and out into the courtyard. Tristan noted the pleasant weight of her arm linked through his, the way the sunlight pulled amber threads through her dark hair. As they walked, he found himself drawing her steadily closer, until she leaned against him. He was pleased when she didn't pull away, instead curling her fingers around his forearm.

Tristan stopped outside of the stable, and Sarah turned questioning eyes on him.

"Horses?" Sarah asked when a whinny sounded from within the building.

Noting the trepidation in her voice, Tristan asked, "You don't ride?"

"Not that often." Sarah shrugged and pulled free of him. "But I can hold my own."

He smiled, knowing she was lying.

"It's a simple enough challenge," Tristan said, walking into the stable. "All you have to do is keep up with me on a ride around the island."

His original intention had been to challenge Sarah to a race, but her wary approach to the stable made Tristan think a flat-out race might be too dangerous. He wanted to win this challenge, but had no desire to put Sarah at risk. And though he was reluctant to admit it, Tristan knew what he wanted most was simply the chance to spend the day with Sarah riding around the island.

"Can I pick our horses?" Sarah asked. She tried to make the question playful, but Tristan picked up the nervous edge of her voice.

"If you like."

Sarah walked along the stalls, gazing up at the curious heads that poked over their stall doors to greet the newcomer. Ares, who occupied the farthest stall in the row, heard Tristan's voice and bellowed.

"Do you have an elephant in here too?" Sarah glanced at Tristan over her shoulder.

"Just a horse that wants to be one," Tristan said, tracing her steps. "Pay no attention to Ares; he likes to put on a show for visitors."

Reaching the end of the stable, Sarah stopped to observe Ares. The stallion was pitching and turning in his hall. He fixed his bright eyes on Sarah and bellowed again.

"He's beautiful," Sarah said.

Tristan smiled at her. "I agree."

Sarah admired the stallion another minute and then gave Tristan a knowing glance. "He's yours, isn't he?"

"They're all mine."

Sarah shook her head. "I meant he's the horse you prefer to ride."

Tristan nodded, pleased and surprised that she'd arrived at that conclusion.

With a teasing smile, Sarah said, "Anything you can do . . ."

Her eyes returned to the stallion.

When Tristan realized that Sarah intended to choose Ares, he reached out to pull her back.

"Sarah, no!"

In her determination, however, Sarah had already opened the stall door and stepped inside. Within the small space, Ares was agitated, blowing and stomping. The sudden appearance of a stranger invading his stall pushed the stallion's restlessness over the brink. He reared up, striking the air with his hooves, missing Sarah's face by inches. She screamed and lost her footing. When she fell, Ares lunged toward the open gate. Without thinking, Tristan dove forward, grabbing Sarah and rolling her beneath him, as the stallion's hooves came crashing down.

Air rushed out of Tristan's lungs when Ares's weight came down on him. He heard the crack of bones, followed by waves of pain. He forced himself to hang on to Sarah until the stallion had trampled over them and bolted from the stable. When Ares's hoofbeats began to fade, Tristan let himself slide off Sarah and onto his side. His lungs wouldn't draw breath. His body, from chest to back, felt as though it was wrapped in iron bands.

"Tristan!" Sarah scrambled to her knees, and Tristan was relieved to see she appeared unharmed. "Oh God."

He couldn't answer her. His back and chest began to burn and throb. Dark spots crept into the edge of his vision. He dug his fingers into the stone paving of the floor, fighting to remain conscious.

"Help!" Sarah shouted. "Someone help us!"

Tristan heard a snarl, followed by a long howl. Sarah turned at the sound of toenails clicking on the cobblestone of the stable floor. She gasped when the hulking shape of Seamus's wolf form bounded toward them.

Seamus snapped his jaws inches from her face, forcing her away from Tristan and back against the stall. Tristan tried to speak, wanting to tell the wolf that Sarah wasn't responsible for his condition, but all that came out was a painful wheeze.

It was enough to get Seamus's attention, however. The Guardian turned from Sarah to Tristan, sniffing at his fallen master. Two more wolves appeared behind Seamus. Some silent orders passed between them, and the newly arrived wolves shifted into human form, each man taking one of Sarah's arms and dragging her from the stable.

"Wait!" She struggled against them. "I need to know how badly hurt he is! Just tell me that he'll be all right!"

The Guardians ignored her pleas. When they were out of sight, Seamus shifted forms and lifted his forearm to his mouth. Then he turned his arm to face Tristan, placing the fresh puncture wound against the Keeper's lips.

"Drink." Seamus watched as Tristan swallowed the wolf's blood.

It had been some time since Tristan had last needed this service from his Guardians, but taking the blood wasn't unfamiliar to him. Since the first skinning of his knees as a boy, Tristan had benefited from his predecessors' careful engineering of their Guardian warriors to serve as formidable soldiers with unique blood flowing through their veins—blood that could heal their own wounds and the wounds of fallen comrades within moments.

Tristan pushed Seamus's arm away when he felt warmth spreading through his limbs, drawing the pain from his body.

He rolled onto his back, welcoming the air pouring into his lungs. Tristan lay there until his pulse had quieted and his breath was steady.

When Tristan sat up, Seamus said, "You want to tell me how that happened?"

"She spooked Ares."

"*She* spooked Ares?" Seamus frowned. "Then how come it's

you who had broken bones and hoof-shaped bruises all over your back?"

Tristan cleared his throat, looking away. "I threw myself on top of her."

"You—" Seamus stared at him. "Bloody hell, Tristan."

"I couldn't let him run her down," Tristan said. "He could have killed her."

"But you *could* let him stomp all over you." Seamus half laughed, half growled. "Because you're immortal and impervious to harm . . . except you're not."

Tristan climbed to his feet. "I'm fine now. Let it go."

"You were seriously hurt," Seamus pointed out. "It's not your job to be chivalrous. All you're supposed to do is stay safe. That's why you're here."

"That's why *you're* here," Tristan replied bitterly. "And you've once again kept me safe. Good work."

Seamus shook his head, sighing. "There's honor in wanting to protect the girl, but not to the point of being reckless."

Tristan didn't answer, turning his gaze to the courtyard.

"We'll get that ill-tempered beast back into his stall," Seamus said. "I'm sure you want to reassure the lady that you've suffered no permanent damage."

"She did seem quite concerned, didn't she?" Tristan said, recalling the stricken expression on Sarah's face as the wolves dragged her away from him.

"That she did."

"Very concerned, even." A smile crept over Tristan's mouth.

"Yes, sir." Seamus scratched his thick sideburns. "What are you getting at?"

Tristan faced the wolf. "Don't tell her."

Seamus frowned at him.

"Don't tell her I'm healed," Tristan said, still smiling. "I'd like to see how this plays out."

Seamus regarded Tristan curiously. "Isn't that a bit cruel?"

"Don't forget what you just said, Seamus," Tristan replied. "It's not my job to be chivalrous."

18

HOURS HAD PASSED since Sarah had seen Tristan, and her throat felt raw from shouting at the Guardians who'd manhandled her back to her room. Though she'd yelled and pleaded, they'd waited until her stomach had tied itself in knots before Seamus finally arrived at the door, first to dismiss the sentinels and second to inform Sarah that while Tristan was injured, his life was not in immediate danger. Sarah had surprised herself by asking the wolf how soon she'd be able to see Tristan, to which Seamus had answered, "Sunset," which Sarah found to be an utterly nonsensical and random time for a visit, but since Seamus was likely to be the one watching over Tristan, she had no choice but to comply.

It had taken Sarah a ridiculous amount of effort to convince Moira that she could manage to bring the silver service to Tristan's room on her own. Once Sarah was crossing the hall bearing a tray laden with a teakettle, cup and saucer, creamer, and sugar bowl, however, she had to admit the whole business was both heavier and more awkward than she'd anticipated.

But cumbersome as her burden might be, it set the stage for the next scene of her plan. Sarah couldn't ignore the truth: she wanted Tristan more with each passing day. Accepting that fact, she'd decided to use it in her favor. She recognized the recklessness of this new plan, but it was the only way she could justify a possible usefulness for her unrelenting desire for Tristan.

It's not as if there aren't precedents for this: Samson and Delilah. Judith and Holofernes. Catwoman and Batman. How often is sex the only weapon left available for a woman to wield?

Her attempts to rationalize the choice made Sarah feel rather empty but did nothing to weaken her resolve. She was also uncomfortably aware that sex wasn't the only issue in play. Her terror when Tristan had rolled beneath the hooves of the stallion had been visceral. That feeling had nothing to do with desire, but Sarah couldn't bring herself to name its source. Focusing on the physicality of her attraction to Tristan was Sarah's only way to keep her aims clear. The rest of it could only lead to confusion and disaster. Sarah couldn't completely ignore that, beneath the surface, troubling emotions bolstered her desire for Tristan. But those were feelings she wasn't yet ready to face. For the moment, Sarah chose to put blinders on regarding anything other than sheer desire and its own means to an end.

As she'd anticipated, Sarah found Seamus standing watch outside Tristan's bedroom door.

He raised his bushy eyebrows at the tea tray. "How thoughtful."

"It's sunset," Sarah replied, suddenly defensive.

"That it is." Seamus opened the door for her with a smile. "He'll be glad to see you, miss. But if he's sleeping, please don't wake him. He needs the rest."

"Of course." Sarah nodded. The old man was so kind for a Guardian. She wondered how many years Seamus had served in the Keepers' packs. Given his age, and that the Keepers extended the lives of their wolves beyond normal human expectancy, she guessed he'd seen at least a century—which meant he likely didn't have much time left.

Seamus closed the door behind her and she crossed to the bed, where Tristan lay very still with blankets drawn up to his neck and his hands folded over his heart. His repose was far too similar to that of a body laid out for mourners' viewing, and Sarah felt a stab of relief when she heard his deep, steady breathing and saw the rise and fall of his chest.

This is a strategy, Sarah tried to convince herself as she carried tea to Tristan's bedside table. *I wanted him to fall in love with me, so he'll trust me and tell me what I need to know. Patients fall in love with their nurses, right? All part of the plan.*

A much more persuasive thought butted in: *That's not a plan. That's a subplot of* Back to the Future, *moron.*

Setting the tray on the bedside table, Sarah bent down and whispered, "Tristan?"

His eyes opened slowly. "Sarah?"

A lump formed in Sarah's throat. She reached out and took his hand. "I'm so sorry. Are you in much pain?"

"A bit." His fingers wrapped around hers. "Nothing I can't bear."

"What can I do?" Sarah couldn't stop the words from spilling out. "This is my fault. You probably saved my life. How can I make it up to you?"

Embarrassed by her outburst, Sarah lamely added, "I brought tea."

"I don't think I'm in the mood for tea." Tristan's other hand shot out, grasping her arm. He pulled her off her feet and on top of him.

Sarah gave a startled cry as Tristan flipped them over, pinning her to the bed. Now that he wasn't hidden beneath the sheets, Sarah saw that he was shirtless but wearing jeans. Half-dressed and far too agile for an injured man, Tristan could barely contain his laughter, and Sarah knew she'd been had.

"You're not hurt!" Eyes wide, she gazed at his bare skin. She could find no bruises. No marks. No sign at all that he'd been stomped on by that stallion when he'd shielded her body with his.

"No." He smiled down at her. "I have exceptional healers at my disposal. And now I'm good as new. Sweet of you to bring tea, though."

"I was *worried* about you," Sarah told him, still shocked by his sudden and total recovery.

"I can tell, and I appreciate your concern."

"You're a jackass." Sarah struggled against him to no avail.

Tristan laughed. "Maybe, but if I am, why did you bring me tea?"

"Fine." Sarah gritted her teeth, anger at the deception seeping through her veins. "Joke's on me. Now, let me up."

"Why would I do that?" Tristan asked. His voice had gone low, quiet in a way that made Sarah's pulse jump. "You said yourself you want to make this up to me."

"There's nothing for me to make up for," Sarah said. "You're fine."

"But I was hurt," Tristan replied. "Ares takes his tramplings quite seriously."

Tristan's grip on her wrists was unyielding but not painful. Where his fingers wrapped around her skin warmth began to spread—up her arms, over her shoulders, spilling through her chest.

Sarah swallowed hard, but her voice came out hoarse anyway. "What do you want?"

Why the hell did I ask that?

His smile somehow managed to be gentle and wicked at the same time. "I have another challenge for you."

"I'm tired of your challenges." Sarah tried to wriggle out of his grip, but he held her down.

"Really?" Tristan's gold-flecked eyes teased her. "But you've done so well. I've barely had the chance to question you."

Sarah pulled her gaze from his, hoping that might help her

focus on something other than how warm she felt. She tried to shut out the image of the taut muscles of his arms and shoulders. The way his jeans hung loose on his narrow hips so that they slid dangerously low when he moved.

"If I accept this challenge, will you let me up?" she asked, still looking away.

"Possibly."

Bringing her narrowed eyes back to his, Sarah snapped, "Why should I accept, then?"

"My answer was 'possibly' because of the nature of the challenge." Tristan surprised her when he released one of her wrists. He touched her cheek. His fingers trailed over her jaw and stroked her neck.

"What's the challenge?" Sarah's pulse was dancing at her throat. She wondered if Tristan could feel it.

"Kiss me," Tristan said, running his fingers lightly over her collarbone. "But that's all."

"That's all." Sarah stared at him. Her breath was coming in shallow pulls. "How is that a challenge?"

Tristan leaned down. His breath caressed her ear when he murmured, "Because I think you'll need more."

As her eyes closed, Sarah didn't doubt that he was right. If she did kiss Tristan, she'd want much more from him. But that didn't mean she couldn't overpower her own desires with the force of her will. If Sarah was anything, she was stubborn.

How hard could it be to stop at one kiss?

"Fine," Sarah said, but angled her neck away from his face. "I accept."

Tristan moved so he hovered over her once more. "Good." His teasing smile was gone, and there was a softness in his gaze, but behind that Sarah saw hunger.

He bent toward her, but Sarah put her hand firmly against his chest.

"I thought you were taking on the challenge," Tristan said.

"I am," Sarah replied, giving him a push until he was kneeling above her instead of pressing her into the mattress. "But the challenge is for me to kiss you. Not the other way around."

Though he frowned, Tristan let Sarah slide up until she was seated beside him.

Grasping the small advantage she'd gained, Sarah told him, "If I'm kissing you, I get to decide how it happens."

"Fair enough." Tristan shrugged, a curious smile flitting over his mouth. "So, how do you want me?"

Sarah swallowed a groan but didn't take the bait. "Right there is fine," she answered, keeping her tone nonchalant.

She moved into a kneeling position that mirrored Tristan's. Facing him, she leaned forward slightly. As she closed the small distance between them, Tristan's gaze slipped from her eyes to her mouth. He reached for her.

"No." Sarah grasped Tristan's wrists and placed his hands at his sides. "I'm kissing you, and that's all."

He laughed quietly but nodded.

Drawing a long breath in a vain attempt to slow her heartbeat, Sarah rested her fingers lightly on either side of Tristan's jaw. She let her eyes close just before her lips touched his, feather soft—it was the barest whisper of a kiss.

Even from that slight contact, Sarah had to quell the shudder of intense pleasure that wanted to grab hold of her. Knowing that if she pulled away now, Tristan would argue she hadn't managed a real kiss, Sarah parted her lips. Tristan's mouth opened in reply, and Sarah took his lower lip between her teeth.

The sheets beneath her rustled, and Sarah opened her eyes

just enough to glimpse Tristan's fists clenched around the bed-clothes. Smiling, she released his lip and slipped her tongue into his mouth.

She almost lost control.

He tasted extraordinary. Warm and rich, with an enticing bite. Sarah's hands left Tristan's face to slide around his neck. She pulled him closer, wanting a deeper kiss. A kiss that reached inside her to touch the heat pooling so low and sweet in her body.

It was the sound of her own small sigh of pleasure that brought Sarah back from the brink. Tristan was doing a fine job of keeping himself in check. His fingers still dug into the sheets, and he returned her kiss, his tongue gently stroking hers, his lips responding to each new touch, but he didn't try to make the kiss his own.

Summoning the small shred of will she had left, Sarah gentled the kiss. She unlaced her fingers from Tristan's neck and touched his face in a reversal of the way their kiss began. She parted their lips, put her hands beside her knees, and, keeping her eyes closed, pushed back from him.

After taking another deep breath, Sarah opened her eyes. Tristan was staring at her, disbelief naked on his face. Under any other circumstances Sarah would have laughed at his stunned expression, but she barely could keep herself from reaching out and pulling Tristan back into her arms. Moving with deliberate slowness, she uncurled her legs and swung them over the edge of the bed, praying she didn't teeter when she stood up.

Sarah rose, straightened her shoulders, and was thankful for every steady step she managed to take until she reached the door. Her hand was trembling as she reached for the knob and turned it. She'd opened the door just a crack when suddenly Tristan was behind her.

He reached over Sarah with one hand and slammed the door shut. His other hand grasped her hip, turning her to face him.

"You win." Tristan's eyes were alight with something Sarah couldn't name. Anger? Lust? Both?

Whatever it was, it emanated from him in waves, and Sarah wondered if she should be frightened.

"I win," she whispered, staying very still.

Then Tristan's mouth was on hers and there was nothing gentle in this kiss. It was rough and demanding, and exactly what Sarah wanted. She wrapped her arms around his shoulders and he lifted her up, carrying her across the room to lay her on the bed.

Tristan stretched over her, and Sarah let her hands roam the way she'd wanted them to when she'd been kissing him moments ago. Her fingers tangled in his hair, traced the shape of his strong shoulders. She pressed her palms flat against him to skim over the carved lines of his chest and the ridges of his abdomen, then slid her hands around his lower back.

Her lips were swollen from his kisses, but she met the force of his tongue and teeth eagerly, her mouth asking for more in turn. Tristan broke their kiss to trail his lips along her throat. His hands slid from her waist, up her ribs, and paused at the swell of her breasts.

Sarah moaned and arched up into his palms, feeling her nipples harden at his touch.

This is too much, too much. Her mind was a storm of sensation. *It's not enough. Not nearly enough.*

Her fingers dug into his back and Tristan reached up to grasp the sides of her blouse. With one hard tug, buttons went flying, exposing the delicate lace of her bra. Tristan bent to kiss the tops of Sarah's breasts, at the same time reaching behind her. Sarah arched up again to accommodate his hand and gave a cry of anticipation and relief when he unhooked her bra, freeing her breasts. Lifting her partly off the bed, Tristan used his free hand to pull her blouse off, then her bra, tossing both aside.

Holding Sarah tight to his body, Tristan moved to a kneeling position that left Sarah straddling him. His hands gripped her lower back and rocked her into his hips. She gasped when the softness between her legs met with the hard length of Tristan's cock. His hips thrust forward as his mouth covered the tip of her breast. Tristan's tongue circled her nipple, and a rush of heat and dampness at her core made Sarah whimper.

She was no longer holding Tristan but clinging to him, desperate for him to relieve the ache building inside her.

"Tristan."

Something in her voice made him pull back to look at her face. What he saw there enticed a slow, dangerous smile across his mouth.

Tristan didn't say anything as he leaned forward, pushing Sarah back onto the mattress while he stretched over her. His lips returned to hers, his kisses slow and deep.

He reached between them to unbutton and unzip her jeans. Without prompting she raised her hips so he could slide them off. Then his palm pressed between her legs. Sarah arched up against his hand and he groaned, slipping his fingers beneath the silk of her panties.

"Christ," he whispered, finding her hot and slick under his touch. "You're so wet."

Words seemed lost to Sarah; all she could do was writhe against Tristan's hand as he stroked her. She'd never thought an ache could be so unbearable and feel so good at the same time. Her body seemed to know that it needed something from Tristan, something she'd never had but wanted desperately. And it wasn't that Sarah didn't grasp the concept of fucking. But understanding the mechanics and living the sensation were more different than she ever had imagined.

"Please." She managed to get one hoarse word out.

Still caressing her with one hand, Tristan's other hand moved to the fly of his jeans. Sarah watched, riveted, as Tristan freed his cock, which had been straining against the fabric. Her moan of pleasure at the sight of his arousal surprised her, but Tristan smiled as he kicked off his jeans.

Taking one of Sarah's hands, Tristan guided it to his erection. When her fingers closed around the length of him, Tristan closed his eyes and groaned. Sarah's breath came faster. His cock felt more than good in her hand—thick and strong, straining against her touch. His skin was like silk, so surprising in contrast to how hard and insistent his erection was.

Sarah took a firmer grip, moving her hand up and down his length, and Tristan clenched his jaw. He caught Sarah off guard by slipping a finger inside her. Her hips bucked up instantly and she cried out, another rush of hot dampness flooding through her.

Withdrawing his hand, Tristan brought his finger to his mouth and Sarah shivered as she watched him.

"I want to spend a long time tasting you, Sarah." Tristan bent over her and nuzzled her belly. "But I think it will have to be later. Right now I can't wait."

Sarah's hips bucked again; the ache between her legs had taken her body hostage. "No waiting. I need . . ."

Her voice trailed off. Her body knew what it wanted, but her mind balked. Did she need this? All her instincts were screaming yes, but what little rational thought lingered reminded her that she didn't actually know. She'd never been there before.

Tristan kissed his way up her body, lingering at her breasts until she was writhing beneath his weight. She let go of his cock, burying her fingers in his hair and cradling his head as his tongue flicked over her nipples.

Screw rational. Sarah parted her mouth for Tristan when he bent over her again, kissing him eagerly. *I want this. I want this so much.*

Still kissing her, Tristan stripped off Sarah's panties and then his fingers delved back into her wet folds. His thumb found her clit and began to stroke it. Sarah's limbs trembled, sounds emerging from her throat of their own volition. She no longer had a sense of reality, only the waves of pleasure Tristan's touch evoked.

He kissed her earlobe, whispering, "Do you want me to make you come first? Or do you want this now?"

Tristan nudged her thighs farther apart and she felt the head of his cock press into the slick heat just shy of her opening.

"Tell me." Tristan pushed a bit farther and Sarah felt a surprising tension, and sudden awareness that there would be more than pleasure when he entered her.

Of course she'd known that. But tangled in Tristan's embrace, Sarah had forgotten that this moment would be weighty with trepidation as well as desire.

Tristan was smiling down at her, waiting for her reply. A part of her wished he would just thrust into her, even if it meant pain now and an uncomfortable explanation later. But his eyes were locked on hers, and she knew he wouldn't go on until she asked him to.

"I want—" Sarah couldn't break her gaze from Tristan's. "I don't know. I haven't—"

"Haven't what?" Tristan's smile faded. "Sarah, you're not . . . Are you telling me you're a virgin?"

Sarah didn't answer. She didn't have to. Tristan's eyes widened and his face paled slightly. Without warning he jerked back from her, as if she'd put a lit match to his skin. He swung his legs over the edge of the bed and stood up, his fists clenching and unclenching. Startled, Sarah grabbed the edge of the sheet and drew it up to cover herself to the waist.

"Bloody hell." Tristan grabbed his jeans from the foot of the bed. "Bloody fucking hell, Sarah."

His movements were stiff with anger. He tugged his jeans on while she watched in stunned silence.

Without another word, he was across the room and out the door, slamming it shut behind him.

19

TRISTAN BLEW PAST Seamus and down the hall. He didn't
stop until he reached the small bathroom attached to his study.

Fuck. Fuck. Fuck.

He was too furious to think, not too mention still so hard it
made his teeth hurt.

Gripping the marble basin with one hand, Tristan opened his
fly and drew out his swollen cock. He began stroking himself with
long, swift pulls. When Tristan closed his eyes he could still see
Sarah, panting beneath him; feel the weight of her breasts in his
hands when he kneaded them. He gritted his teeth, fully aware
how heavy his balls were, how his cock grew even stiffer as he
remembered being on the verge of pushing inside her.

God. She'd been so ready for him. So wet. He could only imagine how tight she would have been when he . . .

Tristan let out a groan as he came, his hot spurt of semen hitting the bathroom wall. He leaned against the sink, having found
the release he needed. But it was a bitter way to get off, considering he'd been about to have a beautiful woman whom he wanted
far more than he should.

"You know, I could have helped you with that."

Tristan looked up and saw Lana's reflection in the bathroom
mirror. Her wings gave an irritated little flutter.

"I'm not in the mood, Lana."

Lana stepped forward and ran her hands along his bare shoulder blades. "You *were* in the mood, but you finished without me. I bet I could bring you back though, so it's not a total loss."

One of her hands slipped around his waist to where his fly was still open. She grasped his cock that, while recently spent, was still half-erect. He clenched his jaw when he felt himself twitch with arousal at her touch. Tristan had no doubt that Lana could have him hard again in a matter of seconds. He also knew he could turn around and tell her to get on her knees and stay there until he had his satisfaction.

But it wasn't Lana who had gotten him so riled up he'd had to jerk himself off in the bathroom like some randy teenager. It wasn't Lana he wanted. He knew he would never want the succubus in his bed again.

Tristan swatted Lana's hand away from his cock and buttoned up his jeans. "If I need something from you, I'll ask."

A growl drew Tristan's gaze beyond Lana. Seamus stood just outside the bathroom door. Tristan was glad to note that the wolf's angry gaze was for Lana and not him.

Lana's nose crinkled up. "When was the last time you had a bath, dog?"

Seamus ignored her, turning his attention to Tristan.

"What it is, Seamus?" Tristan asked.

"The young lady has returned to her own room," Seamus replied. "I thought you'd want to know that."

"Thank you," Tristan walked around Lana, who remained stubbornly between him and the door. "Lana, please tell the kitchen staff that I'll expect dinner at the usual time tomorrow."

"You'll be dining alone I assume?" Lana asked.

"No," Tristan said. "They should prepare a meal for two."

Tristan hesitated when he passed Seamus. He wanted to ask if Sarah had seemed all right when she'd left his room, if she'd been upset. But he could do no such thing with Lana hovering nearby.

Though he knew it could only be an uncomfortable conversation, Tristan made up his mind to confront Sarah rather than delay the inevitable. He stopped to pull on a T-shirt before heading to her room.

When he reached her door and lifted his hand to knock, Tristan froze, realizing he had no idea what he planned to say. His thoughts remained scattered. What if she'd gone to bed and he was about to disturb her?

Tristan was still standing outside Sarah's room, debating what his first words should be, when the door opened.

"Tristan." Sarah's eyes widened. She'd changed into a long, silk robe that clung to her curves. Tristan's jaw clenched when he felt his cock stir simply from the sight of her.

Fucking hell.

But upon seeing Tristan at her door, Sarah clutched the robe's neckline, hiding any bare skin, and shrank away.

Is that what I've done? She's afraid of me?

"I—I was going to the baths before I turned in for the night." Sarah sounded as frightened as she looked.

Tristan coughed, trying to clear the tightness in his throat. "I don't mean to disturb you, but I was hoping we could talk."

"I don't—" Sarah took another step back. "I'm not sure that's a good idea."

Her eyes were downcast, unwilling to meet his gaze.

With a sigh, Tristan raked his hand through his hair. "I shouldn't have left like that. It was a damn fool thing to do. You have every right to be angry with me."

"But you were angry with me," Sarah said quietly. "Because I—"

Her voice died and Tristan realized with horror that Sarah wasn't afraid; she was ashamed.

What kind of a monster am I?

"No," Tristan said, clenching his fists to control the rising anger he felt at himself. "I was just . . . taken aback. But the way I behaved . . . Sarah, that wasn't your fault."

Sarah finally looked up at him, but what he saw in her face wasn't reassuring. She remained wary, confused, and worst of all, hurt. Tristan loathed himself for making her feel that way.

"I didn't mean to mislead you about . . . " Sarah said quietly. "I just didn't expect . . . I'm not . . . I don't—"

"Please don't apologize." Tristan tried to reach for her, but Sarah shrank from him again. He felt sick. "You have nothing to be sorry for. I'll leave you alone now, but I hope you'll join me for dinner tomorrow."

Sarah remained silent for several beats in which a cold fist seemed to grasp Tristan's lungs. Then she nodded and he could breathe again.

"Good, I mean, thank you," Tristan said. "Till dinner, then."

Sarah nodded again. "Till then."

She closed the door and Tristan turned away, acknowledging to himself that he'd become entangled with his prisoner in a way well beyond his intentions. More than that, he feared he'd already passed the point of being easily freed.

20

SARAH WAS AFRAID, but of what she could no longer be sure. Tristan didn't frighten her—at least, not in the sense that she thought he might do her physical harm or treat her with malice. The way he'd held her, touched her—the look in his eyes when he came close—all of these things bespoke an attachment that ranged beyond simple lust.

But that realization was frightening enough—more so because her own feelings reflected those she saw in Tristan.

Amateur. Sarah cursed her naïveté. She sat before the mirrored vanity, lost in thought as Moira brushed Sarah's hair and hummed dreamily.

How could I ever have thought I could seduce a man without consequences when I've never done it before?

Sighing, Sarah shook her head. *And now I'm obsessed with Tristan—a man who I humiliated myself in front of and I'm sure doesn't want me at all now. God, I'm an idiot. What was I thinking?*

"Did I pull too hard, miss?" Moira asked, frowning at Sarah in the mirror.

"Oh, no, Moira." Sarah waved her hand, bidding Moira to continue with her task. "It's not you."

Moira pursed her lips. "If you don't mind, miss, may I ask what's wrong? You seem so troubled."

Sarah met the girl's inquiring gaze. For a moment, Sarah was tempted to blurt out all her feelings. It would have been a relief to have someone to confide in. But just as quickly, she tamped down that notion. Not only was a young girl like Moira ill equipped to take on the burden of Sarah's troubles, but Moira was also technically among her enemies. All the servants in Castle Tierney had loyalty to the Keepers and were terrified of angering their masters. One wrong word and Moira might be frightened enough to repeat everything Sarah said to one of the older servants—no matter how poorly they treated the girl.

What a fucked-up place this is. Maybe that's why I'm fitting in so well. Because what else could I be but a total head case, given that I'm falling for my jailor?

And there it was. Sarah hadn't let herself fully admit where her feelings had been leading. But there was no use denying it anymore. Whatever excuses she'd made to justify her actions, the past twenty-four hours had laid stark her desire for Tristan—a longing that had nothing to do with her mission and everything to do with him.

"I'm just tired," Sarah told Moira. "But I'll be fine."

"Would you like some tea before you go downstairs?" Moira asked brightly.

Sarah smiled despite her nerves. Moira was always so eager to help—the girl's earnestness offered Sarah a nice dose of comfort.

"Thank you, Moira," Sarah replied. "But I'll just wait for dinner."

Though Sarah hadn't particularly expected Tristan to appear that evening and escort her to the dining hall, she nonetheless felt like she was walking to meet her doom as she descended the castle stairs alone. She entered the hall quietly and found Tristan already there. His back was turned to her as he paced before the fireplace. Sarah caught his expression in profile and saw her own anxieties captured on Tristan's face. She drew a sharp breath and Tristan turned at the sound.

"You came," he said, surprised and clearly relieved.

Sarah nodded, moving to her usual place at the table. "I said I would."

"I know, but—" Tristan sat beside her, still agitated. After a long sigh, he said, "I'm just glad you're here."

Sarah didn't reply. "Glad" wasn't a word she would use to describe her feelings about being there. She couldn't pick out a specific emotion from the turbulence that filled her mind. A part of her wanted to be near Tristan, hoping to sort through the confusion of thoughts with his help. But Sarah was hesitant to open up to him. His rejection of her the night before remained a fresh wound, perhaps too tender for close examination.

The meal presented was light—broiled fish and wilted greens—which came as a relief. Sarah didn't think her stomach could have taken heavy, rich foods. They both ate quietly until Tristan set his fork and knife down.

"Sarah, I—" He paused and then reached for her hand. She watched as he turned her wrist over and rested his fingertips against her palm. "I'm so sorry."

A lump formed in Sarah's throat so suddenly that she had to close her eyes. She refused to shed even a single tear in front of Tristan. The last thing Sarah wanted was for him to see any weakness on her part.

"Last night I was just . . . surprised," Tristan continued. "But that's no excuse for how I acted."

When she'd reined in her emotions, Sarah looked at him. "Thank you for apologizing." Sarah hesitated, her pulse quickening as she said, "I don't blame you for not wanting—"

I should have just slept with Jeremy. If I had, then I wouldn't be sitting here, humiliated.

Sarah ground her teeth, chastising herself for the hasty thought. *You didn't fuck Jeremy because it didn't feel right. Because you didn't know how much you could want to be with someone until . . .*

Watching the way the evening light softened the hard lines of Tristan's face, Sarah's chest cramped, making her wince. It didn't matter how much she wanted him. Not anymore. He'd made that clear.

"Not wanting?" Tristan frowned at her. "Sarah, if you think for a minute that I walked out last night because I didn't want you, you couldn't be more wrong."

"But when you found out that I haven't . . ." Her voice trailed off as she watched Tristan's jaw clench.

"I was a complete ass," Tristan said. "But that has nothing to do with how I—"

He fell silent and pulled his gaze off of her.

"How you what?" Sarah wrapped her fingers around his.

When he looked at Sarah again, the intensity in his eyes stole her breath. "I still want you. There was never a moment when I didn't want you."

"Then why did you leave?" Sarah whispered.

"Because I'd presumed things," Tristan told her. "And that meant I approached you in a way that wasn't . . . What I'm trying to say is that your first time should be handled with more finesse."

"I thought you had plenty of finesse," Sarah replied, and was immediately mortified. *What the hell did I just say?*

Startled, Tristan opened his mouth to reply, but then began to laugh. A momentary flare of anger lit Sarah's veins, but then she giggled and soon she was laughing so hard that her sides ached.

When she finally caught her breath again, all the tension gripping Sarah's body had ebbed away and she offered Tristan a genuine smile.

"I don't know what to make of you," Sarah said. "Aside from

the wealth and the Guardians, you're not at all what I've always been told Keepers are."

"Maybe that's because I've been kept apart from the other Keepers." Tristan threaded his fingers through hers.

Sarah shook her head. "I don't think that has anything to do with it. I think it's simply a matter of who you are."

"Do you like who I am?" Tristan asked softly.

"Yes," Sarah replied. "I shouldn't, but I do."

"Why shouldn't you?"

"You know why." Sarah frowned. "I'm a Searcher. We're enemies."

"You didn't know anything about me when you came here," Tristan said. "Now you do. Doesn't that change things?"

Sarah pulled her hand free of his. "It has changed how I feel about you. But it doesn't change how I feel about the war."

Tristan sat back in his chair, regarding Sarah for several moments. "What if you weren't fighting the war?"

"Impossible scenarios aren't helpful," Sarah said.

"It's not impossible," Tristan replied. "You've said yourself that your companions won't come looking for you. That they'll assume you're dead. What if you simply let them believe that . . . and stay here with me."

"No." Sarah didn't even allow herself to consider that option. "That would be a lie. I couldn't live with myself for turning away from people I love."

Tristan flinched at her words. "But you will turn away from me."

"That's different," Sarah told him. "This place, everything that's happened between us—it's a fantasy. The outside world is real."

"This is my world," Tristan countered. "And now you're part of it."

"I'm not."

"I want you to be."

"I can't stay," Sarah whispered. "I can't willingly be your prisoner."

"And I can't let you go," Tristan said. His voice became so soft, Sarah had to lean toward him to hear what he said next. "Not yet."

Sarah could barely breathe. "Not yet?"

Tristan moved so quickly, Sarah didn't have time to register that he'd gone from sitting beside her to standing over her. His hands cupped her face and he bent to kiss her. His lips were gentle, as though he worried she'd push him away. Sarah grasped the collar of Tristan's shirt. She opened her mouth to taste his tongue. Tristan slid one of his hands down her neck and Sarah sighed with disappointment when his palm barely skimmed her breast. His hand kept moving, tracing the curve of her waist and out again over her hip. When Tristan touched her thigh and his fingers slipped into the high slit of her gown, Sarah took his lower lip between her teeth, biting gently to urge him on.

A low sound, nearly a growl, emerged from Tristan's throat and Sarah bit harder, teasing the edge between pleasure and pain. She got the response she wanted when Tristan palmed her leg and his fingertips grazed her inner thigh. Sarah shuddered when his hand brushed against the silk of her panties. His fingers fluttered along her sex, the light touches sending flares of pleasure up to the crown of her head and down to the tips of her toes.

Sarah kissed Tristan harder. Undoing the top buttons of his shirt, she ran her palm along his collarbone. She held him closer as she inched along the seat of her chair, wanting more pressure from his hand against her. But Tristan pulled back, taking his hand out from beneath her dress. Sarah almost swore at him; her bruised lips wanted his kiss again and it was all she could do not to writhe in the chair in an attempt to ease the ache between her thighs.

Tugging on his shirt, Sarah said. "Don't stop."

"I'm not planning to." Tristan kissed her cheek, then whispered, "But we shouldn't stay here."

He stood, offering Sarah his hand. She took it.

Their fingers laced together. It was a simple act, but it was a way of clinging to each other as Tristan led Sarah out of the dining hall and up the staircase. The upper floor of the castle was quiet, for which Sarah was grateful. All she wanted to think of was Tristan. No doubt. No distractions. No fear of being watched.

He paused in the middle of the hall, leaving it to Sarah to choose their destination. Sarah squeezed his hand, pleased, and tugged him toward her bedroom door. Tristan pulled her into the room, shutting and locking the door behind them. He turned to face her. They stood in silence for a moment, breathing hard, gazing at each other. Tristan moved first, stepping forward and sliding his arms around Sarah's back. He pulled her against him, molding her curves to the hard lines of his body. Sarah could feel how taut he was, the power in his limbs. His hands moved to cup her ass and he lifted her up. She moaned when she felt the hard outline of his erection pressing into her.

Holding Sarah tight, Tristan carried her across the room to the bed. Rather than laying her down, Tristan set Sarah on her feet. He reached around and found the zipper of her dress. He pulled it down slowly, then took a breath and stepped back.

Sarah kept her eyes on Tristan's face as she slid the straps of her dress from her shoulders and down her arms. The bodice dropped away, and Sarah pushed the dress down her hips and let it fall to the floor. She stayed still as Tristan's gaze drank her in.

Taking a step toward him, Sarah reached out and finished unbuttoning his shirt. She waited as he shrugged the crisp cotton from his shoulders and chest. Unable to resist touching him,

Sarah laid her hands against his golden skin, feeling the warmth of his body and the rise and fall of his breath.

In a tender gesture, Tristan lifted one of her hands to his mouth and kissed her fingertips. When he released her hand, he wrapped his arms around her waist and pulled her close. He bent to kiss her and ran his hands up her spine, pausing to unclasp her bra. Sarah let the bra fall away and then arched up when Tristan lowered his head and took the peak of her breast in his mouth. She cradled his head as his lips and tongue caressed her skin. Her fingers slid through his hair and she gave a small cry of pleasure when his teeth gently closed on her nipple.

Tristan lifted his head and kissed her on the mouth again. His lips trailed over her cheek and he murmured, "Lie on the bed."

He watched as Sarah stretched out. Then she watched as he unbuckled his belt and shed his pants and boxers. She drew a quick breath of anticipation when she saw how aroused he was. When he came to the bedside, Sarah reached for his cock, but Tristan caught her wrist.

"Not yet."

Keeping Sarah's wrist in his hand, Tristan took her other wrist as he knelt above her, then pinned both her arms above her head while he kissed her. She loved the taste of him, the way his tongue stroked over hers, and the teasing nips of his teeth on her lips. Heat was building low in Sarah's body, her hips arched up toward Tristan's, but he kept his body above hers.

"I'm going to move," Tristan said, releasing her arms, "but I want your hands to stay above your head."

Sarah nodded, closing her eyes as Tristan's mouth and hands made their way down her body. He took his time enjoying her breasts. His palms cupped their weight, his fingers toyed with her hard nipples. He licked and sucked until Sarah was calling out his name, begging for relief.

She looked down at Tristan and met his eyes. He smiled and trailed kisses down her stomach. His forearms pressed her thighs apart. When Tristan's mouth brushed over the hem of her panties and she felt his warm breath between her legs, Sarah's heart jumped, making her wonder if she could handle what was about to happen.

Tristan pressed his lips against her sex through the fabric and Sarah gasped and then shuddered. She felt his hands at her hips, pulling her panties down. Though her pulse was racing, she didn't resist as he slipped her underwear off. She could barely breathe when his gaze fixed on her sex. Tristan glanced up at her and smiled again. Then he lowered his head.

⚘

Tristan had known Sarah's taste would be intoxicating. When his tongue flicked over her, the delicate skin already slick with desire, he was reminded of salt and honey. He glanced up at her and reveled in her expression of wonder and desire. It was still unbelievable to Tristan that he would be the man to teach her this pleasure. He moved his lips along her damp folds, building pressure, exploring her and gauging her reactions. When his tongue stroked her clit, Sarah bucked up with a startled cry.

She looked down at him, her cheeks flushed with lust and a little embarrassment at her body's instinctive reactions. Tristan smiled and kissed her inner thigh, then bent to suckle the most sensitive part of Sarah's body. She shuddered and sighed, but finally let herself ease into the strokes of Tristan's tongue.

His body felt like a coiled spring. The scent of her, the taste, made Tristan want Sarah more than seemed bearable. He wanted to be inside her, to feel her sheath clenching around his cock. Instead he held his instinct in check and concentrated on Sarah. Her hips began to rock against his mouth and she moaned.

While he continued to lick her clit, Tristan caressed Sarah's opening and then slipped a finger inside her. She drew a sharp breath and arched up. Working her clit with his lips and tongue, Tristan slid a second finger into Sarah's core and began to stroke her from within.

She was so hot and tight, and so goddamn wet, it made Tristan's cock ache and his ball sac grow heavy, insisting on relief soon.

Fucking hell. Hold it together.

It wasn't like Tristan to feel like he might lose control. He'd never wanted a woman as much as he wanted Sarah. The need to claim her, to ride her until he'd taken his pleasure, was wild within him. But he was determined not to rush her. Since Sarah was a virgin, he couldn't avoid causing her pain in this, their first time together. Tristan could, however, ensure that she experienced pleasure as well.

Tristan felt Sarah's body tighten around his fingers. Her breath came in shallow pulls and her skin was hot. He increased the pressure of his mouth on her clit and sped up the thrusts of his fingers. Sarah was rocking into his mouth and fingers, matching the rhythm. She arched up and cried out at the same moment that hot, liquid silk rushed over Tristan's fingers and her sex pulsed its climax.

Kissing his way up her body, Tristan let his hips settle between Sarah's thighs. The head of his cock slid against the heat of her wet cleft and Tristan gritted his teeth against the overwhelming urge to thrust into her.

Sarah was breathing hard.

"Tristan." She reached up to hold his face in her hands. "Oh my God."

He bent and kissed her mouth, letting his weight press her into the mattress. He felt the swell of her breasts, soft and heavy against his chest and he rocked his hips forward, letting his cock nudge into her slick opening.

Sarah kissed him harder, lifting her hips to meet him, and he pushed farther, sliding inside her until he felt resistance. Sarah felt it too and tensed. Her fingers dug into his shoulders.

"Tristan?" she whispered.

Tristan pulled back from their kiss, looking down at her. Her eyes had widened slightly and they were searching his for reassurance.

"Are you all right?" he asked. Propping himself up with one arm, Tristan cupped her breast with his other hand, teasing her nipple with his fingertips.

"Yes." Sarah arched up into his hand. "I want you. Please. I want you inside me."

Tristan bent to kiss her again. Sarah's arms slid around his neck and Tristan pushed into her, hard and deep. He felt Sarah's breath catch with pain. He continued to kiss her, easing her into the slow rhythm of his thrusts as her body stretched to accommodate him.

When he felt Sarah's hands slide down his back to grasp his hips and her legs wrapped around him, Tristan let himself stroke deeper and faster. She was tightening around him and he knew Sarah was close to another orgasm. She moved with him, lifting her hips to let him thrust deeper still.

Sarah's fingers dug into his hips and she cried out. Her body shuddered and her sex pulsed around his cock. As Sarah came, Tristan finally let himself ride her as hard as he wanted to. He reached beneath her, lifting her hips so he could bury himself deep within her over and over. Then he was coming, his seed spurting inside her and an accompanying tide of pleasure washing through his body.

Tristan groaned as he spent himself. Sarah clung to him,

holding his body close as she felt him climax. He rolled to the side, pulling Sarah into the curve of his body.

He stroked her hair and kissed her shoulder. Sarah tangled her arms with his.

"I don't know what to say," she murmured.

Tristan laughed quietly. "You don't have to say anything."

"But I—" Sarah hesitated.

Tristan tightened his arms around her.

"I want you to know," Sarah whispered. "I didn't know what it would be like."

Smiling into her hair, Tristan asked, "What was it like?"

"Beautiful," Sarah replied, tucking her chin into her chest as if embarrassed.

Tristan ran his hand down the length of her body. "For me, too."

Sarah rolled over so she was face-to-face with him. When he met her eyes, looked at her face, the flare of emotion was so sudden and intense, Tristan felt like he'd been socked in the gut.

Damn.

He'd been worried about control when he was fucking her, but Tristan saw now that where he'd really lost control was in another arena entirely.

Noticing the changed expression on Tristan's face, Sarah frowned. "Is something wrong?"

"No," Tristan said quickly. He brushed his lips across her forehead.

She watched him for a moment, then said, "Things have gotten very complicated, haven't they?"

Tristan swallowed hard and laced his fingers with Sarah's. "Yes. I think they have."

21

FOR A LONG time Tristan and Sarah lay together, each watching the other. Neither speaking. Then Tristan unlaced his fingers from Sarah's and stroked her cheek. Cupping her face, he kissed her, tenderly at first, but then parted her lips with his and tasted her mouth and tongue.

Sarah's body warmed, her muscles becoming pliant as Tristan's hands followed the curve of her waist and hip. His fingers slid over her ass and her body arched toward him. Gripping her hips, Tristan held Sarah slightly apart.

"Are you sore?"

Sarah frowned, then blushed when she understood his meaning. She shifted her weight, considering the question. "Maybe a little, but not enough to . . . I mean, I want to . . . if you—"

She blushed again, feeling both shy and ridiculous. *What am I, sixteen?*

Tristan kissed Sarah's forehead and her cheek. Now that he was closer, Sarah felt his stiff cock press into her thigh.

"Oh." She glanced down at his erection.

"As you've noticed," Tristan said, smiling at her, "I want to."

Returning his smile, Sarah said, "This time, there's something I want to do."

"Whatever you like." Tristan bent to kiss her, but when he started to push her down, Sarah resisted, rolling him onto his back.

"You said, whatever I like," Sarah said, leaning over him. "I like this."

She pressed her lips to his collarbone. His chest. Her tongue circled his nipple and then flicked lightly along his abdomen. She smiled when Tristan's body tensed with anticipation.

"Sarah." His hips rocked up slightly and the tip of his cock brushed her chin.

Turning her face, Sarah let her lips brush against the head of his rigid length. He shifted his weight and groaned as she traced the outline of his erection with whispered kisses. With each touch of her lips, Sarah felt him harden more. His cock twitched up, seeking the heat of her mouth and the grip of her hands.

Sarah ran her tongue along Tristan's full length and then took him into her mouth.

"Oh my God." Tristan's thighs flexed under Sarah. She tasted salt and spice at the tip of his cock.

Taking a firm grip at the root of his erection, Sarah stroked him while her mouth and tongue matched the pace of her hand.

Tristan began to thrust into her mouth. He swelled against her lips. Suddenly he grasped Sarah's upper arms and pulled her away from his cock and onto his chest.

"If you keep going I'll come in your mouth," he said.

"Would that be such a bad thing?" Sarah smiled down at him.

"Not at all," said Tristan with a smile of his own. "But I'm not ready for this to be over yet."

Cupping the nape of Sarah's neck, Tristan drew her down into a kiss. His other hand slid between their bodies. Pressing his palm against the shape of her sex, Tristan let his fingers begin to delve between her folds.

Sarah made a small sound against Tristan's mouth and moved against his hand.

Tristan broke their kiss. "You're already so wet."

"Yes." Sarah kissed him again, a little surprised herself that going down on Tristan had made her so ready for him. Then again, having his cock in her mouth was something Sarah had fantasized about. So was what she wanted to do next.

Sarah grasped Tristan's wrist and pulled his hand away from her. Straddling him, she lowered herself until she felt the head of his cock pushing into her slick opening. Her body was electric with the power she felt as he watched her. She reached for Tristan's hands and curved them over her breasts. Sarah closed her eyes as he cupped them and felt their weight.

Slowly, she lowered herself onto Tristan's cock. Her eyes opened wider, as the feeling of him so deep inside her was almost startling. Tristan made a low sound and propped himself up on one elbow. His other arm wrapped around her, pulling her close so he could draw her breast into his mouth.

Sarah tangled her fingers in Tristan's hair. Her other hand gripped his shoulder as she lifted her hips and began to ride him. His teeth grazed Sarah's nipple and she gasped, driving her hips down hard. Tristan continued to suckle her breasts and she moved, stroking up and down his cock with more urgency.

Heat and friction built an extraordinary pressure deep within Sarah. She let her head drop back, her silken hair touching the bare skin of her shoulders. No longer fully controlling the rise and fall of her hips, Sarah let her body take over. The base of Tristan's cock rubbed her clit, while inside her the head of his erection stroked hidden sites of intense pleasure.

Crying out as she came, hard and sudden, Sarah's fingers dug into Tristan's shoulders. She felt her sex rippling around him, clasping his cock with pulse after pulse of overwhelming sensation.

She was still dizzy from her climax when Tristan's mouth covered hers and, still inside her, he rolled Sarah onto her back. She gasped, ready to protest. Even his slow strokes felt like too much for her to take. But Tristan's lips and tongue coaxed her into the new rhythm. Soon she felt her hips lifting to meet his thrusts as that now-familiar tension stirred in her core. Tristan began to move faster and Sarah slid her hands over his back to cup his ass, loving the way his muscles flexed under her touch with each stroke.

Sarah could feel that Tristan was holding back, keeping himself in check for fear of hurting her. But she wanted him to let go. To feel the wonderful abandon she'd experienced when he'd turned control over to her fully.

"I want you to take me," she murmured into his neck. "Take me now. As hard as you want."

Tristan's body tensed and he kissed her temple. "Are you sure?"

"Yes."

He reached beneath Sarah, tilting her hips up, and thrust. Sarah bucked against him, crying out from the sheer pleasure of having him buried to the hilt inside of her. Tristan braced her hips against him and stroked in and out of her. Sarah ran her hands up his arms, reveling in his taut muscles, in his sheer male power. The tension building in her clit crested and washed over her. Sarah gasped and let the tide of pleasure carry her.

Tristan's cock grew even harder inside her as he thrust again and again. With a groan of pleasure he came and Sarah felt his cock pumping Tristan's seed deep inside her.

After pushing the damp hair from Sarah's forehead, Tristan bent to kiss her. He pulled out of her and rolled onto his side, drawing Sarah against him. Tucked against Tristan's body, Sarah found herself adrift in unexpected emotions.

How can I be so comfortable here? Feel so safe?

She tried to remind herself that Tristan was still her enemy.

That all of this was a bizarre twist in the plans she'd laid. But lying to herself was no longer viable. Tristan had become something wholly unanticipated. She was in the arms of a man she trusted. And whom, though the very notion still struck her as impossible, she'd begun to love.

22

SARAH SLEPT WITH her head resting against Tristan's chest. Tristan had woken some time ago, but he hadn't wanted to disturb Sarah. Her lips were slightly parted, her breath a warm caress on his skin. She'd wrapped one arm around him, and though she slept, her embrace remained strong, as though she needed him to stay close.

The sheets had slipped down in the night, baring one of Sarah's breasts for Tristan's admiration. He'd been resisting the temptation to trace the curve of her skin and tease her nipple until it hardened under his fingertips. Now that the full light of day spilled through the room, Tristan decided to indulge his urge.

He stroked Sarah's shoulder and collarbone, slowly moving his hand down and then cupping her breast. Tristan smiled when Sarah gave a sigh of pleasure and arched her back so the fullness of her breast filled his hand. Squeezing the soft flesh, Tristan circled her nipple with his thumb until it became erect. Sarah stirred but didn't wake.

Carefully lifting Sarah, Tristan bent his head and took the peak of her breast into his mouth.

"Tristan."

He looked up. Her eyes were open, her cheeks flushed. Sarah's hands cradled his head, her fingers tangled in his hair. Tristan teased Sarah's nipple with his tongue. Her breath came faster.

Still suckling Sarah's breast, Tristan reached beneath the sheets and pushed her thighs apart.

"Yes," Sarah breathed as Tristan began to massage her clit. Her hips rocked against his hand, encouraging him to increase the pressure of his touch.

Tristan rubbed the hot, sensitive nub, using the rhythm of Sarah's movement to gauge the speed of his strokes. She was panting now, her body writhing against his touch. Her hands moved from Tristan's head to grip his shoulders. Sarah's nails dug into his skin as she cried out, her hips thrusting forward and slick heat spilling onto his fingers.

Sarah was still trembling from her climax when Tristan gently pushed her onto her back and pushed his stiff cock inside her. His head dropped forward as he fought to control himself. Her sex was still rippling from her orgasm, pulsing around Tristan's cock.

Gritting his teeth, Tristan forced himself into a slow, steady rhythm, wanting to bring Sarah back to the brink before he came. Sarah reached up to wrap her arms around Tristan's neck. She pulled him down into a kiss, tasting him as her hips arched up to match his thrusts. Their kiss deepened as he stroked deeper and harder inside her. When Tristan felt Sarah's sharp pull of breath as her sex tightened around him, he let himself give in and fuck her the way he needed to. He rode her faster, thrusting to the hilt. Sarah broke from their kiss and shouted Tristan's name as another orgasm overtook her. Tristan groaned and bit her shoulder as he came, stroking deep until he was fully spent.

Tristan rolled onto his side, propping himself up on one elbow so he could look down at Sarah. He cupped her jaw, stroking her cheek with the pad of his thumb.

"Good morning." Sarah smiled, reaching up to touch his face. "It is morning, isn't it? Or am I just having a really great dream?"

Tristan kissed her forehead. "It's morning. Unless we're dreaming the same dream."

"That would be quite the trick." Sarah stretched beneath Tristan and he felt a wave of happiness as he witnessed her contentment.

"What would you like to do today?" he asked her.

"You mean you don't have a challenge ready for me?" Her tone was light, but the question made Tristan uneasy.

"I think perhaps we've moved past challenges," he said.

Sarah looked at him, silently running her hand over his neck and shoulder, down his arm.

"Yes," she said quietly. "But I'm not sure what that means."

Tristan nodded, his gut clenching as their easy mood ebbed away. "Would you like to take a walk outside the castle grounds? It looks like the weather will hold today."

"A walk would be nice," Sarah said, though her body had tensed much like Tristan's had. "Maybe a bath first."

Unwilling to lose all of the happiness they'd been enjoying until now, Tristan said, "Would you mind company?"

"In the bath?" Sarah's mouth twitched into a smile. "That has potential."

"I thought so too."

Her smile became a frown. "But . . . won't we be seen?"

"Sarah, if you were hoping to keep our tryst a secret, you picked the wrong place and the wrong lover," Tristan said. "My movements are always tracked."

"I know," Sarah said, shifting beneath him uneasily. "But don't you find that a bit uncomfortable?"

"Of course," he replied. "But I don't have a choice in the matter."

"And why is that?" Sarah asked.

Tristan hesitated, taken aback by how much he wanted to tell her. Everything. But how much of a risk would that pose? Despite his feelings for this woman, Sarah was still a Searcher, and still a threat. Wasn't she?

Opting to dodge the question, Tristan said, "That's a conversation better suited for our walk."

"All right." Sarah gave him a skeptical look that quickly became mischievous. "But first the bath?"

"First the bath." Tristan bent to kiss her.

Smiling, Sarah rolled from the bed and Tristan enjoyed his view of her walking naked across the room to the alcove. When she reemerged, Sarah had donned a silk robe.

Tristan left the bed and pulled on his trousers. "If you don't mind stopping by my room, I'd much rather wear a robe to the baths than the bottom half of my suit."

"Is your robe rose silk, too?" Sarah grinned at him. "I'm sure you're stunning in it."

Laughing, Tristan took her hand and they left Sarah's room behind, crossing the hall to Tristan's door.

Tristan pulled Sarah into his room, and close to him. He kissed her neck and earlobe.

"You know, we could stay here for a bit before we go to the baths."

But Sarah had gone stiff in his arms. She was staring at his bed. Tristan turned and his blood went cold. His bed wasn't empty.

"There you are." Lana sat up, not bothering to cover her bare breasts when the sheet dropped away.

Tristan froze. "What are you doing here?"

Her laugh crackled with delight. "Waiting for you, of course." Her eyes grazed over Sarah. "I didn't know you'd be bringing company. Though your little pet is welcome to join us. I know we talked about a threesome—this is a fabulous opportunity, don't you think?"

Tristan took a step toward the bed but stopped because of the sound that slipped from Sarah's throat. It was a sort of cry, terribly soft and cracking.

"Sarah." Tristan turned, reaching for her.

Sarah jumped back to avoid his touch. Her eyes were fixed on his face, and the look Tristan found there robbed his blood of its heat. All the color had drained from Sarah's face. Her green eyes were wide with disbelief and a desperate hope. She stared at him, waiting for the denial he couldn't offer.

When Tristan didn't speak, Sarah's gaze left him and settled on Lana once more. After a moment, Sarah closed her eyes. Tristan watched her shoulders begin to tremble. He took a step forward, but she backed away without looking up.

"No." He barely heard her whisper.

Without warning Sarah bolted from the room, and Tristan heard the slamming of her bedroom door from across the hall.

A throaty laugh glided across the room. Lana slouched onto the pillows, running her hands over her bare skin.

"Mmmmmmm. That was perfect. Just perfect."

Tristan went to the door and closed it. He wanted to go after Sarah, but this disaster had to be dealt with first.

Lana rolled onto her side as Tristan crossed the room. She stretched her hand toward him. "Come here, lover. That little scene has left me in the perfect mood to please you. I'll do whatever you like."

"I don't want you here, Lana," Tristan said. "Get dressed and get out. You aren't welcome in this room or my bed without an invitation."

"So formal." Lana twirled her fingers through her ebony curls. "Don't you like surprises anymore?"

"I said, get out."

Lana sat up, her playfulness vanishing. "I came to take what was owed me. You said the Searcher would suffer for my pleasure. Instead you act as if . . ." Her eyes narrowed and she drew a hissing breath. "You're in love with her."

"I see jealousy addles your mind, Lana," Tristan said, ignoring the thud of his pulse. "Love? You know that's a child's game."

"But you are a child, Tristan." The rage in Lana's face gave way to a cool smile. "Do you think she belongs to you? That she could love *you*?"

Tristan returned her gaze steadily. "That's not a concern of mine."

"I think it is." The growing pleasure in her voice made Tristan's fists clench. "And I wonder how Bosque will take the news. His progeny ensnared by the charms of not only a simple human, but a Searcher."

"I'm sorry you've grown so bored that you need to spin these mad tales," Tristan said. "And I doubt that Bosque will appreciate being so misled."

"That stoic façade of yours doesn't fool me, Tristan." Lana rolled off the bed. She walked toward him, naked and uncaring.

Tristan went very still as Lana gripped his shoulders and leaned in, whispering, "Do you think he'll approve? Do you dream that he'll elevate her when you ask? You know that will never happen. Not after Marise."

Tristan hunted for a cutting retort but could find none. Lana's verbal blow struck true and its pain lingered. Marise Bane, like Tristan, had been a direct descendant of Eira—the first Keeper. Matriarch of all Bosque Mar's followers. And just as what would one day be expected of Tristan, Marise's marriage and her production of further heirs of the original Keeper line should have been overseen by Bosque himself. But that was not what had happened.

Cloaked in rumor and speculation, the tale of Marise's rebellion was considered a blatant lie by some Keepers and storied truth by others. If the gossip was true, Marise had won the love of a fellow Keeper—another direct descendant of Eira, in fact—but Marise's paramour had been a woman: Lumine Nightshade. Unwilling to tolerate their relationship, Bosque commanded that the lovers be separated. Though Marise couldn't defy Bosque's direct order, she retaliated by quickly engaging in a sordid affair with a human. A rakish gambler brought to the American West by the Colorado Gold Rush, Efron LaSalle bore no resemblance to the type of mate Bosque would have picked for Marise. By the time Marise's act of retribution came to light, she was carrying Efron's child. Though Bosque held only disdain for Efron, Marise's pregnancy kept the Harbinger from ridding his house of the undesirable rogue. Thus, Efron the gambler had been elevated from shiftless wanderer of the frontier to husband of one of the most powerful Keepers alive. Marise's vengeance cut deeper still upon her death in childbirth, leaving Efron alone to raise the new heir to Bosque's legacy.

Lana's questions struck at the heart of Tristan's predicament. Even if Sarah could be persuaded to stay at Tristan's side, Bosque would never brook a Searcher for his heir's wife. At best Tristan's master would tolerate Sarah as a mistress, but even that small mercy seemed uncharacteristic of the Harbinger.

Tristan had no choice but to glare at Lana and remain silent while she smirked.

After kissing his cheek, Lana walked away from Tristan and opened the door.

"Don't leave your clothes here," Tristan called after her. "I don't want you or anything of yours in this room."

"I didn't wear any when I came," she answered, and paused to look over her shoulder at him. "You should remember something, Tristan, or you might get yourself into real trouble."

"What's that?" Tristan asked stiffly.

"Keepers aren't meant to love, they're meant to rule."

Tristan waited until she was gone, then he dropped into a crouch and buried his face in his hands. He'd broken into a cold sweat and he was dizzy to the point of not being certain he'd stay on his feet if he stood up.

He had to go to Sarah, but what could he say to her? How could he explain?

Gritting his teeth, Tristan realized he couldn't justify, apologize, or rationalize anything. Not until he knew what Sarah was feeling, what she thought of him after . . .

He shuddered and forced himself to stand. Quivering on the floor like a coward accomplished nothing. He stumbled into the bathroom and splashed icy water on his face until his mind cleared and the trembling of his limbs ceased.

The trepidation Tristan experienced as he crossed the hall and knocked on Sarah's door was damn near paralyzing. When she didn't answer, Tristan knocked again.

"Sarah?" he called.

No response.

Tentatively, Tristan turned the doorknob. At least she hadn't locked him out. Tristan entered the room and closed the door behind him. Sarah wasn't immediately in sight.

"Sarah?"

"Go away!" Her voice was slightly muffled behind the half-open door to the alcove bathroom.

"We need to talk." Tristan paused outside the alcove. "May I come in?"

"No!" A violent retching sound from the other side of the door alarmed Tristan enough that he pushed into the bathroom.

Sarah was kneeling beside the toilet. Sweat had matted her

hair to her forehead and temples. She averted her eyes from Tristan, but not before he saw how bloodshot they were. Tears streaked her cheeks.

"I don't remember inviting you in," she said, scooting along the floor so she could lean against the alcove wall.

"You're sick." Tristan bent on one knee, peering at her.

"Something like that." Sarah turned her face away from him. "Stop it."

"Stop what?" Tristan asked. "Stop looking at you?"

"Stop pretending you care whether I'm sick or not," Sarah replied. "Stop acting like you have any regard for how I feel at all."

"Sarah—"

Her head snapped up. "Do *not* say my name like that."

Tristan frowned as he stood up. "I don't understand."

"You have no right to speak to me as if there's something between us," Sarah said.

"There is," Tristan said. "If you just let me explain—"

"Explain that you prefer fucking monsters?"

"I don't." Tristan bristled at her tone.

"Then you haven't fucked her?"

He didn't answer. Sarah drew up against the wall, shrinking farther from him.

"Things were different before you came here. I didn't know—" he began, then sighed. "Sarah, it's not—"

"I told you not to say my name like that," she said. "And I don't care what it is or is not. I know all that I need to. Now, get out."

The derision in her voice was so similar to his own toward Lana that Tristan balked despite his desire to argue. Had Sarah's perception of him changed so drastically?

Do you think that she belongs to you? That she could love you?

Tristan took a step forward, reaching for Sarah. "You know who I am. The past doesn't matter."

"The hell it doesn't!" She knocked his hand back. "I hate myself for letting you near me. You will never, ever touch me again."

It felt as if the floor suddenly heaved beneath him, and Tristan grabbed the doorknob to steady himself. Sarah was on the bathroom floor, vomiting, not because she was sick but because of her revulsion—revulsion toward him.

"Leave," Sarah said. "If you're going to kill me, kill me. Otherwise, stay away."

With a nod Tristan pushed himself out of the alcove. Unsteady steps carried him across the room and into the hall, where he stumbled into Seamus.

"Is everything all right, Tristan?"

You are a child.

Something splintered inside Tristan. Something old and long-buried. He collapsed against the wolf, his body quaking with silent sobs.

"Ah, lad." Seamus shouldered Tristan's weight, helping him across the hall and into his room. "It was bound to happen. There's no shame now. No shame."

But it wasn't shame that wrung sorrow from Tristan's body. It was fear, a slow spread of horror through his limbs, for he knew that he'd found something he desperately needed. Something he hadn't known he was searching for but that he'd just as likely lost forever.

23

SARAH DIDN'T REMEMBER when she'd dragged herself out of the alcove and into bed. She must have fallen asleep at some point, because a knocking at her door woke her. Her head throbbed and her body felt bruised and knotted. She rolled over, willing the interruption away. All Sarah wanted was to forget everything that had happened the night before, to hide from the world as long as she could. But whoever was at the door refused to give her respite and the loud banging persisted.

When it became clear that the knocker wouldn't be giving up, Sarah forced herself out of bed and went to the door. Her hands were shaking. It could only be Tristan, and she didn't know how to face him. Her chest cramped, full of pain and longing. She didn't understand how it could be possible to want someone so much and yet hate him with equal vigor.

Leaning her forehead against the hard surface, she spoke into the solid wood. "Tristan, I'm sorry. I just . . . I can't . . . not yet."

"It's Seamus, miss," a gruff voice answered.

Sarah straightened, suddenly more alert than she'd felt all night. The wolf was at her door and fear began to cool her blood.

"Is Tristan all right?" Sarah cracked open the door. If Seamus was there and not Tristan, did that mean something had happened to him in the few hours since she'd banished him from her room?

"That's what I'd like to speak with you about," Seamus replied. "May I come in?"

Nodding, Sarah stepped back to let him through the door. They regarded each other warily. Searcher and Guardian both knew that in most situations their encounter could only result in a fight to the death. Yet nothing that had taken place in Castle Tierney seemed to follow the rules that Sarah had learned about her world and this war.

"Would you like to sit?" Sarah gestured to the high-backed chairs near the bedroom's fireplace.

Seamus shrugged and took a seat while Sarah settled into the chair opposite him.

Clearing his throat, Seamus said, "I understand you and Tristan had a falling-out."

Sarah stared at the wolf for a long moment and then laughed harshly. "I don't know that a 'falling-out' is how I'd describe it."

"How would you describe it?" Seamus asked, unruffled by her irreverent reaction.

"I believed Tristan was something other than what he truly is." Sarah straightened in her chair, defensive under the wolf's judgmental gaze. "I blame myself for ignoring the fact that he's a Keeper. And my enemy."

She added, with a glare, "Like you."

Seamus nodded, one corner of his mouth tilting up. "And yet, we're sitting here peacefully, not fighting."

"I don't have any weapons," Sarah told him.

"So you'd just attack me if you did?" Seamus countered. When Sarah didn't reply, he said, "Things are not as they seem in this place. You know that. You've lived it."

"I've been a fool." Her voice was low and accusatory, but only toward herself.

Seamus leaned forward, resting his elbows on his thighs.

"You're not a fool. You're young. So is Tristan. And there are greater things at work here than what side of a war you're fighting on."

"What's greater than a war?" Sarah asked.

"I think you know."

Sarah looked away from the wolf. Her fingers curled tight around the chair arms. "I can't love him."

"You do love him."

"It doesn't . . . How I feel is . . ." Sarah hated how her voice was shaking. She couldn't stop seeing Lana's bare flesh tangled in Tristan's sheets.

Seamus's nose crinkled up. "I know what you saw last night, and you shouldn't dwell on it. Lana did it to provoke you."

"She succeeded," Sarah murmured.

"She's very good at it," Seamus replied. "But don't blame Tristan for Lana's cruelty."

"But—" Sarah couldn't finish the sentence. It was too humiliating. Maybe Tristan hadn't intended for Sarah to know about his trysts with Lana, but that couldn't erase the fact that they'd happened.

"He hasn't been taking the succubus to his bed," Seamus said, surmising the direction of Sarah's thoughts.

"Since I've been here," Sarah replied, her glance challenging the wolf to argue with her. Tristan had told her the same, but that knowledge did little to assuage her injured feelings.

Seamus shook his head. "You can believe what you want, but I swear to you it stopped well before you showed up. He never had much of a taste for the hell bitch. He was fucking her because it was expected."

"How would fucking a succubus ever be something that's expected of a person?" Sarah half laughed, half choked in disbelief.

"You're not a Keeper. You haven't lived in his world," Seamus said. "Who Tristan is meant to be weighs heavily on him. He's been trying to fill that role, but his nature isn't suited to it. Even so, when Bosque Mar sends you a toy, you play with it and offer your gratitude."

Sarah shuddered at the implications, feeling a wave of nausea course through her. When she'd taken a few breaths to calm her roiling stomach, she paused, considering the wolf's words, and asked, "Who is Tristan meant to be?"

Seamus's lip curled back, revealing sharp canines, and Sarah rose from her chair, taking a step back.

"You started this," she said. "If you don't want to tell me, why did you come here?"

The wolf growled at her but didn't move to attack. "I probably shouldn't have come to you. But the lad deserves better than this fate, and as far as I can see you're the only thing that might save him from it."

Sarah stared at Seamus, barely able to breathe. *What fate?*

Reading the question in her eyes, Seamus said, "I think it's best for you to find out for yourself. Ask Tristan about his parents. I think he'll be ready to tell you now . . . if you're ready to let go of what came to pass before you were in his life."

"And if I'm not?"

"Then you've condemned the both of you, and you have my pity." Seamus stood up and gave a slight bow. "Miss."

He paused at the door, saying over his shoulder, "If you do decide to speak with Tristan, you'll find him in the stables."

When he was gone, Sarah went to the alcove and splashed cold water on her face.

The lad deserves better than this fate.

Sarah gripped the sides of the basin, letting water drip down her cheeks and into the sink.

What was happening within these cold stone walls? More was

at play than her unwelcome attachment to Tristan. Much more. And Seamus—who should show an interest in Sarah only as far as ripping her throat out—had just urged her to delve deeper into the castle's secrets.

They both manage to escape.

Did Tristan want to escape his fate as much as Seamus hoped the Keeper could avoid it?

Sarah made up her mind and quickly dried her face with a towel. The wolf had played his cards wisely; Sarah's curiosity was piqued. She wanted to know what was keeping Tristan in this place and, more than that, she hoped the answer to that riddle would offer her a way to justify her feelings for him.

After dressing in a simple cotton shirt and jeans, Sarah went in search of Tristan. Warm spring air suffused the courtyard as she arrived at the stables. The sun peeked through a light veil of clouds, muting the colors of an otherwise fine morning.

She found Tristan fully consumed by his labors. His shoulders flexed as he forked hay into the stall, his skin glistening with a soft sheen of sweat. Sarah watched him work, taking in the fluid lines of his body. Even the brief glimpse of his taut arms and back heated Sarah's blood.

"Tristan." Her voice cracked when she said his name, and she bit her lip with chagrin.

His movements became stiff, but he didn't turn to face her. "What is it, Sarah?"

Though Tristan kept at his task, his anger was clear in the way the pitchfork jerked in his hands.

Sarah's fingernails dug into her palms. She'd come to try to untangle her knot of confusing impulses, but how could she when he wouldn't even look at her.

"Are you just going to stand there?" Tristan's laugh was disdainful. "Feel free to pick up a fork and lend a hand."

Heat flooded her cheeks. "I wanted to talk to you."

"Talk, then."

Edging toward him, Sarah said, "About last night . . . I shouldn't have said those things about you."

His jaw clenched, but he didn't speak. His cold demeanor made Sarah's chest cramp.

"Tristan, please." She'd come up beside him. "I want things to be right between us." *Right between us? I don't even know what that means.* She doubted any words would suffice to describe the mess she'd found herself in.

Tristan paused and then set the pitchfork down. At first Sarah was relieved, but when he looked at her she was filled with dread. The bitterness in his gaze made her take a step back.

"How can things be right between us, Sarah?" He snapped. "Ever? Have you forgotten who I am? Who you are?"

"Of course not."

"You didn't have to come down here to apologize," Tristan continued. "What you said was true. And it did a fine job of reminding me where I belong. I am nothing more than your enemy. I'm everything you hate."

"Don't say that," Sarah whispered. Her chest cramped at the implications of his words. She couldn't blame him. Hadn't she been the one to say she never wanted him to touch her again? Those words had been fueled by grief and fear, but she didn't know how to take them back.

"Why not?" Tristan's mouth hooked into a cruel smile. "Would you rather I lied to you?"

Sarah stared at him. She was tempted to run, as she felt tears threatening. Instead, she forced her chin up, facing her own fears as much as his obstinacy.

"Why are you saying this?" Sarah asked. "I know I made you angry and I'm sorry for that. But this isn't you."

"Because you know me so well." Tristan started to turn away, but Sarah grabbed his arm.

He went very still. "Don't."

Sarah didn't let go. She moved closer to him, reaching up to touch his cheek with her other hand.

"Don't," he said again, closing his eyes. "You asked me not to touch you again. If you meant that, walk away now."

She stroked her fingers along his temple and jaw. "I'm not walking away."

"Sarah," he said.

She rose onto her tiptoes and kissed him. His body didn't yield to her touch, and he remained stiff, inflexible.

"Tristan, I—" Her throat wanted to close, but she forced the words out. "I know exactly who you are . . . and I'm in love with you."

Tristan went very still, and Sarah stood watching him. She'd never intended to confess so much, and suddenly she could hear only the hammering of her pulse as she held her breath.

Then Tristan groaned and wrapped his arms around her. He lifted Sarah up and carried her into the stall, laying her upon the fresh bed of hay. She opened her mouth when he bent to kiss her. His lips and tongue met Sarah's with a force that verged on desperate.

Sarah gasped when Tristan's arm slid beneath her and rocked her hips up against him. His erection was already straining against his jeans, pushing into the softness between her legs. The strokes of his hands and the hunger in his kiss made it plain how much he needed her.

"I thought I'd lost you," he whispered. "I can't lose you, Sarah."

Molding her palms to the hard muscles of Tristan's upper back, Sarah pulled him down onto her body, welcoming his weight and the thrust of his hips against hers.

"I need to fuck you hard." His teeth grazed her neck. "Now."

At the raw edge of Tristan's voice, Sarah felt a sudden, clenching heat between her thighs. She didn't trust herself to speak, so she nodded.

Tristan rose to his knees and tugged off Sarah's jeans and panties. Leaving her shirt on, Tristan grasped Sarah's hips, turning her onto her hands and knees in one smooth motion.

Sarah was breathing hard as she heard Tristan unzip his fly. She felt his hands gripping her hips and then she cried out as the hard length of him thrust inside her.

He pulled back and thrust again. Sarah moaned, dropping her head as heat washed over her body. Tristan's fingers took a near-bruising grip on her skin as he found his rhythm, pounding into her, each thrust of his hips harder, faster.

Sarah dug her nails into the ground, feeling her body tense as pleasure welled deep inside her. Tristan's balls slapped against her with each thrust of his cock, making her tremble and then shudder as her climax came in waves. She felt Tristan grow even harder as she came, then he groaned as he spent himself inside her.

After quickly pulling out of her, Tristan drew Sarah's body against his and rolled them over to lay curled in the sweetly scented hay. He pushed her hair aside and kissed the back of her neck and her shoulders.

"Get dressed," Tristan murmured, "and come with me to the baths."

24

STEAM CLOUDS BILLOWED around Tristan and Sarah as they sank into the hot water of the bath. Tristan was grateful for the quiet and privacy offered by the thick heat of the room. He needed to feel apart from the madness that his world had become, even if it was only for a little while.

He settled onto the bench in the deeper section of the bath while Sarah submerged, soaking her hair and face. She languidly floated in the water while Tristan watched steam silhouette her body like silken gauze. His gaze followed her movements and he resisted the urge to go to her and take her in his arms. Tristan regarded the intensity of his feelings with deep wariness. He didn't deny their existence, but he wasn't entirely comfortable claiming them either. To want someone as much as he wanted Sarah left Tristan uneasy. His life had always been carefully controlled; what he felt for Sarah was unpredictable, almost wild, both addictive and alarming.

"I am a fan of these baths." Sarah swam up to Tristan and nestled in the curve of his arm. Tristan pulled her close, running his fingers over her wet skin. The water cradled her breasts, and Tristan drew her onto his lap so he could fondle them. His cock grew hard at the thought, seemingly never sated even after having so recently taken her.

Sarah shifted restlessly against Tristan, but not in a way that signaled she was feeling amorous.

Reining in his ardor, Tristan asked, "What is it?"

"Seamus told me to ask about your parents," Sarah said.

"Seamus said that?" Tristan's arms tightened around Sarah. Why would the old wolf be pushing Sarah to learn about his past?

"Yes." Sarah turned so she could look at him. "What do you think he wants me to know about them?"

"I'm not sure." Tristan sighed. He usually avoided giving too much thought to his childhood. "He was never fond of my parents, but then again, neither was I—at least not of my father. Truthfully, Seamus took care of me more than either of them."

"Why is that?"

Tristan leaned forward, placing a gentle kiss on Sarah's damp mouth. He needed the reassurance of her closeness before he traversed any further into this conversation.

"How much do you know about Keeper lineage?" Tristan asked.

"Very little." Sensing his uneasiness, Sarah wrapped her arms around Tristan's neck. "I know that Bosque Mar, the Harbinger, made the first Keepers way back when and there have been more ever since."

"Not many more," Tristan told her. "We keep our numbers small so we don't have to share too much power. And we only have children as we are bidden."

"As you're bidden?" Sarah's brow furrowed. "You have children when you're told to. Who does the bidding?"

"Bosque."

She drew back from him, and Tristan saw fear in her eyes. "He has that much control over your lives?"

"Those of us he deems important enough." Tristan shrugged to hide the tension building beneath his ribs.

"And what makes one Keeper more important than another?" Sarah asked. "You aren't all the same?"

Tristan shook his head. "Our world is very hierarchical, much like the one in which we first came to power. Bosque favors Keepers who can trace their lineage back to Eira, and demands they carry on his legacy in this realm."

"And you can?"

"Yes." Tristan tangled his fingers in Sarah's wet hair. "Eira is my grandmother."

He felt Sarah tense. "Your grandmother was the first Keeper."

"And my parents married and produced an heir when Bosque dictated that they must," Tristan said quickly. "No sooner."

"Were they in love?" Sarah frowned at him.

"No," Tristan answered. "They came from the proper families."

Sarah touched his cheek. "That's awful."

He laughed roughly. "I suppose it is."

"Not to get too Freudian," Sarah said carefully, "but you don't believe your parents didn't love *you,* do you? Because I'm sure they must have."

"I'm not so sure," Tristan replied, smiling at how convincing Sarah had tried to sound. "My mother did, but she was always brusque with me—concerned that I not be coddled. My father treated me like a business transaction. He had very little to do with raising me. If I give them the benefit of the doubt, I'd say that perhaps they didn't want to encourage me to become attached because they knew they weren't long for the world. And I'd be alone."

Sarah shivered and Tristan pulled her onto his lap. She tucked her head beneath his chin.

"Will you always be alone here?" Sarah asked him.

"Bosque sends visitors on occasion," Tristan replied. "But no one will come to stay until—" He stopped, not wanting to upset her, but Sarah finished the thought for him.

"Until he sends you a wife."

"Yes."

Sarah became very quiet.

"I don't want it," Tristan murmured. "I've never wanted it."

"What do you want?" Sarah's lips brushed his throat when she spoke.

Tristan pushed her away from his chest and tipped her chin up. "I want you."

He bent to kiss her, but Sarah turned her face away.

"Tristan, I can't be that to you," she said. "I love you. But I won't become a Keeper."

"I'm not asking you to," Tristan said quietly. "Even if I was, Bosque would never allow it."

"But before now you've asked me to stay," Sarah said.

"I know." Tristan dropped his gaze. "That was before . . . when it was all part of a game."

He glanced at Sarah, expecting her fury, but she was nodding. "I understand. It was a game for me, too . . . at first."

Relieved, Tristan continued. "I told you that Keepers have children when bidden, but we aren't like Guardians, whose reproduction is wholly regulated by Keepers."

"I don't follow." Sarah tilted her head, waiting for his reply.

"Accidental pregnancies happen," Tristan said. "Keepers elope. It's rare, but there are those who have risked Bosque's anger to pursue their own desires."

"And what happens to them?" Sarah asked.

"It depends." Tristan smiled ruefully. "Sometimes on Bosque's mood, sometimes on the offender. He's more likely to let things slide with the lower-ranking Keepers. There will always be a punishment, but its severity ranges widely."

"All right, but what does that have to do with you?"

"It has more to do with my cousin, Marise, but it affects me," Tristan answered. "Marise Bane can trace her lineage back to Eira, just as I can. And Bosque had specific designs for her family's future. But it was rumored that Marise had fallen in love with another Keeper in Vail, where she lived, a woman: Lumine Nightshade."

"That's quite the rumor." Sarah raised an eyebrow.

"Even more so in the nineteenth century, which was when they met," Tristan said. "How they were discovered and what Bosque did about it is all speculation. But the relationship was quashed and Marise rebelled in the way she knew would hurt Bosque the most. She eloped before he could marry her off."

"With who?"

"With a literal gold-digging card player at one of the Colorado mining camps," Tristan said. "And now Efron Bane is one of us— though Bosque still dislikes him."

Sarah laughed. "Who knew the lives of Keepers were so scandalous?"

Tristan smiled, but his mirth quickly faded. "Obviously Marise is much, much older than I am. All of this had taken place before I was born, but once I was, Bosque made it clear that no such mishaps would be taking place in my future. That's why I'm on this island."

"You're fucking Rapunzel," Sarah said, rather stunned.

"Yes." Tristan sighed. "Yes, I am."

Her startled expression became troubled. "So you were sent here with the aim of keeping you free of worldly entanglements."

Tristan nodded.

"There's something I need to ask you." Sarah shifted away from him, anxious.

"Of course." Tristan watched her agitation with growing alarm. "What is it, Sarah?" Tristan grasped her upper arms. "You're trembling."

"I . . . I was sent here because we learned that something important to the Keepers was hidden in this castle," Sarah whispered. "My mission was to find it."

"That's what you want to know?" Tristan's mouth twisted into a wry smile. "There's nothing hidden here."

Sarah rested her palm against Tristan's chest. "That's what I was afraid of."

"You need better spies."

"It's not a thing, Tristan," Sarah said slowly. "It's you."

Tristan's brow furrowed. "What does that mean?"

"I think it means I need to get you off this island."

He released her arms and climbed out of the bath. "That's impossible."

"Have you ever tried to leave?" Sarah asked as Tristan wrapped a towel around his waist.

Bitterness crept up Tristan's throat. "Do you even have to ask?"

He didn't want to think about how many times he'd imagined what it would have been like to leave the island and seek another life. But he'd always known such thoughts were fantasies, indulged at one's own peril.

Sarah exited the bath and came to face him. Water dripped down her naked body and Tristan felt his cock stir again. The determination on her face made him certain that he needed to dissuade her from this nascent plan.

"Leaving the island isn't an option." He handed her a towel so he could focus on their conversation.

"You can't know that," Sarah replied.

"Of course I can," Tristan said, feeling a twinge of disappointment when Sarah covered herself with the towel. "My entire life is designed around my not leaving the island."

Sarah shook her head. "But you've never been in this position before."

"What position?"

"You have help." Sarah put her hands on her hips. "I can help you."

Tristan laughed. "You. As in, my prisoner."

Sarah's face fell and Tristan immediately regretted his words. "I shouldn't have said that, Sarah. It's just a difficult subject for me. I can't leave. No matter how much I want to."

"It's ridiculous to abandon the idea out of hand," Sarah shot back. "And yes, I know I'm your prisoner. But if you took a moment to think this through, you'd see that it's not just me who would help us."

Tristan frowned at her and Sarah threw up her hands in exasperation. "Seamus! Seamus obviously wants to help you get out of here. Why else would he have me digging into your past?"

"Seamus is a Guardian," Tristan said. "Their loyalty is absolute."

"Perhaps," Sarah replied. "And I know that's why Keepers use them as soldiers, but in this case I'd say Seamus's loyalty isn't to the Keepers. It's to you."

Tristan drew a long breath. "Maybe."

Sarah grasped Tristan's hands, squeezing his fingers tightly. "Talk to him. Please. That's all I'm asking."

"That alone could be a great risk," Tristan answered. And the risk wasn't to him. Bosque wouldn't kill someone of Eira's line; Tristan knew that much. But he'd eliminate Sarah without hesitation.

"Think about who Seamus has been to you, Tristan," Sarah

urged. "Do you really think he'd do anything that would cause you harm?"

"Fine." Tristan leaned down and kissed her gently. "I'll talk to him. But I can't promise anything more."

"I'm not asking for anything more." Sarah smiled against his lips. "Yet."

☙

Tristan left the baths before Sarah, who decided she needed time in the heat and steam to actually relax. Despite the soothing touch of the water, Sarah found it difficult to release the tension that knotted her limbs.

Sarah didn't doubt that Tristan loved her. But when it came to abandoning everything he'd ever known, she worried that his love might not be enough. Sarah knew what she was asking of him: that he give up his world in order to join hers. Of course Tristan would balk at the suggestion. Even if he did claim that he wanted no part of his Keeper inheritance, joining the ranks of his long-time enemies was another matter altogether.

It would take time to persuade Tristan that leaving was their only option. The idea of extending her stay at Castle Tierney didn't appeal to Sarah, but she didn't see another way forward.

Seamus might at least give Tristan a nudge in the right direction.

Sarah knew there was another option: she could tell Tristan about the bodies in the dungeon, about the macabre feasts that Lana and Owen indulged in unbeknownst to their master.

That revelation would make Tristan revile his life in the castle even more, but Sarah was reluctant to play that winning card. Though she preferred to tell herself that she kept this secret because it would devastate Tristan to know the torment of inno-cents that had been taking place in his home, Sarah knew that protecting him from that knowledge was only part of her hesitation.

I want him to choose me.

Sarah sank deeper into the tub, so only her eyes and forehead cleared the water's surface, as if to hide from the embarrassing admission.

How ridiculous, to stop myself from telling Tristan something that could be the key to convincing him to leave. For what? Vanity?

It was selfish and reckless, and Sarah could afford to be neither.

As she climbed out of the tub, dripping water onto the marble floor, Sarah resolved to tell Tristan everything. She toweled herself off and found an array of robes hanging along the wall. She'd just slipped the cotton robe on when she whirled around, the back of her neck prickling.

Out of the corner of her eye Sarah had caught a movement, the flickering of a shadow. Or so she thought. Scanning the room, Sarah couldn't see anything, though her vision was somewhat obscured by thick clouds of steam. Nor did she hear any sounds of movement.

After waiting another few minutes to be certain she was alone in the room, Sarah dismissed the sensation and walked from the steam-filled room to the broad chamber that held the swimming pool.

Sarah pulled up short, staring at the man who stood alongside the pool. He was very tall—lean but broad-shouldered. His dark hair was combed back from his olive-skinned face and its sharp, angular features. But it was his eyes that stopped Sarah's breath. They were silver.

"I thought I'd give you some privacy," the man told her. His voice was cold and smooth and very low, like a thin sheet of ice over deep waters. "I'd hate for you to feel exposed upon our first meeting."

It didn't matter that Sarah pulled her robe tighter around her body. She felt horribly vulnerable. Every fiber of her being screamed that she was in danger.

"Tristan so rarely has guests that I haven't invited to the castle myself," the man continued. "When Lana told me of your . . . stay, I came at once."

"You're Bosque Mar." The lingering heat of the baths seeped from Sarah's skin.

Tristan's affront to the succubus had been too much for her to bear and she'd called the Harbinger back to Castle Tierney.

Oh God. Sarah went rigid because her body threatened to quake with terror. She desperately fought to control her panic.

"And you're a Searcher," Bosque replied. "Forgive me for being surprised to find you luxuriating in Tristan's home, rather than wearing manacles."

"There were manacles," Sarah said, finding courage in a tart response. "At first."

Bosque laughed. "Ah, yes. Lana informed me of the evolution of your status here. I'm intrigued. Of course, I have my reservations as well."

"Of course." Sarah glanced around the room. Bosque stood between her and the door.

Following her gaze, Bosque smiled slowly. "So rude."

Sarah didn't see him move or hear him speak, but she sensed movement behind her, accompanied by a squelching sound. She turned just in time to throw her arms out, but the huge tentacle had strength a hundred times her own. Black and stinking of brine, the snakelike appendage continued to unwind itself from one of the columns that framed the pool. The tentacle coiled around Sarah's body, constricting just enough to make breathing painful but not impossible.

"I merely ask for a brief conversation," Bosque told her. "And I merit your attention."

"Go to hell." Sarah struggled against the tentacle, and it squeezed tighter until she screamed.

"You'll find that provoking me earns you only pain." Bosque strolled toward Sarah, his gaze sweeping up and down her body. "I suppose you're attractive enough, but that hardly explains Tristan's wayward attachment to you. You do realize I cannot allow his dalliance to continue; as much as I'd like to indulge my ward, it will only cause him harm in the future."

"So are you going to have your tentacle squeeze me into jelly or are we still getting to know each other?" Taunting Bosque was the only thing keeping Sarah's fear from overwhelming her.

Bosque shook his head. "You misunderstand me. I have no intention of killing you. That is Tristan's work. I came to find you only out of curiosity."

Sarah wanted to scream, *Tristan would never hurt me.* But Bosque's confident smile and easy manner sent chills spiraling through Sarah's veins.

Sensing her doubt, Bosque's smile broadened. "It was a pleasure."

And suddenly he was gone and Sarah lay in a heap on the cold floor. The tentacle that held her was once again only a carving around the column. For a moment, Sarah let herself believe she'd imagined it all—a hallucination born of stress and exhaustion. But when she crawled to her feet, the pain in her ribs made Sarah gasp. Opening her robe, Sarah looked down to see the blue and purple marbling of bruises.

She sank back to the floor, the trembling in her limbs rendering her unable to stay upright.

I have no intention of killing you. That is Tristan's work.

Sarah huddled on the floor, growing colder by the minute but feeling too weak to move. *He won't hurt me. Not after everything.*

She closed her eyes and tried to conjure Tristan's face and the love she'd seen in his eyes. But in the darkness of her mind, the only eyes Sarah remembered were silver.

25

TRISTAN HAD JUST emerged from his room, dressed and ready to seek out Seamus, when the wolf found him first.

"We need to talk," Seamus said.

Tristan nodded. "Where?"

"Ride out to the edge of the eastern wood and tether Ares there," Seamus replied. "Walk along the forest line toward the coast. I'll meet you."

Without another word Seamus shifted form and slunk away. Tristan had never seen the wolf so agitated, and that couldn't be a good sign. He wasted no time getting to the stables and taking Ares out of the castle grounds. The stallion sensed Tristan's restlessness and responded in kind, making a wild dash to the eastern side of the island. Ares bucked and snorted his disapproval when Tristan reined him in at the edge of the woods, making it clear that the horse had a mind to take a run around the whole of the island.

"In a bit." Tristan patted Ares's neck, slowing the stallion to a walk to cool him down before they stopped.

Taking Ares just inside the line of trees, Tristan dismounted and unbridled his horse. He replaced the bridle with a halter and used a lead line to tie Ares onto a low-hanging branch. While Ares contented himself with snuffling out sweet spring shoots from the undergrowth, Tristan went in search of Seamus.

Tristan stayed close to the forest's edge as the wolf had instructed, and after he had walked a quarter of an hour, he heard Seamus call from deeper within the woods. He found the wolf sitting atop a boulder in a small forest glen. When Tristan approached, Seamus jumped down from the giant rock and walked over to meet him.

"Has something happened?" Tristan asked.

"I'm of a mind to ask you the same thing, lad," Seamus replied. "But yes, I overheard a conversation between Lana and Owen."

Tristan's mood darkened instantly. "And?"

"Lana wants to summon Bosque to the castle," Seamus growled. "Owen was trying to talk her out of it. Protocol and such."

"Yes," Tristan said. "If she summons Bosque without my consent, she's circumventing my authority."

"I think she'd like nothing more at the moment." Seamus rolled his head from side to side, cracking his neck loudly. "You've managed to get quite the rise out of her."

"She had no right to—" Tristan stopped himself. He didn't want to waste energy on Lana's behavior.

"It's not about what Lana thinks she's entitled to," Seamus told Tristan. "Her jealousy is simply a front because she senses what's really going on."

Tristan asked warily, "What do you mean?"

Seamus gave him a long look.

"I'm in love with Sarah," Tristan said. It was strange to say it out loud, frightening even.

"Of course you are. You'd be a fool if you weren't." Seamus's growl was followed by a sigh. "But if Lana goes through with her plan, which she will, then when Bosque returns, he'll make you kill Sarah. No—he'll more likely let Lana kill her and make you watch. You must know that."

Tristan's fists clenched, but he nodded. "What can I do?"

"There's only one thing you can do. You can run." Seamus turned his gaze toward the sound of crashing waves in the distance. "Go to her people. They're the only ones who might be able to hide you away."

"How can we run?" Tristan asked. "I'm always watched."

Seamus grinned at Tristan, revealing a wolf's sharp canines. "Well, first you'll need a distraction."

Tristan laughed at the wolf's eager expression. "Why am I inclined to believe you've thought about this before?"

"I've just been itching for a real fight." Seamus shrugged. "All the wolves have."

"You think the whole pack will side with us?" Tristan asked with surprise.

Seamus paused, scratching at his beard. "Not all, but most. Even those not overly fond of you have a sense of loyalty to me. Even if they don't aid us, they won't interfere, either."

"I've done a piss-poor job of ruling this place, haven't I?" Tristan rubbed his temples, suddenly bone weary.

"You arrived here a boy and never became a tyrant." Seamus clapped Tristan on the shoulder. "That's a feat most Keepers I've known can't manage."

"That's not the most flattering measure of success," Tristan said wryly.

"It's not the worst, either," Seamus said. "The truth is you've never been given the chance to find out who you are—you've only been told. But I'd wager that you'll be a good man once you're free of this place."

Tristan looked closely at Seamus and frowned. "But if you help us escape, what will happen to you and the other Guardians?"

"It depends on how the fight goes down," Seamus told him. "If it's staged as a Searcher attack, we might be able to give you the time you need to run without giving our involvement away. If that doesn't work . . . well, I'd rather go down fighting."

"You'd take that risk for me?" Tristan murmured.

"That question can only be answered with acts," Seamus said. "Not words."

Tristan crouched on the forest floor and bowed his head. "Your courage only makes my cowardice more shameful."

"You've never been a coward, Tristan." Seamus paced alongside the Keeper.

"You might not say that if you knew what I'm feeling," Tristan replied.

"Why don't you tell me and we'll find out," Seamus said.

Tristan forced himself to stand up. He might feel like a cowering child, but he at least could act like a man. "I'm afraid."

"Of what?" Seamus asked.

"Of life," Tristan said, then laughed at the absurdity. "Of her. Of happiness." Tristan swept his hand through the air. "This is all I've known. What if I go with her only to prove that I'm worthless without all the trappings and protections Bosque has always provided?"

Seamus stood face-to-face with Tristan. "You're afraid. But you want to go nonetheless?"

"I can't lose her," Tristan said. "That's all that matters. Wherever she goes, I'll go."

"A true coward never admits fear," Seamus said. "Recognizing fear is the only way to overcome it. You'll be fine, lad."

"Thanks . . . I think." Tristan smiled at the wolf.

Seamus returned Tristan's smile. "Don't worry about what happens outside the island until you've managed to find a way off it. The Guardians can help you fight, but the leaving is another matter."

"I know," Tristan told him. "I don't know how any of this can possibly work, but she's determined that it will."

"Quite a remarkable lass you've found." Seamus chuckled.

"I know," Tristan replied. "Believe me. I know."

As he rode back to the castle, Tristan was overwhelmed by a strange emotion that he soon realized was contentment.

He laughed aloud, prompting a snort of suspicion from Ares.

"Don't worry, lad." Tristan leaned forward to pat the stallion's neck. "I'm just surprised to be so happy, given that I'm about to run away from home."

That made Tristan laugh again, and Ares tossed his head, annoyed by his rider's odd behavior.

When they arrived at the stables, Tristan dismounted and led Ares toward the outbuilding that held the horses' stalls. Without warning, Ares gave a high-pitched whistle and reared, almost tearing the reins out of Tristan's hand.

Tristan wheeled around to face the panicked stallion. "Whoa. Easy, lad. What's the matter?"

"Some animals find my presence unsettling."

The voice made Tristan's heart seize up. Gripping the reins tight, Tristan turned to face Bosque. The tall man blocked the entrance to the building and he was holding a pitchfork. The sight was such a caricature of a devil lying in wait that Tristan could have laughed if not for his horror.

"This is a surprise," Tristan said, forcing a pleasant tone.

Bosque returned his smile. "I'm sure it is. Lana sent for me."

"I figured as much." Tristan's mind was racing, scrambling for the right word or action to prevent impending disaster.

"Have you also guessed why I'm here?" Bosque asked. His voice was soft as velvet, but Tristan knew that meant only bad things lay ahead.

"My prisoner." Better not to name her, Tristan thought. Better to project nonchalance, indifference.

Tristan's pulse bespoke his lack of indifference, barreling as it was through his limbs, making him dizzy as blood rushed to his head and heart.

"Yes," Bosque replied. "You have a Searcher in your house. I've met the girl. Quite feisty, isn't she?"

Tristan couldn't stop himself from blanching, and Bosque tilted his head, regarding his ward curiously.

"Tell me, Tristan," Bosque said, "do you think it wise to give a Searcher free run of the castle?"

"She's being watched," Tristan answered. "The Guardians—"

"Yes, yes," Bosque interrupted. "I suppose she is on a short leash. And what she's done and seen here are of little concern to me."

"I'm glad to hear it." Tristan stepped back to stroke Ares's bowed neck. The stallion was blowing hard and stomping his feet.

The poor creature is desperate to get away from Bosque.

"What I am concerned about," Bosque said, "is Lana's assessment of your feelings for the Searcher."

"Lana is jealous because I've been fucking the other girl." Tristan tried to make his tone as harsh as possible.

You have to play this off as a petty thing.

Bosque seemed to give Tristan's assertion some consideration. After a few minutes, he said, "Lana is a creature of impulse, and she could very well be swayed by jealousy."

Holding Tristan's gaze, Bosque continued, "But tell me, Tristan, what then are your plans for this Searcher?"

"I hoped to gather information about the Searchers from her after she came to trust me." Tristan drew a quick breath. "I've found seduction to be a rewarding form of entertainment."

With a chuckle, Bosque said, "I suppose that's fair."

Tristan's frenzied pulse began to ease. "You have nothing to worry about. I assure you."

Bosque nodded, drawing closer to Tristan. Ares jerked back on the reins and almost pulled Tristan off his feet.

"Easy," Tristan murmured to the horse, but kept his eyes on Bosque.

"I want to believe you, Tristan," Bosque said, walking alongside Ares. "But I worry that perhaps I've been too lax in my attention to you."

"You've given me everything I could have ever wanted," Tristan said quickly. "I'm indebted to you."

"Yes," Bosque said. "You are. And you'll pay that debt by continuing the legacy of your grandmother Eira."

"I intend to." Tristan watched Bosque walk in a slow circle around Ares. He worried that the stallion might strike at Bosque with his hooves, but Ares stood still, his entire body quivering with fright. Lather had formed on his neck and shoulders. Tristan had never seen the stallion in such a state.

"Good." Having made a full turn around them, Bosque paused in front of Tristan and Ares. "Because you've spoken the truth, Tristan. I have given you everything."

"I know." Tristan had the sudden urge to flee.

Bosque smiled slowly. "But I wonder if you don't understand that I can also take things away."

Without warning, Bosque hefted the pitchfork and drove it into Ares's chest. The stallion squealed, rearing with such force that he ripped the reins from Tristan's hand, tearing skin off his palm.

Bosque struck again and again. Ares's breath became wet wheezes. The stallion groaned, falling to his knees and collapsing onto his side. Tristan stood paralyzed by disbelief and anguish as he watched the horse drown in his own blood.

Tossing the bloodied pitchfork aside, Bosque said quietly, "That was a merciful death. Your Searcher's end will not be so swift if you disobey me."

"What do you want me to do?" Tristan whispered, his voice hoarse.

"I'd be happy if you killed her," Bosque replied. "But if your carnal appetites demand she be available to you, I'll allow it. However, she must become a true prisoner under Lana and Owen's guard. Do you understand?"

Tristan nodded. Ares had stopped moving. The stallion's eyes had become flat and glassy.

"It's time for you to accept your place in this world," Bosque said. "Don't disappoint me, Tristan."

"I won't."

And Bosque was gone.

Tristan stared at the dead horse for a long time. Turning his back on Ares, Tristan walked away from the stable and toward the castle, knowing he could no longer escape his fate.

⚘

Sarah stripped the covers from her bed, wrapped them around her body, and sat in front of the fireplace. She couldn't seem to get warm. It felt as if Bosque's presence had taken her body temperature down several degrees. Gazing into the ruddy glow of the flames, Sarah tried to rid her mind of Bosque's words.

That is Tristan's work.

The Harbinger used words like an expert torturer used a knife, cutting but not killing—maximizing pain without taking life.

The sound of the door opening made Sarah jump to her feet in alarm.

Tristan came through the door and closed it behind him.

The rush of relief that Sarah would have anticipated upon

seeing Tristan never came. Instead her heart beat at a slow dirge of a pace and she still felt cold.

Tristan approached her slowly, warily, which only made Sarah's blood frigid.

He stopped a short distance from her. Close enough to reach out and just touch her but not within the sphere of intimate space.

"Bosque said he saw you." Tristan's words were stiff, almost mechanical.

Sarah nodded, wanting to ask, *What did the Harbinger say to you?* But her throat was closed tight and words wouldn't come.

"Are you hurt?" Tristan asked.

Shaking her head, Sarah swallowed a few times and managed to say, "I think he just wanted to frighten me." With a harsh laugh she added, "It worked."

"What did he say to you?" Tristan's gaze was cool, distant.

That's what I wanted to ask you. "That your attachment to me couldn't go on."

"What else?"

Sarah drew a sharp breath. "That he wasn't going to kill me. Because you would."

Tristan's eyes hardened, making his features bleak. "Are you afraid of me, Sarah? Do you think I'm going to kill you because Bosque ordered it so?"

Sarah almost retreated, as Tristan's words cut like a blade, but she heard the fear behind his questions. Dropping the blankets that had cocooned her, Sarah shook her head, stepped forward, and took Tristan into her arms.

"Never."

"How can you trust me?" Tristan's arms went around Sarah's waist, but his gaze was troubled. "You've seen what he is. Sarah, that's what I am. I share his blood."

"Your blood wasn't your choice," Sarah said, touching his cheek. "But you don't have to let the Harbinger choose what your future will be."

A bit of the wild panic in Tristan's eyes faded, but the despair remained.

"Do you love me?" Sarah whispered.

"More than anything." Tristan's hand slid up her back. He cradled the nape of her neck in his palm.

Sarah placed a kiss in the hollow of his throat. Looking up at him again, she said, "Then choose me."

Tristan rested his forehead against hers. "We have to leave. As soon as we can."

"I know." Holding Tristan close, Sarah finally felt her body begin to warm.

26

SOME PART OF Sarah had believed that knowing more about the Harbinger would make planning an escape easier, but instead it pushed her toward a dangerous edge of panic. She didn't know how much time they had, but guessed it was very little, at best. Her life rested upon the whim of a petulant and cruel succubus, and Sarah knew that she had to puzzle out some way to mitigate the threat Lana posed.

But Lana wasn't Sarah's only concern. The logistics of getting off the island was still a major obstacle that Sarah needed help dealing with, and that meant she'd have to put more lives in danger.

"I was hoping you'd join me for tea today, Moira," said Sarah, as the girl was about to place the gleaming silver tray on the side table.

This is the only way. And it might save her, too. You have to remember that. It might save her, too.

Moira set the tray down so hard it rattled. "Join you, miss?"

"Yes." Sarah tried to keep her voice even. Though she and Tristan had agreed that this was their best course, her nerves were jangled because of the risk. "There's something I'd like to talk to you about. Please sit."

Moira perched on the edge of her chair and fidgeted. "Have I done something wrong, miss?"

"Moira," Sarah said wearily, "you don't have to assume that you've done something wrong anytime someone asks to speak with you. Since I've been here I don't think you've done a single thing wrong."

"That's kind of you, miss," Moira said, still shifting restlessly in her seat.

"It's not kind, Moira," Sarah told her. "It's true. You need to have more faith in yourself. And that's why I want to talk to you."

Moira looked at Sarah with wide eyes, and Sarah felt a twinge of guilt. On the one hand she was about to offer the servant girl the chance to forever change her life's course; on the other hand Sarah was also offering her the chance to lose it.

Sarah poured two cups of tea. "Sugar? Milk?"

"I should be doing that, miss!" Moira reached for the pot, but Sarah shook her head.

"You're my guest today," Sarah said. "Just tell me how you like your tea."

"Two sugars, miss," Moira replied with a shy smile. "And a splash of milk."

After preparing Moira's cup and handing it to the girl, Sarah said, "Moira, do you ever think about leaving Castle Tierney?"

Moira jerked in surprise and some of her tea sloshed over the side of the cup. "Of course not, miss," she said. "This is where I belong."

"Moira," Sarah said carefully, "I'm asking you to tell me what you truly feel and not what you think I want to hear."

The cup trembled in Moira's hand.

"I know it's a difficult question." Sarah leaned forward and touched Moira's arm. "But I would be greatly indebted if you'd answer me honestly."

Moira whispered, "Sometimes I think about it. But it's all foolishness and daydreams."

"What sort of daydreams?" Sarah asked, offering Moira a sympathetic smile.

"I think I would like to travel," Moira said, gaining confidence as she spoke. "And meet different people. Everyone here is the same. The families never change and—"

She broke off and blushed scarlet.

"And?" Sarah urged.

Keeping her eyes downcast, Moira said, "I don't fancy any of the lads from the other families, miss."

Sarah managed to stifle her laughter. "Well, that would be frustrating."

"Oh, it is!" Moira blurted, then blushed again.

"Moira, I'm going to tell you something, and the reason is that I've come to trust you," Sarah said. "And I hope that you trust me and that you'll help me."

"Is something wrong?"

Sarah took Moira's no longer addressing her as "miss" to be a good sign. "Yes. I'm in danger. So is Tristan."

The pink hue of Moira's cheeks drained away.

"I need to get a message to the mainland," Sarah continued. "And I hope that you'll deliver it."

Moira chewed on her lower lip. "I don't go to the mainland."

"Tristan can arrange it so that you will," Sarah told her. "He'll send you along on the supply trip tomorrow morning with instructions that you've been asked by him to pick up a special gift for me. You'll do that, of course, to make sure your reason for going isn't suspect, but I need you to do something else as well."

Sarah stood up and went to the vanity. Opening one of its drawers, she withdrew a sealed envelope.

"When you're in the village, I need you to bring this letter to the fishmonger," Sarah said. "And when you give him this letter, you must say this: 'I'm here for the midnight catch.'"

"What's the midnight catch?" Moira asked.

"It's a signal to the fishmonger that you need to see the people who can help me," Sarah answered. "Moira, I won't deceive you. What I'm asking is very dangerous, but you're the only one I trust to do this."

"Why do you need help, miss?" Moira put her tea aside and worried at her apron. "You seem to be much happier here. I thought maybe . . ."

"What?"

"I hoped that you'd come to like it," Moira said softly. "That you and Master Tristan . . ."

Sarah took Moira's hands. "I am in love with Tristan, but that's why I have to go."

"Leave?" Moira's face fell. "You're leaving?"

Sarah nodded, dropping her voice to a whisper. "Not just me, Tristan must leave too. It's the only way we can be together."

"Why can't you be together here?" Moira frowned. "This is Master Tristan's home."

"Not by choice," Sarah told her. "Tristan is like you. He's here because his family has been told they have to be here."

"You don't love him enough to stay with him?" Moira's voice was almost accusing.

"If I stay, I'll die." Sarah squeezed Moira's fingers. "That's the truth. You know I'm a prisoner here, and how I feel about Tristan doesn't matter to the one who put him on this island."

"Lord Mar," Moira said in a frightened whisper.

"You know who he is?" Sarah asked.

Moira nodded. "He's something terrible."

"Yes," Sarah said. "That's why Tristan and I have to leave."

"I don't want you to leave, miss." Moira sighed. "If you'll excuse me for speaking above my station, you're my friend. My only friend, really."

"Oh, Moira." Sarah laughed. "Of course you're my friend too. I wouldn't ask this of you if you weren't."

"Thank you." Moira beamed at her.

"And that's the other part of this," Sarah continued. "Tristan and I have to leave, but I want you to come with us. Will you?"

Moira gaped at Sarah.

"This is your chance to have a different life," Sarah pressed. "To travel. To make your own choices. I want that for you, Moira. You deserve more than this."

"You'd take me with you?" Moira's voice was thick and her eyes began to glisten.

"I would never leave you behind," Sarah said.

Moira jumped up and threw herself into Sarah's arms. The girl's body shook as Sarah held her and Sarah couldn't tell if Moira was laughing or crying. But when Moira lifted her face and smiled, Sarah saw that it was both.

❧

Sarah found playing her new part much more of a challenge than she'd expected once a plan for escape had been set in motion. Over dinner, her conversation with Tristan had been trying, to say the least, even though Sarah knew every word to be a fiction. In earshot of the servants, Tristan had belittled her, made casual reference to locking her in her room or even keeping her in chains, and passing comments about Lana's comeliness. Sarah's heart didn't stop aching until they'd retired to her room for the night.

"That was unbearable," Sarah said as Tristan closed the door.

"I'm so sorry." Tristan took her hand, squeezing her fingers so hard that Sarah had no doubts he shared her distress. "It gutted me to speak that way to you. Are you going to be all right?"

"Yes," Sarah told him, meaning it, though she wished she

wasn't finding it so difficult to meet Tristan's eyes. "I know that wasn't you. We have to make this look convincing, or it could all fall apart."

"I would kill anyone for treating you the way I just did." Tristan released her hand and paced through the room. "*You* must want to kill me."

Sarah managed a quiet laugh. "I don't want to kill you, though I came close to slugging you a few times."

"I'll give you a free shot." Tristan came to stand in front of Sarah and offered her his cheek. When she shook her head and smiled at him, he led Sarah across the room and they sat together on the edge of her bed.

"Don't be too hard on yourself. This was my idea, remember?" Sarah said.

Tristan let out a long sigh, but he nodded.

"And Moira has agreed to help," Sarah told Tristan. "She wants to come with us when we go."

Tristan ran his hand through his hair. "That sentiment seems to be catching. Maybe we don't need to bother with a covert escape; it sounds like I could just let the servants stage a coup."

"Moira's an exception," Sarah said. "I'm guessing the woman who beats her is pretty invested in the system here."

Nodding, Tristan added, "And while Seamus says otherwise, I wouldn't be surprised if the Guardians who aid our cause do so only because they're bored with their lives here. Not the greatest vote of confidence."

"At least we won't be fighting them." Sarah kicked off her heels. One, maybe two Guardians she'd stand a chance against, but facing a pack of wolves would be suicide.

"It's not the wolves I'm worried about," Tristan said. The edge in his voice drew a questioning glance from Sarah.

"Even if our little act tonight was a success, I don't think we have much time before Lana will summon Bosque again," Tristan told her. "If he returns while we're still on the island . . . Let's just say it wouldn't be a good thing."

"Tristan." Sarah steeled herself as she spoke. She'd been rehearsing this conversation in her head all day. "If Lana is the problem, there's a way to stop her. Or at least to buy us more time than our show of domestic unrest will."

"If you've thought of a way to take Lana out of play, I'd love to hear it."

Sarah grimaced when she said, "You could sleep with her."

"What?" Tristan's voice was flat.

"That's what started this." Sarah pressed on, despite the hard cast of Tristan's gaze. "She's jealous. If you persuade her that I'm just a passing interest, she might not summon the Harbinger."

Sarah tried to keep her expression blank, but her fingers dug into the sheets. The thought of Tristan taking Lana to bed filled Sarah's stomach with pins, but there was so much at stake.

"That's not an option," Tristan said. "I'm not going to fuck Lana."

"I don't like it either," Sarah told him. "But can we risk Bosque suddenly appearing again? How could we escape then?"

Tristan took Sarah's face in his hands. "No."

Sarah's throat closed as her skin heated. The way Tristan was looking at her . . .

"I will not touch another woman," Tristan said. "Only you. No matter the cost."

Sarah placed her hands over Tristan's. He leaned forward and kissed her. His lips were warm on hers. His tongue slipped into her mouth, tasting her.

"You're the only woman I want," Tristan murmured. "I'm going to show you how much I want you."

"Yes." Sarah ran her hands up Tristan's neck and curled her

fingers in his hair. All thoughts of strategy and sacrifice bled away as Sarah surrendered to Tristan's will.

Tristan grasped Sarah's wrists and pulled her hands away from him. "Stand up. I want you beside the bed, facing me."

Quietly, Sarah moved to the side of the bed and stood up.

"Take off your dress."

Her heart rate climbed as she undid the clasp of the halter dress and let it fall to her waist, baring her breasts. Then she bent forward to push down the skirt. The silk jersey pooled at Sarah's feet. She stood facing Tristan, wearing only a thong of ivory silk and lace.

Sarah didn't speak as Tristan took his time looking at her. His gaze raked over her body, making her breath come faster. Her skin began to ache for his touch.

Unable to bear it, Sarah reached for him.

"No."

Sarah went rigid.

"You were ready to ship me off to bed Lana," Tristan told her. "You will not touch me until I tell you to."

"Tristan, I didn't want you to go." Sarah's stomach clenched. "I would hate it, but I thought the only . . ."

At her pleas, the corner of Tristan's mouth twitched into a half smile, and Sarah realized he was provoking her for his own pleasure. What a wicked man he was. The tightness in her stomach eased and in its place a sudden spike of desire made her shudder.

"I will not touch you until you tell me to," Sarah whispered.

Tristan nodded. "Good. Now spread your legs."

Widening her stance, Sarah gasped when Tristan cupped her sex. He turned his hand over, rubbing his knuckles along her shape so the silk of her thong stroked sensitive skin.

Sarah's thighs began to tremble and she reached for the bed-post to steady herself.

"No."

"I'll fall," she half moaned as Tristan's hand moved faster and with more pressure, focusing on her clit.

"I'll catch you," he said quietly.

Clenching her fists, Sarah's nails dug into her palms as Tristan continued to stroke her. Her hips rocked back and forth against his fingers. She gave a throaty cry when his other hand came up to cover her breast, kneading the tender flesh. Tristan leaned forward and took her other breast in his mouth, teasing her nipple with his teeth and tongue.

It was too much. Sarah shuddered violently as Tristan brought her to a swift, sudden climax. Her legs quaked and folded and she fell, but Tristan's arm caught her around the waist as he lifted her onto the bed.

Sarah was still riding the crests of pleasure from her climax when she felt Tristan strip off her thong, and then his cock was pushing into her wet folds. He filled her slowly, drawing a low moan from her throat.

Tristan pushed Sarah's arms above her head, pinning her by the wrists as he rode her. Her hips bucked up to meet his thrusts and she wrapped her legs around his hips, urging him deeper inside her. Tristan held her down as his cock filled her, friction building hot tension within Sarah's core. She writhed under him as he rammed harder and faster, and then she screamed as she fell apart, coming in wave after wave. Sarah heard Tristan's shout match her cry and felt his climax pumping inside her.

Releasing her arms, Tristan didn't pull out of her, but propped himself on his elbows and gazed down at Sarah.

"May I touch you now?" Sarah asked, breathless.

"Yes." Tristan smiled. "But no more talk of trysts with succubi to further our cause."

She reached up to trace his jawline. "If you'd agreed, I wouldn't have let you go through with it in the end."

"I love you, Sarah," Tristan said. He turned his cheek to lay a kiss on her palm.

Sarah nodded, whispering, "And I love you."

Shifting his weight off her, Tristan rolled onto his side. Sarah turned to face him.

"What now?" she asked.

"Now we wait until Moira returns tomorrow afternoon." Tristan pulled the covers over them. "And hope she brings good news."

"I don't think I'll be able to sleep," Sarah said when Tristan turned out the light.

In the darkness Tristan's lips brushed over her throat. "Then we won't sleep."

27

THOUGH TRISTAN BROUGHT her over the edge of ecstasy twice more before Sarah settled against his chest for the night, sleep eluded her. She listened to the slow, steady beat of Tristan's heart while he slumbered but could find no such peace of her own.

Her restlessness finally drove her out of bed. Sarah slipped into her robe and stole from the room. She knew she'd been wrong to suggest Tristan be the one to deter Lana from summoning the Harbinger, but Sarah couldn't put the threat from her mind. Leaving it to chance was too great a risk. She had to do something.

A growl rumbled from the shadows.

"You should be in bed." Seamus came to stand beside Sarah.

"Do you always keep watch?" Sarah asked him.

"Not always," Seamus replied. "But the way things stand now, I'll not trust the task to anyone else. I'll be here, but you belong with him. Go back inside."

"There's something I need to do," Sarah said.

"At this hour?" Seamus peered at her. "What are you up to?"

"I need to find Lana."

"That's trouble if I've ever smelled it," Seamus said gruffly. "You can't be thinking of taking on a succubus on your own. You do know she can breathe fire, don't you?"

Sarah hadn't known that, and she shuddered at the thought. "I'm not planning to fight her. I just need to convince her that she's in control of the situation with Tristan."

"She brought Bosque here," Seamus said. "If you provoke her, she'll do it again. And then you'll be dead."

"Yes," Sarah replied. "And you know as well as I do that keeping Lana from summoning the Harbinger again is the only way Tristan and I can have a chance to escape."

Seamus fell silent, but after a few moments said, "You'll find Lana's room near the top of the east tower. Be careful."

"Thank you."

Leaving the wolf to his watch, Sarah went to the tight spiral of stone steps that gave entrance to the eastern tower. She climbed in darkness until she spotted a thin sliver of light that escaped through the crack of a thick wooden door. Not bothering to knock, Sarah pushed the door open.

The sudden bright light made her squint and cover her eyes. When her vision adjusted, Sarah went rigid in the doorway. The small room she'd entered had characteristics of both a brothel and a torture chamber.

A strange assortment of furniture occupied the space: a velvet divan, a silk-upholstered chaise, a narrow wooden table that featured shackles bolted at each end, a wheel strewn with leather straps. Whips, cudgels, hooks, and knives accented the shelves that framed a fireplace much smaller than those found in Tristan's and Sarah's rooms. Spread on the floor in front of the flames was a large wolf pelt surrounded by dozens of pillows. Sarah's chest cramped as she speculated that the rug was courtesy of some Guardian's ill-timed disobedience.

Lana was sprawled before the fireplace, her wings outspread, reminding Sarah of the way a cold-blooded creature might bask in the sun.

"I suppose I should say 'welcome.'" Lana rose from the mound of silk pillows. She wore a strapless leather bustier and a sheer silk wrap skirt that did little to obscure the lace panties beneath it. "But you're not, and I'm not interested in lying to you for the sake of appearances."

"I'm sorry for the intrusion." Sarah forced herself to leave the doorway and meet Lana in the middle of the room. "But I need to speak with you."

"Do you?" Lana folded her arms over her chest, and her wings curled in irritation.

Coming closer to Sarah, Lana sniffed the air. "You left him to seek me out. I'll admit I'm interested enough not to throw you down the stairs."

"I left him because I'm afraid he'll leave me," Sarah blurted. "And I don't want that to happen."

Lana arched a brow at Sarah. "From all I've witnessed, our Tristan is infatuated with you."

"There are things you haven't witnessed," Sarah said quietly. "He's been different lately. Tonight . . . I couldn't, I mean he didn't want . . ."

"I'm listening." Lana watched Sarah's face closely.

Sarah knew she had to be very careful, choosing each word and action with precision. Lana would not only sense, but also consume, every emotion Sarah exuded. That meant it was impossible for Sarah to be disingenuous. She had to let her emotions spill out honestly, but in a way that would affect Lana's perception of Sarah and Tristan's relationship.

Letting fear roll through her limbs, Sarah averted her eyes from the succubus's intent gaze.

"Tristan favors me now," Sarah said. "But he won't continue to if I can't keep him interested."

"What makes you think you can't?" Lana asked.

Sarah cringed and from the corner of her eye saw Lana smile. "Before Tristan I hadn't ever . . ."

Lana began to laugh. "Yes, that's right. Tristan took a virgin to his bed."

Grasping Sarah's chin, Lana forced Sarah to look at her. "Tell me, dear, was he surprised?"

"Yes." Sarah gritted her teeth.

Lana released Sarah's chin and laughed again. "What a novel experience that must have been for him."

Sarah nodded. "At first he seemed angry, but then it seemed to excite him. And I'm afraid that what you said is true, that he was only interested because it was novel—something different."

With a shrug, Lana said, "Possibly."

"I'm worried that my lack of experience will mean I can't give Tristan what he wants," Sarah said. "And that he'll soon tire of me. Tristan told me what Bosque's orders were: to kill me or keep me for pleasure."

"That's true. And I assume you're hoping for the latter," Lana replied. "Tell me something else, Searcher, are you sure you don't want Tristan to tire of you? And if not, why? Do you see sex as the only means of saving your skin, or is something else motivating you?"

Sarah retreated until her back was against the wall. She wanted Lana to feel dominant. It would only help her cause.

"I want to stay here. With him."

"Really?" Lana half turned from Sarah and walked slowly toward the fireplace. "That surprises me. Your kind are usually loyal to the marrow. Will you turn on your own so quickly?"

"All I've learned about the war is that it's a lost cause." Sarah wilted against the wall. "Bosque was here. I saw his power myself—there's nothing like it. We can't win this war, and I don't want to die."

"Hmmm." Lana gazed into the flames. "Cowardly, but honest. And you're not wrong. I've always thought the Searchers were honorable morons. This isn't a war that you and your good intentions will ever win."

"I know," Sarah murmured.

"But that still doesn't explain why you've come to me," Lana said.

Sarah pushed herself away from the wall, taking just a few steps toward the succubus. "Tristan said that if I stay, that I'm to be your ward, so that I can learn . . . your art."

"My 'art'?" Lana laughed. "Are you trying to flatter me into helping you?"

"You know how to please men, to please Tristan," Sarah said. "You can show me what to do so he won't put me aside. So he won't kill me."

"Do you think you could handle the knowledge I've mastered?" Lana pulled a black leather bullwhip from one of the shelves.

Sarah answered, "I'd like to try."

Lana pivoted, and the whip's length snaked out. The leather cord wrapped around Sarah's waist. Lana gave the handle a sharp tug and Sarah stumbled toward her.

"Are you sure about that?" Lana continued to pull on the whip until Sarah stood face-to-face with the succubus.

Lana bent her head and kissed Sarah's throat and then the corner of her mouth. Sarah tensed as Lana's fingertips ran along her collarbone.

"You're wise to be frightened of me," Lana murmured. "The things I could show you. How pain is pleasure. How begging can be strength. Nothing is more pure than agony."

Lana took Sarah's lower lip between her teeth, biting hard enough that Sarah tasted blood. Lana's breath tasted of rose petals and spring rain. Sarah's pulse spiked, and a tingling warmth flowed over her skin.

Of course the succubus would have aphrodisiac breath.

Sarah whimpered at the ache that seized her body, but didn't pull away, relieved that she at least managed to stop herself from reaching for Lana the way she suddenly longed to.

Stepping back, Lana gave Sarah a long, sweeping look while licking Sarah's blood from her lips.

"That's it, my lovely," Lana murmured. "Show me what you want."

Sarah felt control slipping away. Her head tipped back and she moaned.

Then Lana sighed. "No." She let the whip loosen; its coils slid off Sarah's hips and onto the floor. "You're a pathetic, simpering girl and for all the spine you've shown I'm surprised you can even stand up straight. I'd much rather have you fearful that Tristan will cast you out of his bed at any moment than teach you tricks to keep him there."

When Lana backed off, Sarah slumped against the wall gulping air until the sensual daze of the succubus's spell had cleared away. Her heart was still pounding, but she'd accomplished what she'd hoped to.

"What a shame." A tall figure stepped through the open door. Sarah stiffened when the firelight revealed Owen's face. "I was anticipating quite the show."

"Learn to live with disappointment," Lana answered him. "I'm not in the performing mood."

Owen ignored Lana and came toward Sarah instead. "So, our little captive is looking for lessons."

He jerked his chin in Lana's direction. "You do know that she's not the only one who can teach you."

Sarah backed away. She'd had a firm sense of how to handle Lana, but Owen was another matter.

He stalked after Sarah until she bumped into the wall. She tried to sidestep, but Owen laid his palms flat against the wall on either side of Sarah, trapping her.

"There's no one better to show you what a man needs than me," Owen said. He leaned closer, and Sarah held her breath, not taking any chances that the incubus could seduce her with the mystical characteristics at his disposal. "In fact, you could get on your knees right now and I'll give you all the pointers you could ever want."

His wings curved around her, taking the place of his arms to cage her while his hands moved to her shoulders, pushing Sarah down.

She brought her knee up hard.

Owen groaned and doubled over. Sarah shoved him aside and bolted across the room.

She turned when she heard the incubus roar and saw a spout of flames jet from his mouth.

Oh God.

"You'll be getting a different kind of lesson for that, bitch." Owen started toward Sarah, but Lana stepped into his path.

"Get out of my way," Owen snarled at her.

"Let her be, Owen." Lana pressed the coils of her whip against his bare chest. "How do you think Tristan will react to news of you coercing his little human for your own pleasure?"

"No more cross than he's bound to be with you," Owen replied.

"Not true," Lana said. "She came to me, but look how she shrank from your touch. I'm afraid you aren't as alluring to her as Tristan—or me, for that matter. You'll just have to nurse your wounds and your ego without the girl."

Still standing between Owen and Sarah, Lana looked over her shoulder at the Searcher. "Run along, now. I'll make sure Owen doesn't give chase. If I decide I want you for a pupil after all, I'll come find you."

Sarah ran. She was breathless by the time she reached the bottom of the steps and raced down the hall, so she wasn't able to scream when someone reached out and grabbed her.

"Keep quiet," Seamus growled. "Did you get what you needed? You didn't come to any harm, did you?"

"I'm fine," Sarah told him, gasping for air. "As far as getting what I needed . . . we'll have to wait and see."

"I suppose that's the best we can hope for," Seamus said.

Sarah nodded. Her panicked heart rate was finally easing off. "I think it is."

She bid Seamus good night, and returned to her room. Relieved to find Tristan still asleep, Sarah shed her robe and slipped beneath the covers.

Though he didn't wake, Tristan stirred and pulled Sarah into his arms. She tucked her head against his chest, letting the warmth of his skin and the comfort of his familiar, masculine scent soothe her.

"I love you," Sarah whispered into his skin. It didn't matter that he wasn't awake to hear her. She simply needed to say the words and know their truth.

28

"YOU WANT ME to tell everyone that you're sick?" Tristan asked Sarah.

Tristan had returned to his room to get dressed but had returned only to be informed by Sarah that she didn't plan to leave hers all day.

"Yes." Sarah was propped up in bed. Her dark hair spilled over the white linens.

"You don't look sick," he told her. Watching her, Tristan thought only of how appealing Sarah looked. He was of half a mind to join her in bed, but Sarah was all business.

"Then don't send anyone to visit me," Sarah replied curtly. "Except Moira. The minute the boat brings her back, send her to tend me. Since she's my usual maid, it shouldn't raise any suspicions."

"What if the other servants want to tend you in Moira's absence?" Tristan countered.

Sarah frowned. "Just tell them that I'm in a difficult mood because I'm unwell and I refuse to have anyone but Moira serve me."

"Fine." Tristan let out an exasperated breath. "You seem to have all the angles covered, but why are you staging this charade?"

"I want Lana to think I'm terrified that she won't help me," Sarah told him. She made a show of stretching and when she arched her back, Tristan's body tightened at the sight of her breasts straining against the fabric of her chemise. "She needs to see me as weak, frightened, and utterly submissive."

"I don't follow." Tristan walked to the bedside. Even if Sarah wanted to feign illness for the day, it didn't mean he couldn't tarry another hour.

"I couldn't sleep last night," Sarah said, "so I went to see Lana."

Tristan had been about to reach for Sarah, but froze. "You what?"

Sarah lifted her hands to placate him. "Look at me, Tristan. Obviously I'm fine."

"Why the hell did you go looking for her in the first place?" Despite Sarah's insistence that she hadn't been in danger, Tristan's blood went cold at the thought of her facing Lana alone. He reached out but only to pull back the sheets, his assessment of her body no longer compelled by desire but fear that she'd been injured.

"Hey!" Sarah snatched the sheets from his hand, burrowing back beneath them. "I'm cold."

"Are you hurt?" Tristan asked.

"Of course not," Sarah replied, fluffing up her pillows again. Tristan frowned; her actions were a bit too casual, and he knew no matter how much Sarah insisted that whatever had happened while he slept, it hadn't all been pleasant.

"Don't be flippant," Tristan said. "Tell me what you did."

"It occurred to me that Lana isn't jealous because I'm sleeping with you," Sarah told him, dropping her façade of ease. "It's about power. She wants to feel that she has some power over you. I got in the way of that."

Tristan made a low sound of disdain. "Lana never had power over me."

"I know that," Sarah said. "But she believes otherwise. I needed to convince her that my relationship with you was tenuous and that she still has the ability to obliterate it at any time."

"And how did you manage that?" Tristan's brows knit together.

"I just played on what you'd told me—that Bosque's condition for keeping me alive was that you hand me over to Lana." Sarah smoothed the sheets on her lap, averting her eyes from Tristan's. "So I went to Lana begging her to help me."

"You've got to be joking." Tristan scowled. "What kind of help could Lana give you?"

"I, um, told her that I was afraid I couldn't please you . . . sexually. And that I worried you'd grow bored with me and kill me instead of keeping me."

"Bloody hell." Tristan sat on the edge of the bed and covered his face with his hands. "Of all the things . . . why in God's name would you say that *to Lana*?"

"Because I knew it was the one thing that would provoke her. And I think it worked, Tristan." Sarah touched his arm. "When I asked her to teach me what she knew, she refused. She taunted me. And it delighted her."

"Wait." Tristan looked at Sarah sharply. "You asked her to what?"

"To teach me how to please you." A light blush crept along Sarah's cheeks.

Tristan cleared his throat. "And what if she hadn't refused?"

"Then . . ." Sarah had trouble holding his gaze. "I suppose I would have learned some things?"

"Sarah!" Tristan stood up and paced beside the bed. "Is there anything else you'd like to tell me about your escapades last night?"

"No," she said quickly. "But if you see Lana today, let her believe you might be feeling restless about me. She wants to believe I'm too insipid for you. The more she's convinced of that, the less likely she'll be to summon the Harbinger again. At least, I hope so."

Tristan gave Sarah a long, measured look. "You're impossible. You know that, don't you?"

She beamed at him until he shook his head and laughed.

"I want you to tell me that none of what you said to Lana last night has any real foundation." Tristan leaned over her, smiling. "There is nothing about you that doesn't please me."

"I know," Sarah said, and pulled Tristan down to kiss her. "But thank you for saying it."

She gave a sigh of pleasure when Tristan's hand slid beneath the sheets to cup her breast, finally touching her the way he'd been wanting to. He loved the way her body reacted instantly, yielding to him. He was already hard.

"Maybe I should be sick too." His thumb rubbed her nipple and Sarah shivered.

She arched into his palm as he squeezed her breast, but then said with regret, "If you stay with me, it will contradict the narrative of conflict I've constructed about us."

"We're a constructed narrative now?" Tristan laughed, pulling his hand away.

"Only temporarily." Sarah offered him an impish smile. "Now, go spread the word of my declining health and ill temper."

"With pleasure," Tristan said, heading for the door. He tried not to think about how long his balls would ache after that unfinished encounter. "I can't get away from you fast enough, wretched woman."

"Hey!" Sarah threw a pillow at him.

"Just getting into character," he replied, flashing a wicked smile at her before he left the room.

❧

Tristan tried to approach the day as if Sarah had never come to Castle Tierney, deciding that tactic offered the best means for conveying a detached attitude toward her presence in his life. He followed old routines—a light breakfast followed by an hour of reading in his study. A late-morning walk to the cliffs. Lunch. An early-afternoon ride to the eastern shore of the island.

As the hours passed, Tristan marveled at and was more than a little troubled by how empty his life seemed without Sarah. Had he really spent so many years passing day after day like this?

What disturbed him the most was the knowledge that he could have—no, *would* have—gone on like that for years.

For the first time Tristan could remember, he felt sympathy for his father. Though Tristan had always resented the man's perceived indifference toward his son, Tristan was suddenly forced to consider the way his own life would have followed the same pattern. How could anyone survive such a prescribed existence except through detachment?

With his mood growing more turbulent, Tristan climbed to the top of the battlements. Since the boat bearing supplies for the island, and more important, Moira, was expected soon, Tristan thought he'd undertaken enough quotidian activities to indulge in a little brooding while looking out at the sea.

The only bright spot of his day thus far had been a mid-morning run-in with Lana. Though he'd been dreading such an encounter, Lana merely sashayed past Tristan wearing a smug expression. As much as the idea of Sarah putting herself at risk had dismayed him, Tristan had to admit she'd done a masterful job of mitigating the threat Lana posed.

Tristan leaned against the stone rampart and gazed at the restless sea. Low, sullen clouds banked the distant shoreline. The sea reflected the gray sky, stirring quietly on this day when there was little wind.

"You do know that watching for the boat won't make it come any faster."

"Good afternoon, Seamus," Tristan greeted the wolf.

Seamus mirrored Tristan's stance and gazed toward the shore. "She's not really ill, is she?"

"No." Tristan smiled. "But she'll be glad to know the rumor has spread. It's what she wanted."

"Then I suspect she'll also be happy to hear that the staff is abuzz with news that Sarah has fallen out of your favor," Seamus added.

"Already?" Tristan glanced at Seamus, surprised by the news.

"There's rarely gossip in this castle," Seamus chuckled. "Two pieces to gnaw on at once and they don't know what to do with themselves."

Spotting a small object that broke the monotony of gray waves, Tristan grinned at Seamus. "You were wrong about watching. There's the boat now."

The wolf shrugged and nodded. "Can't be right about every-thing."

"Seamus." Tristan turned to face his old friend. "When the boat docks, go down and escort Moira to Sarah's room to nurse her through this illness."

"So it's the girl who's helping you." Seamus eyed Tristan thoughtfully. "Yes, I see it. She's the best choice."

"I'll have to keep my distance for a bit," Tristan told him. "But I'll make a cursory visit later this evening."

Tristan's jaw clenched. Keeping the rest of the castle convinced that a rift now existed between he and Sarah meant he would likely have to sleep in his own room, without her. He had a miser-able night in store.

"That should keep everything in order," Seamus replied. "At least until you're ready to act." He rolled his shoulders back. "I guess I'll make a run down to the dock."

"There's one more thing," Tristan said.

The wolf threw him a questioning gaze.

"When we leave the castle, we're taking Moira with us," Tristan told Seamus. "And I think you should come as well."

"You want to take me with you," Seamus said with a frown. "To the Searchers."

"I know it's a difficult prospect to swallow," Tristan said, "but if they're going to offer me—a Keeper—some sort of amnesty, they'll certainly do the same for you."

"No." Seamus let his gaze wander back to the open water. "I'll not be leaving this place."

"Do you have a reason to stay?" Tristan asked. He'd anticipated some hesitation on Seamus's part, but not an outright dismissal.

"I'm an old wolf." Seamus kept his eyes on the sea. "Too old to begin again. Your story is just beginning, but mine has reached its final chapters. I'll help you escape, but that's your future and none of mine."

"You're awfully fatalistic, Seamus," Tristan said. "This is not a ship, and you're not a captain. There's nothing noble about staying here to sink."

Seamus's mouth crinkled into the hint of a smile. "That's not what I'm doing, lad. I just know where I belong. My pack may be a ramshackle lot, thrown together because we didn't fit into the Keepers' plans elsewhere, but they're still my pack and I'm their alpha. I'm no lone wolf."

Tristan fell silent. Seamus had risked everything by colluding with Tristan and Sarah, and Tristan hated the thought that he'd be abandoning his oldest friend.

"I can smell the grief on you, lad," Seamus told him. "There's no call for it. The only tragedy here would be for you to stay on this island. And don't try to understand what I've said about my reasons for staying. There are some things only wolves know."

"If you say so," Tristan replied, still uneasy.

"I do," Seamus said. "Now I'll be off. You're right to keep your distance from the lass for a few more hours. The castle will be in a complete tizzy by the end of the day. If there's something you need to know about Moira's trip, I'll find you."

"Thank you, Seamus."

Seamus nodded, and then a wolf trotted along the battlements before disappearing into one of the castle towers.

Tristan returned to his thoughts and the company of the sea. He watched the boat grow slowly larger as it approached the island. Its arrival heralded momentous change for everyone to whom the island was home. Seamus had spoken true. Here were so many beginnings and endings, and nothing would remain the same.

29

WIIEN MOIRA DREW a folded slip of paper from her apron pocket and handed it to Sarah, the girl's hands shook. Even so, Sarah thought Moira had never seemed more alive. Moira's eyes gleamed with excitement and she couldn't stop smiling.

"I did it, miss," Moira said breathlessly. "I did it!"

"I knew you could, Moira," Sarah replied. "And please don't call me 'miss' anymore. We're friends, remember? You're not my servant."

"Yes, m— Sarah." She hovered over Sarah's shoulder. "What does it say?"

Sarah unfolded the note and read. "Oh my God."

"What's wrong?" Moira asked, too polite to read the note herself.

"Tonight," Sarah said, putting the note aside. "They want us to leave tonight."

Fear crept back into Moira's voice. "So soon? Can we do that?"

"Can we?" Sarah turned her gaze to Seamus, who had stayed in the room but kept silent.

"Yes," Seamus answered.

"They think it's too great a risk to delay even a day more," Sarah told the wolf. "They'll be waiting for us between midnight and three a.m. If we don't make that window, they'll assume we failed to escape."

"And if that happens, will they come for you?" Seamus asked.

"No." Sarah picked up the note and gave it to Moira. "Burn this."

Seamus gave a derisive snort. "Not long on courage, your friends, are they?"

"Courage isn't the issue," Sarah replied. "They won't come after us because I told them not to."

"There are no guarantees you'll get away," Seamus said, bristling. "Why not have a fallback?"

"I think I've stalled Lana, but there's no guarantee," Sarah told him. "I won't ask my friends to face the Harbinger just to save me."

"What about Tristan?" Seamus growled. "He cannot stay here. I'm risking myself and my pack for him, not for you."

Moira gasped, looking from Seamus to Sarah in horror.

Sarah addressed the wolf calmly. "Then you and your pack should do your best to make sure he gets off the island. Don't you think?"

With a snarl, Seamus left the room.

Moira edged across the room. "Do you think it was wise to provoke him?"

"I wasn't trying to provoke him," Sarah said. "I was telling him the way things are."

Moira quickly nodded, but her sudden paleness betrayed her nerves.

"Are you all right?" Sarah asked her. She guided the servant girl to a chair.

"I'll be fine, m—" Moira twisted her fingers together in her lap. "It's just tonight . . . that's so soon."

"I know," Sarah replied. "But I think they're right to push us into action. The longer we wait, the more danger there is of discovery."

"What should I do?" Moira asked.

"There's not much we can do at the moment." Sarah rubbed the back of her neck as she felt tension build there. "We have to go on as if nothing has changed."

Moira murmured, "Oh, dear."

"I know it's difficult," Sarah told her. "But we have no choice."

Watching Moira fidget, Sarah offered, "You could escort me to the baths, and while I'm there you could go to the kitchen and prepare some hot compresses for me. I know it's not much, but I need to clean up and it will at least give you something to do."

"And keep the house thinking that you're ill," Moira said, brightening up. "Yes. I'd like that."

Sarah hoped she'd let herself become haggard enough to appear ill, or at least upset, as she took Moira's arm and let the girl lead her through the castle. Moira left her at the entrance to the baths and scurried back up the stairs. Pushing through the wooden door, Sarah ran past the pool into the steam-filled room that housed the deep soaking tubs. The memory of that tentacle was too fresh in Sarah's mind to make her want to linger near the pool. If there had been baths anywhere else in the castle, she'd have gone there rather than return to the site of her encounter with Bosque Mar.

Letting steam wrap around her and soothe her tense limbs, Sarah shrugged her robe off.

A cough made her yelp and jump back. *Why the hell did I think it was okay to come down here again?*

Sarah scrambled to pick up her robe and cover herself as she heard the splash of water. Someone was in one of the far tubs, but their presence had been hidden by the thick steam.

"Sarah?"

"Tristan." Limbs going weak with relief, Sarah dropped her robe again. "I didn't know you were here."

He materialized out of the steam, naked and dripping water. "We seem to have had the same idea."

"Should I leave?" She didn't move, riveted by the sight of him.

Tristan kept coming toward her. "I don't think I'd like that."

"But we're supposed to—"

He silenced her with a kiss, then whispered, "I came here alone. So did you."

"But if someone puts it together that we're both here . . ." Sarah's pulse jumped at her throat when Tristan touched her bare skin, pulling her against him. His long, hard cock pressed into her stomach and she gasped at her sudden rush of desire.

"Who's to say that we did anything other than argue," Tristan said, kissing her cheek, then her neck. "Though that isn't what we're going to do."

Sarah slid her arms around his neck as his lips moved down her body. "Tristan, wait."

Tristan's damp hair brushed along her shoulder. "I really don't think anyone will suspect—"

"It's not that." She forced herself to push him away. "Moira's back, and the Searchers are ready to take us out of the village, but they've asked for it to happen tonight."

"Tonight?" Tristan frowned. "Why hasn't Seamus told me this yet?"

"I think he's probably telling his pack first," Sarah replied. "Since they're responsible for setting up a distraction while we make our escape. By the way, how are we making our escape? The boat?"

"No," Tristan told her in a hesitant voice. "There's another way. A faster way."

"Why do I get the feeling you don't want to tell me what it is," Sarah said.

"Because I don't," Tristan admitted. "I think it would be better if you found out when we reach that point."

"I don't understand."

"If you know, you might try to talk me out of it," Tristan said. "And I know it's our best chance."

"But—"

"Do you trust me?" he asked her.

"Yes."

"Then trust me."

When Sarah didn't argue, Tristan said, "I should find Seamus and see if he knows what kind of distraction the wolves will create."

"Yes, you should." Sarah's chest tightened with disappointment.

"I will," Tristan replied. "After."

He lifted Sarah and carried her into one of the steaming pools. When the water reached Tristan's waist he turned Sarah to face him. Understanding what he wanted, Sarah kissed him and wrapped her legs around his hips. She reached between them to grasp his erection and guided it between her legs.

He hesitated when she began to draw him inside her. "Are you sure you're ready?"

"I was ready the minute I saw you come out of that pool naked." Sarah gently bit Tristan's earlobe and drove her hips down, sheathing his full length.

She shuddered as he filled her. Tristan groaned and gripped Sarah's ass. Sarah held his shoulders and began to slowly move up and down Tristan's cock. She reveled in the sensation of him hardening even more as she rode him.

Tristan's mouth covered Sarah's. His tongue slipped inside to stroke hers. Sarah tightened her sex around his cock, driving down hard. Tristan made a low sound against her lips and she began to move faster. She locked her arms around his neck, letting the tension build, hot and insistent, within every nerve of her sex. Her nails dug into Tristan's skin and she gave a small cry as she came. As Sarah's core rippled around Tristan's erection, she melted into the pleasure. She clung to Tristan as he thrust hard, riding her climax until he came into her with a groan.

Easing them both down into the water, Tristan drew Sarah into a tender kiss. They remained entangled, holding and caressing each other quietly until their breath had eased, pulses slowing.

"Now I should go," Tristan said, kissing Sarah's cheek. "You should stay in your room and keep Moira with you. When it's time, I'll come for you. But I should keep a distance until then."

Sarah nodded. She didn't trust herself to speak because fear had suddenly taken hold of her and she wanted to beg him to stay with her.

Tristan kissed her again and then gently extracted himself from their embrace, setting Sarah on the bench at the pool's end. Beneath the water's surface Sarah gripped the edge of the marble bench, forcing herself to be still, biting her tongue so she wouldn't call out to him.

When he was gone, Sarah bent her head and let the tears come. She didn't weep for grief, but from the terror born at the prospect of losing everything so suddenly and violently as might happen in a mere matter of hours. She wept until fear's cold grip loosened and her body unwound from its knot of anxiety.

When it was over, she felt stronger than before, knowing that hesitation and doubt were monsters she couldn't have chasing her that night. Free of them, Sarah climbed out of the hot water and put on her robe. She found Moira awaiting her outside the baths.

How long Moira had been waiting, or if she'd seen Tristan, Sarah didn't know, and neither did she ask. Nor did Moira speak to either question, simply saying, "I'm ready, Sarah."

Sarah smiled at her. "So am I."

30

"I THOUGHT YOU were a wolf," Tristan said to Seamus. "Not a stubborn ass."

They'd returned to the top of the battlements, but this time they were facing away from the sea instead of looking down on the courtyard. Gazing upon the space in which his whole world had been contained, Tristan couldn't help but notice how small it seemed. How limited.

"You're the one who's being stubborn," Seamus argued. "I'm the one who has to pull this off; let me do it as I see fit."

Tristan shook his head. "Can't you set a fire somewhere else? What about the kitchen? Kitchen fires are a common enough occurrence."

"The stables not only offer the easiest target—lots of flammable material—but they also will cause a panicked reaction," Seamus said. "More than other parts of the castle would."

"Why?"

"Because everyone here knows how important they are to you," Seamus told him.

"I don't like it," Tristan said sourly. As eager as he was to leave Castle Tierney, Tristan would take no joy in seeing it destroyed. Especially not its best features.

"All of the horses will have been turned out for the night," Seamus said. "They'll come to no harm."

And your favorite horse is already dead. The wolf didn't have to say it. Part of the reason Tristan didn't want to see the stables burn was because they'd been home to Ares.

"It's the principle," Tristan said, arguing simply to indulge his foul mood. "They're exceptional stables. And I've spent more time there than anywhere else in the castle."

"That's the point," Seamus replied. "It will draw suspicion from you. We don't want anyone thinking you could be behind the fire."

"I would never set fire to the stables!"

Seamus's grin revealed his sharp canines. "You do realize you're making my argument for me."

"You don't have to gloat." Tristan pivoted to look at the tower on his right.

Seamus followed Tristan's gaze. "That's the other thing. If you're using this tower, the stables are in the right position to obscure anyone's view. Particularly since you'll have a smoke cover as well."

Tristan winced but nodded. "It's a good plan."

"Now, about your end of things," Seamus continued. "Are you sure you want to summon the Morrígna? I agree they'll get the job done, but calling upon them . . . You've never done anything like it, Tristan."

"I know," Tristan said. "But that power is my birthright. What good am I in this if I don't use it?"

Seamus's burly shoulders bunched up with tension. "Keep in mind it's your birthright that you're trying to get away from."

"If we try to use conventional methods to get off the island, we're more likely to be stopped." Tristan crossed the battlement to look toward the mainland. "A boat would be too slow. And I don't have a helicopter." He laughed. "And if I ordered one, that might be a little suspicious."

"I know," Seamus said, but his expression remained troubled. "But the sort of magic you'll be calling on is unpredictable. Always."

"I'm aware of that," Tristan replied. "But it's a risk I have to take."

"And Sarah agrees?"

When Tristan didn't answer, Seamus chuckled. "And here I thought the best relationships were founded on trust."

"They are," Tristan said. "This isn't about trust. We trust each other enough to risk our lives for one another."

Seamus cast a skeptical gaze on Tristan. "Then what is it about?"

"The war," Tristan answered. "The power I'm going to use is the very reason that Searchers and Keepers have been trying to destroy each other for centuries. I am leaving it behind, but I don't think Sarah would be pleased to know that our escape hinges on my calling upon the forces of the nether."

"She seems like an open-minded lass." Seamus grinned.

"I don't want her to be afraid," Tristan told him. "At least, not any more than she already is."

"Fair enough," Seamus replied. "But you may not be giving her enough credit. She's a brave one."

"I know that." Tristan leaned out over the battlement and looked down. Far below, waves crashing upon the rocky shoreline appeared small, but Tristan knew that anyone caught in that surf unprepared would be crushed in a matter of minutes. Sarah would need all her courage for later. They both would.

"What time do you want the ruckus to begin?" Seamus asked, following Tristan to the opposite side of the battlement.

The wind picked up and Tristan buttoned his coat to keep out the chill. "We have a three-hour window to rendezvous with the Searchers." He gave Seamus a wry smile. "It still sounds wrong to say that."

"Can't disagree with you," Seamus said with a laugh.

"It is what it is," Tristan said. "Start the fire just before midnight."

"You don't think that's cutting it a bit close?" Seamus said with a low growl. "Doesn't your date with the enemy start at midnight? I don't think there's anything to be gained by being fashionably late."

"I know," Tristan replied. "But you're right about summoning the Morrígna. It takes a lot of power, and I'll have the most at the turning of the day. It's called the witching hour for a reason."

Seamus nodded, his face grim. "Just before midnight, then."

❧

Sarah had never considered how cruel time could be, but as she sat in her room with Moira—neither of them able to speak, muzzled as they were by anxiety—Sarah came to the conclusion that anticipation offered much greater torment than fear.

The day waned and the sun disappeared. Moira built a fire and fetched a light supper for them, but the food went untouched. Sarah developed a monotonous pattern of moving her gaze from her uneaten dinner to the door, to the fireplace, and then to her plate again.

She forced herself to break the cycle by looking at Moira, who was sitting quietly, staring at her fingers, which she'd twisted together in her lap.

"Maybe you should change," Sarah said.

After so much silence, Moira jumped at the sound of Sarah's voice.

"I'm sorry, miss," Moira said. "I mean, Sarah. You startled me. What did you say?"

"Your clothes." Sarah gestured to Moira's uniform. "A dress and apron don't seem like the most practical wardrobe for traveling."

Moira frowned at her. "These are the only clothes I have. I mean, other than my nightgowns."

Sarah grimaced, though she should hardly have been surprised that even Moira's clothing was designed to remind the girl of her purpose in life—to serve in the castle.

"You may not have other clothes"—Sarah rose and went to one of the armoires—"but I do."

Relieved to have even a simple task, Sarah hunted through drawers until she found an outfit more suited to the night's coming work. She paused, turning to wave at Moira.

"You really don't need anyone else picking out clothes for you," Sarah said. "Find something you like and put it on."

Moira joined Sarah and began to rummage through the drawers.

"I'm not sure what would be best," Moira said with a frown. She glanced at Sarah. "Something like what you're wearing?"

Sarah nodded. She'd selected clothes that were the closest she could find to Searcher gear: dark riding breeches, a close-fitting but comfortable knit shirt, and a suede vest.

Moira's mouth twisted and Sarah asked, "What's wrong?"

"It's just . . ." Moira suddenly laughed. "I've never worn men's clothes."

"I'm sorry?" Sarah looked down at herself. She hadn't thought she looked particularly manly. "Hold on. Do you mean you've never worn trousers?"

Moira nodded, still giggling.

"Thank God we're getting you out of here," Sarah said, releasing an exasperated breath.

"Sarah."

Sarah looked up to find Moira's eyes shining with laughter, but also tears.

"What?" Sarah asked, suddenly worried.

"Thank you." Moira flung her arms around Sarah's neck.

Sarah hugged the girl back, her throat too thick to speak. They both gave in to laughter as they tore through the carefully folded clothes in the armoire, tossing rejects aside until it looked as if a tornado had whipped through the room.

"Is everything all right?"

Tristan stood in the doorway, gazing in alarm at the chaotic state of Sarah's bedroom.

Not trusting herself to answer without devolving into another bout of hysterical laughter, Sarah simply nodded.

"If you say so." Tristan closed the door behind him. "It's time."

Sarah said to Moira, "Get changed in the alcove."

Moira nodded, quickly scooping up leggings and a shirt.

Tristan crossed the room to meet Sarah. He kissed her and she leaned her head against his chest.

"Did you know that Moira's uniform is the only type of clothing she has?" Sarah asked.

"I didn't know that," Tristan said with a sigh. "The more I've learned since you arrived, the more I realize what a poor job I've done here. Meaning that I've done nothing at all but think of myself."

"You were taught that this way of living was meant to be." Sarah looked up at him. "But that's not who you are. You're already changing."

Tristan kissed her again. "You don't think I'm a lost cause, then."

"Never."

"I brought you a gift." Tristan shrugged off his coat and Sarah gasped. Her harness, filled with gleaming knives, was slung over his shoulder.

He handed Sarah the leather harness and she immediately strapped it on. "You do know how to win a girl's heart."

"I'm glad you like it." Tristan smiled.

Her gaze moved to Tristan's waist, where a sword hung in its scabbard, and her heart gave a hard thud against her ribs. If all went well that night, Sarah reminded herself, neither her knives nor his sword would be painted with blood. If all went well.

Though muffled, Sarah started as a wolf's howl pierced through the castle walls. A chorus of howls soon joined the first, the Guardians' voices raising the alarm.

Tristan's smile faded. "They've begun."

31

TRISTAN LISTENED AT the door, waiting for the shouts and the rush of panicked footfalls to fade, signaling the moment they might slip into the castle halls without being noticed. Sarah and Moira hovered nearby. The ginger-haired girl wore a determined expression, but she had Sarah's hand in a tight grip.

When he turned the doorknob, Sarah said, "Tristan?"

"Just a moment." He opened the door a crack. The hall was quiet and appeared empty. Tristan stepped into the hall and glanced back at Sarah and Moira. "Let's go."

They moved swiftly and quietly, Tristan leading the way. Even through the stout stone walls, cries and howls reached them. As Seamus had intended, the castle's inhabitants had rushed outside to battle the fire, and Tristan let himself hope that they could slip away without a fight.

When he reached the entrance to the eastern tower, Sarah said, "Tristan, wait."

"What's wrong?" Tristan stopped and glanced over his shoulder at her.

Sarah nodded at the dim spiral staircase. "Do we have to go this way?"

"Yes," Tristan told her. "We need to reach the top of this tower. Why?"

With a shake of her head, Sarah replied, "Nothing. Never mind."

Troubled by her hesitation, Tristan was nonetheless aware that they had no time to delay. He turned back to the tower steps and started the climb. It wasn't long before Tristan pinpointed the source of Sarah's question. As he approached the wooden door that led to one of the tower chambers, he remembered that Sarah had been in the tower before. In that room. Lana's room.

Tristan wished he had time to reassure Sarah that when the alarm had been raised both Lana and Owen would have been among the first to respond. The tower, despite being the home of both the castle's resident succubus and incubus, still offered the best means for escape. Tristan kept climbing.

The staircase came to an end in a small armory. Tristan went to the ladder that led to a trapdoor that accessed the tower's battlements. He climbed up quickly and threw the door open. The smoke hit his lungs and he began to cough.

Looking down at Sarah and Moira, he told them, "Cover your mouths with your shirts and stay low when you come off the ladder."

Tristan crawled onto the battlements, turning to help Sarah and Moira exit the tower. Plumes of oily smoke rose from the courtyard. Sarah scrambled to the edge of the tower, peeking out at the sight of destruction.

She turned to Tristan with a horrified expression. "The stables?"

"The horses were turned out," Tristan answered, though his chest constricted. He couldn't bring himself to look at the burning building. "It's just the structure."

"It looks like the whole of the castle is down there," Sarah said. She began to cough and covered her mouth again.

"Good," Tristan said. He stood up, hoping he could keep from coughing long enough to get through the incantation. "Stay down. I'll tell you when it's time to move."

Sarah nodded and crawled over to Moira, shielding the girl with her body.

As Tristan lifted his arms, the trapdoor banged open and a figure surged out of the armory.

Tristan went for his sword, but then shouted, "Wait!"

Fortunately, Seamus jumped aside just in time and one of Sarah's knives clattered against the battlements. The wolf shifted into his human form.

"What's wrong?" Tristan crouched down.

"Lana left the courtyard," Seamus told them. "I don't know where she's gone, but it's likely she's looking for you. I thought you should know, and I wanted to lend a hand if there's trouble."

Tristan nodded, rising again to begin his spell. There could be no more hesitation. Seamus, a wolf once more, stalked in front of Sarah and Moira, his hackles raised.

As Tristan's fingers began to dance through the air and he whispered words that belonged to no human tongue, he heard Sarah draw a hissing breath. He guessed she'd been about to object, to try to stop him, but instead she began to cough. He forced himself to ignore the sound, concentrating on the symbols that snaked from his fingertips to hang in the air around him. Unlike the ritual that summoned a wraith, these symbols didn't manifest as fire but as shadow. Spooling from his hands like ethereal thread, the smoke from the stable fire camouflaged the intricate design he created. For that, Tristan was grateful—he hoped Sarah would see as little as possible of the dark magic he worked. He was ready to leave that life behind, to forsake his inheritance for her, but in this moment his legacy was what could save them. Tristan could only hope that Sarah would understand.

The smoke stabbed at Tristan's eyes, stinging and blurring his vision. He forced himself to keep the incantation going despite the feeling that dozens of razor-sharp barbs were ripping up his lungs.

When the last word of the incantation left his throat, Tristan fell to his knees.

"Tristan!" Sarah left Moira huddled against the battlement and crawled to his side.

Coughs wracked Tristan's chest until his muscles cramped. Sarah wrapped her arms around him, holding him tight while he struggled for breath.

"So this is where you've gotten to."

Seamus snarled, pinning his ears back as he glared at Lana. The succubus was perched atop the battlements, her wings framing her body as if she were a stone gargoyle, perfectly placed to watch over the courtyard.

Lana gazed at Tristan. "Pulling the temple down on our heads, are we? A clever ploy. Too bad I sensed your spell as if it were being written on my very skin the moment you began to cast it. I should have persuaded Bosque to stay for a few days. He's going to miss all the fun."

Sarah's arms tightened around Tristan. He gave a slight shake of his head and pushed her away, whispering, "Get to Moira. Be ready."

He sensed Sarah's reluctance, but she released him and scrambled over toward Moira and Seamus. As she moved, Sarah's hand dipped to her knives and a blade flashed out toward Lana.

Lana caught the glint of the knife and dodged, but not quickly enough. The blade buried itself in her shoulder and she screeched.

Tristan jumped to his feet, ignoring the burning of his lungs. Lana rose from her crouch and tugged Sarah's blade from her flesh.

"I was going to make you a deal, Keeper," Lana told Tristan. "A small mercy of killing your bitch quickly, but I'm afraid she's just taken that off the table."

Tristan didn't answer. He needed to conserve what little breath he had for when it was truly needed. He kept his eyes on Lana but also on the dark sky at her back.

Lana turned her accusing glare on Seamus. "As for you, dog, I'm willing to name this foolishness an act of misguided loyalty. If you prove your loyalty to Bosque now, I won't tell him of your treachery."

Seamus bared his fangs at the succubus, answering her with a vicious bark. The wolf's hulking form shielded the two women.

"How disappointing." Lana stretched her hand out. A whip appeared in what had been her empty palm. Its length danced through the air, formed from shadow rather than leather.

Seamus lunged at Lana and her whip lashed out, striking his flank. The wolf yelped, faltering, but he feinted from her next strike. Lana leaped from the battlement to meet Seamus' next attack. He slipped beneath the snaking shadow whip and clamped his jaws around her calf.

Lana screamed and fell back onto her elbows. She shrieked again when two more of Sarah's knives lodged in her waist and thigh. Turning toward the women, Lana opened her mouth.

"No!" Tristan shouted.

A spout of flame jetted toward Sarah and Moira. Sarah turned, covering Moira's body with hers, but the blaze didn't reach them.

Seamus snarled and leaped, throwing himself between the spear of flame and its target. The wolf's growl died in a whine and his huge body dropped to the ground. Tristan gazed in grief and horror at the exposed bones and charred flesh revealed by the gaping hole in Seamus's side.

"You'll regret that, Lana." Tristan rushed to the fallen wolf, standing over him and taking up the role of shield for Sarah and Moira.

Lana laughed. "I very much doubt that I will."

Behind her, an enormous dark shape came into view and Tristan smiled. "I think you'll find you're very wrong about that."

Tristan lifted his arms and shouted into the night sky. A sudden wind, followed by an inhuman cry, filled the air. Lana whirled around and gasped. With the succubus distracted, Tristan turned to Moira and Sarah.

"Jump!" Tristan shouted over the screaming wind. "Jump from the tower toward the sea!"

Sarah stood up. "Are you insane?"

"You have to trust me," Tristan pleaded. "Jump now!"

Though she blanched, Sarah grasped Moira, who appeared too frightened to resist. Locking her arms around the girl's waist, Sarah nodded at Tristan and then threw herself and Moira from the tower battlements.

Tristan closed his eyes, hearing Moira's scream. Then nothing.

"You wretched child."

Tristan turned back to face Lana. The gaze she fixed on him was beyond hateful.

"How dare you invoke the powers gifted to you by your master to thwart his will?"

The succubus still held the shadow whip. She was bleeding but showed no sign of faltering.

"I can't kill you," Lana snarled. "But I think I'll be forgiven for causing you just a little pain."

She flicked her wrist and the whip coiled around Tristan's arm. He went to his knees. The shadow whip's lash hadn't caused physical pain; instead it filled him with the agony of despair. His mind became a torrent of unbearable images: Seamus staring at him with dead eyes, Moira and Sarah's bodies broken on the rocks beside the crashing waves.

He bowed his head, trying to fight the hopelessness that wanted to consume him.

"You will never leave," Lana said. "And you will never forget that I am the one who's kept you here."

Tristan dared to lift his eyes. What he saw at Lana's back lit his heart with strength.

"You've forgotten something more important, Lana," he said, standing.

She pursed her lips. "Have I?"

Raising his arms once more, Tristan said, "I summoned the Morrígna."

"And little good that trick did you," Lana replied, but her smug expression ebbed.

"Now you remember," Tristan said, taking a step back.

Lana glanced up a moment before it descended upon her. Giant talons seized Lana's shoulders, dreadful pops and cracks sounding as the bones of her wings were crushed in the Morrígna's grip.

As she screamed, flames erupted from Lana's throat. She struggled against her attacker as she was lifted from the tower but to no avail. Tristan listened to Lana's shrieks fade as she hurtled away from the castle and vanished into the night sky.

Another bout of coughs seized Tristan. He doubled over and crawled toward Seamus's unmoving body.

Though the charred crevice in the wolf's side was horrible to look at, Seamus's face remained unscathed. Tristan touched the wolf's soft muzzle.

"I'm sorry, my friend." Tristan bowed his head. "You did more for me than I ever could have deserved. Thank you."

Though he felt such a benediction hardly worthy of Seamus's

sacrifice, Tristan had to use what little strength he had left for his own flight. He crawled to the edge of the tower and pulled himself up onto the battlements. Tristan let coughs wrench through his lungs until he believed himself capable of completing the final incantation.

He stood atop the battlements and dared to look down. Far below the sea roiled, dashing itself upon the shore in an endless assault. One last time, Tristan raised his hands and implored the midnight sky for aid. The wind roared at his back and Tristan let its strength propel him forward. He fell from the tower and into the darkness.

32

THEY WERE FALLING.

They were falling, and Moira was screaming.

Sarah felt a brief stab of thankfulness that when she'd jumped, Moira had been facing the tower. She wouldn't have wanted the girl to see the sea rushing up at them the way Sarah was seeing it. She wondered if she should close her eyes.

Is it better or worse to see your death coming?

Her doom was suddenly blotted out, land and sea obscured by a giant black shape.

Sarah grunted as they landed atop a broad surface covered with a silken substance that mitigated the harshness of their abruptly broken fall. Instinctively, Sarah grasped for something to hold on to. She grabbed handfuls of the strange stuff around her, finding it soft yet strong.

Feathers?

"Are we dead, miss?" Moira still clung to Sarah.

"No," Sarah told her. Assured that they were no longer plummeting to their deaths, Sarah tried to gather some sense of what had happened.

The wind still whipped through her hair and pulled tears from her eyes, but it hit the front of Sarah's body as if they were being propelled forward through the sky. Along with the steady rush of air, Sarah heard another sound, a repetitive low whoosh, forceful as the beating of a drum but larger, its resonance hollow.

The sound was accompanied by movement, slow yet great, on either side of Sarah and Moira. Wings. The powerful stroke of massive wings.

Moira had been looking about with the same puzzlement as Sarah when she suddenly blanched.

"It can't be." Moira began to whisper frantically under her breath. Her words made no sense, and then Sarah realized the girl was reciting the Ave Maria.

Sarah grasped Moira's hands. "What's wrong?"

"It's the Morrígna." Moira's voice shook.

The fact that Moira could be so afraid despite the miracle that they hadn't plummeted to their deaths made Sarah's mouth go dry. "What's the Morrígna?"

"The war ravens," Moira said. "Three goddesses—pagan goddesses—Badb, Macha, Nemain. I thought they were only legends."

Sarah peered into the darkness. She could just make out the head of the great bird that had saved them and was now bearing them toward the mainland.

"Tristan summoned them," Sarah murmured.

"He can command goddesses?" Moira shuddered. "I knew Master Tristan had great power, but not like this."

"They aren't goddesses," Sarah told her. "They're creatures from the nether, from Bosque Mar's realm. Keepers have the ability to summon such beings into our world."

But not usually creatures of this magnitude. A thought Sarah kept to herself. No wonder Tristan hadn't wanted to reveal this plan to her. Knowing that he could wield magic this dark made Sarah uneasy. She'd been right that Tristan was the invaluable object hidden in Castle Tierney, but she was only just beginning to realize what that might mean.

Maintaining a tight grip on the giant raven's feathers, Sarah craned her neck to look back at the island. A sooty, orange gleam silhouetted the castle, but Sarah could see little else.

Where was Tristan?

Fear spiked through Sarah's veins. What if Tristan had never intended to leave? What if he'd arranged for her escape, using himself as a distraction but knowing he wouldn't go with her?

Desperate, Sarah climbed up the raven's neck.

"Where are you going?" Moira cried as Sarah left her behind.

"Stop!" Sarah shouted at the bird. "Turn around!"

"Sarah!" Moira scrambled up beside her. "What are you doing?"

Ignoring Moira's pleas, Sarah yelled again. "We have to go back! The one who summoned you is in danger! Please, we have to help him."

The raven gave no heed to Sarah's commands. The inexorable beating of its wings continued to propel them eastward, away from the island.

Sarah bowed her head, exhausted and defeated. She'd known there would be little chance that the great raven would respond to her. Whatever words Tristan had spoken during his spell were in a language completely unknown to Sarah. And the powers that Tristan—or any Keeper—invoked when calling upon the nether were those rejected by Searchers. No one but the Keepers could access the magic that connected them to Bosque Mar.

Tears slipped from beneath Sarah's eyelids.

She'd lost him. She was free, but she'd lost Tristan.

"Sarah." Moira's fingers dug into Sarah's shoulders.

Sarah opened her eyes and at the same moment her stomach dropped as the raven swooped toward the earth.

"What is it doing?" Moira's eyes were wide with fright.

Leaning forward to see past the bird's hulk, Sarah made out shapes far below. Shapes that were quickly becoming larger and more defined.

"It's taking us to the village," Sarah said. Her heart lay heavy as a stone behind her ribs when it should have been exulting. But Sarah could find no joy in her freedom, only desolation.

As the mainland rose up to meet them, the Morrígan slowed, gliding over the village, then circling, lower and lower. When they hovered just above the rooftops, the raven gave a sudden croak that rattled Sarah's bones.

"I think we're meant to jump," Sarah told Moira.

She looked down. It wasn't a bone-breaking fall, but it would be jarring and Sarah hoped not too painful.

Sarah took Moira's hand, squeezing the girl's fingers tightly. "Together."

Moira nodded.

They scooted to the joint where the raven's left wing met its body and Sarah realized too late that jumping wasn't part of the plan. The Morrígan's silken feathers colluded with gravity to pull them off the bird's back, and then they were falling.

Sarah dropped Moira's hand and shouted, "Crouch and try to roll when you land!"

She hoped the girl had heard and understood. Tucking her body, Sarah hit the earth and let herself roll along the ground. She came to a stop and lay on her back, waiting for her breath to return. Above Sarah, the Morrígan gave another loud call and then its massive shape rose into the sky and was gone.

As Sarah managed to draw her first breath after the fall, another silhouette loomed over her. There was enough light in the village that Sarah could see the crossbow aimed at her heart.

"That was quite an entrance," a familiar voice said.

"Anika!" Sarah's reply was something of a croak, and Anika laughed.

"Give yourself a minute to recover." Anika put the crossbow aside and offered Sarah her hand. "That wasn't a short fall."

"Tell me about it." Sarah found she could breathe more normally as Anika helped her to her feet.

The moment Sarah was standing, Anika pulled her into a tight embrace.

"We thought you were dead."

Sarah wrapped her arms around Anika's shoulders, holding her friend close. "I came pretty close . . . a few times."

"What happened?" Anika stepped back, her gaze searching Sarah's for answers.

"It's . . . There's so much . . ." The joy of seeing Anika ebbed as Sarah's mind sped back to the island. "Tristan."

"Who?" Anika frowned.

From their hiding places within the shadows of the village, more Searchers appeared. All were armed and ready for battle. One of them had Moira by the elbow.

"Sarah!" Moira cried out meekly, casting a fearful glance at her captor.

Sarah was relieved to see it was Patrice who had taken the girl.

"Patrice, she's not a threat," Sarah told the guide. "She helped me escape, and she's a refugee."

Patrice glanced at the frightened girl and nodded. "You understand that we'll have to take precautions."

"She's not a Keeper," Sarah protested.

"I know that," Patrice answered. "But she lived among them?"

"Yes," Sarah replied, throwing Moira an apologetic glance.

"For how long?" Patrice asked, and Sarah's heart sank.

Moira answered before Sarah could. "All my life, ma'am."

Patrice's chest rose and fell as she drew a long, uneasy breath.

"She was born into service," Sarah said, putting her arm around Moira's shoulders. "It's not her fault."

"I assure you she'll be taken care of," Patrice told Sarah. "But until we can get a better sense of who she is, we'll have to treat her as a prisoner."

"Sarah." Moira looked up at her, eyes questioning.

Sarah felt a surge of resentment toward Patrice but had to admit the rationale behind the Guide's decision.

"It will be okay, Moira," Sarah told the girl. "I promise. No harm will come to you and you'll be well treated. We're soldiers, and this is a war. We always have to be careful. Do you understand?"

Moira nodded.

Patrice offered Moira a thin smile. "Brave girl."

Moira lifted her chin. "Sarah taught me how to be brave, ma'am."

Feeling her throat close up, Sarah gave Moira an encouraging nod but couldn't speak.

One of the other Searchers suddenly shouted, "Incoming!"

The group scattered, diving back into the shadows and readying their weapons.

"Come on!" Anika grabbed Sarah's arm and pulled her beneath the eaves of a house.

A familiar, bone-vibrating call sounded above them and then a figure dropped from the sky, hitting the earth hard. Tristan rolled along the ground and then rose to his hands and knees, shaking his head as if to clear it.

"Tristan!" Sarah shouted and rushed to his side.

She fell to her knees and wrapped her arms around him. Overwhelmed with relief at seeing him, Sarah could do nothing more than close her eyes and cling to him.

"It's all right." Tristan folded his arms around Sarah. "I'm here. We're safe."

"Step away from the Keeper, Sarah," Patrice's command sounded at Sarah's back.

Sarah didn't let go of Tristan, but she turned to look at the Guide. Gooseflesh prickled along her skin when she saw Patrice's sword in her hand, ready to strike. "This is Tristan. The one I told you about in my letter. He's what was being guarded at the castle."

"Yes," Patrice replied. "I know who he is. Now step away from him."

The Guide turned a hard gaze on Tristan. "Keeper, I urge you to come willingly and peacefully into our custody. It will go easier if you do."

"Custody?" Sarah's heart was ramming against her rib cage. As much as she didn't want it to, what Patrice was saying made sense. If they were taking precautions with someone as harmless as Moira, of course Tristan would be treated as dangerous. But reason eluded Sarah; her instincts screamed at her to protect the man she loved.

"He is not your enemy." Sarah glared at Patrice. "If it weren't for Tristan, I would be dead."

"Sarah, don't." Tristan carefully extricated himself from her grasp and stood. He addressed Patrice, offering his hands as if waiting for them to be bound. "I understand, and I turn myself over to you."

Sarah moved to step between Tristan and the Searcher who approached with manacles. "No."

"Sarah," Tristan said quietly, "this has to happen. You know that."

Gritting her teeth, Sarah nodded, but before Tristan could be taken Sarah suddenly pulled him close, kissing him. Tristan's arms came around her, pressing her body against his. Sarah heard Anika gasp, but she ignored the sound, unwilling to break the kiss until she absolutely had to.

"Sarah." Patrice didn't have to say anything else.

Releasing Tristan, Sarah whispered, "I love you."

Tristan nodded, and after his wrists were shackled, two Searchers led him away and two others followed with Moira.

Sarah whirled, glaring at Patrice. "If anything happens to them—"

Patrice held up her hand. "Keep in mind who you're speaking to, Sarah. I'm still your commander, and I think it's obvious we need to find out what exactly happened to you."

Still vacillating between outrage and fear, Sarah said, "I'll tell you everything. Just promise me that no harm will come to them. They're . . . I can't begin to explain how important they are to me."

"Sarah," Patrice said gently, "have you forgotten who we are? Who you are? You know we won't hurt him without cause."

Sarah wanted to object, desperate for some further reassurance that Tristan would be safe and that she'd soon be with him again.

"Obviously you've been through some transformative events," Patrice continued. "And we'll take everything you've done and seen into account as we put pieces together. But, Sarah, you must keep in mind that there are greater things at stake right now. We can't be reckless."

Knowing any further arguments would be futile, Sarah's shoulders slumped as she said, "I understand."

Patrice's expression was grim when she said, "Let's get out of here."

Anika took Sarah's arm as they entered the back door of a building, which turned out to be the fishmonger's shop.

"You made it out." Ian stared at Sarah in disbelief. He was standing beside the fishmonger at the shop's counter. "I didn't think I'd ever see you again."

"It came close to that," Sarah told him. "Without Tristan—" Her chest cramped. She wanted to be with him.

"Is he the one who summoned the Morrígna?" Ian's eyebrows shot up. "The few villagers awake at this hour will speak of these things for years to come. The night they saw the Morrígna in the sky."

Sarah met Ian's curious gaze and her mind flashed to the dungeon and the dead woman. Averting her eyes, Sarah dismissed the idea of telling Ian what she'd seen. He knew his wife was gone, and the truth could only cause him more pain.

"A village isn't a village without some good lore to call its own." The fishmonger chortled. "Perhaps it'll bring in the tourists."

"Thank you both for all you've done," Patrice interrupted. "But we can't linger here. You'll send reports of any activity on or related to the island."

"Yes," the fishmonger answered with a respectful nod.

Ian did likewise and said, "I'll take you downstairs."

They descended into the cellar and through the passage that led to the back room that Ian had once described to Sarah.

"Sarah!" Jeremy was waiting for them and he ran to Sarah, wrapping her in a bear hug. "I wouldn't let myself believe it until I saw you."

With more than a twinge of guilt, Sarah returned Jeremy's embrace. At some point an uncomfortable conversation awaited them, but Sarah would initiate it without hesitation or regret. Whatever she and Jeremy had shared had been snuffed out by Sarah's love for Tristan. There was no going back. Sarah hoped Jeremy would understand that and accept it without feeling too wounded.

"It's good to be seen." Sarah wished she could muster more enthusiasm in her voice, but her mind was with Tristan and Moira. She was too aware that she wouldn't be at ease until she saw them again.

"Get us home, Jeremy," Patrice told the Weaver.

Sarah watched as the portal opened and couldn't help but be unsettled by her own detachment. She was free and returning to the Academy—to her friends and companions. Yet she couldn't shake the hollow feeling in her chest.

Yes, she'd escaped. But without Tristan, Sarah realized, it meant nothing.

33

CONSIDERING THEY COULD view him as little other than a mortal enemy, Tristan found the Searchers to be the most civilized warriors imaginable. He'd been raised to view his adversaries as brutish and near-mad with misguided convictions. Instead, he found his captors to be compassionate and patient.

Tristan's "cell" was a sparsely furnished, but comfortable, room. His meals were not only satisfying but delicious. He had daily visits from Patrice and Micah, whom Tristan had come to understand was the current leader of the Searchers. But unlike the unquestioned and permanent rule of Bosque over the Keepers, the role of Arrow, which Micah occupied, rotated among the most skilled and wise of the Searchers.

The Searchers' questions always focused on the same areas: Tristan's past, his ancestry, and what he knew about Bosque Mar. Tristan held nothing back when he answered, so it surprised him that Micah and Patrice revisited questions he'd already addressed time and time again. Tristan worried that they either thought he was lying, or that what Tristan was telling them contradicted other intelligence the Searchers had.

If the latter were the case, Tristan feared he'd remain a prisoner forever. He couldn't offer any information other than what he had, but if what he knew of himself and his world had been a fabrication, manipulated by Bosque, then Tristan would remain perpetually trapped by those lies without any means of escape.

A week had passed when the first change in his daily routine occurred. His door opened, but instead of Micah and Patrice, a Searcher with braided, wheat-blond hair entered the room accompanied by a young girl.

"Moira!" Tristan stood up. In truth, he barely knew the girl but the sight of a familiar face gave him hope in a way nothing else had since he'd arrived.

"Master Tristan." Moira smiled and, out of habit, dropped into a curtsy. It was a bizarre sight, given that Moira no longer wore her servant's uniform but instead was dressed in the leather trousers, shirt, and vest that so many Searchers wore.

The blond Searcher's eyebrows went up and Tristan flinched.

Moira caught Tristan's distressed expression and blushed. "I'm sorry. I'm still getting used to all these changes."

"Don't apologize, Moira," Tristan said quickly. "But please don't call me master. I'm no one's master, nor do I want to be."

The Searcher gave him a wry smile. Moira glanced at her and the woman nodded.

"I asked to visit you because I wanted to tell you that I'm well," Moira said to Tristan.

"I'm glad to hear it," Tristan replied. And he was, but a burr of resentment scratched at Tristan upon knowing that Moira had been freed while he remained imprisoned.

Moira beamed at him. "I'm attending classes."

That surprised him. "Are you? Does that mean you're going to become a Searcher?"

"I'm not sure yet," Moira replied, a nervous edge creeping into her voice.

"It's all right, Moira," Tristan said. "You don't have to tell me.

I'm sure the Searchers would prefer to keep their training methods to themselves."

With a dry laugh, the Searcher said, "You fancy yourself a clever one, don't you?"

Tristan shrugged and went to sit on the edge of his bed. "I don't think stating the obvious makes me particularly clever."

"And funny," the Searcher added. "Clever and funny. No wonder Sarah is so smitten with you."

Tristan gave the Searcher a sharp look as his heart lurched in his chest. "Sarah?"

"I also came to tell you that Sarah is well," Moira piped up. "But she misses you terribly."

Tristan's jaw clenched, but he managed to reply, "I miss her, too. Will you tell her?"

"Of course." Moira nodded eagerly.

"Why don't you go do that now, Moira." The Searcher ushered Moira to the door. "I need a few minutes with Master Tristan."

Moira ducked her head and complied, though she turned to flash a quick smile at Tristan before she disappeared out the door.

When the door was closed, Tristan leveled a steady gaze at the Searcher. "Are you going to tell me your name?"

"I'm Anika," she answered.

"A pleasure to meet you, Anika," Tristan said. "I assume there's a particular reason for your visit, given that I haven't seen you before."

"You've seen me before," Anika replied, folding her arms across her chest. "But you were too focused on Sarah to notice who else was around you."

"Ah." Tristan rested his arms on his elbows. "So you aren't here to ask about me. You're here about Sarah."

Anika grabbed the back of a chair and turned it to face the bed. She sat down.

"Like I said before," Anika said with a smile, "you fancy yourself a clever one."

Tristan returned her stare, waiting.

With an abrupt laugh, Anika said, "Okay then, Keeper, let's get to it."

"Go ahead." Tristan gestured for her to continue.

"Sarah is my best friend," Anika told him. "And she seems to believe you're some kind of wonderful man. I think you're a Keeper."

"And in your mind those two descriptions are mutually exclusive," Tristan said.

"Of course they are," Anika replied. "So the question remains: can you be a good man and a Keeper?"

"I think that's what your bosses have been trying to figure out as well." Tristan sighed. Ever since Anika had mentioned Sarah's name, a burning ache had settled in his chest. Suddenly it was making him irritable.

"You're wrong about that." Anika's smug reply irked Tristan further. "They're after something else and they think they've found it. That's part of the reason I'm here."

Tristan straightened. He hadn't gotten the sense that Micah and Patrice had been satisfied by any answers he'd given them.

His surprise made Anika's smile widen with pleasure. "They may be right," she continued, "but that doesn't change what matters to me."

"And that is?" Tristan asked.

"What your intentions are toward Sarah."

Tristan stared at her, then he began to laugh. Anika stood up, her hands going to the dagger hilts at her belt.

"You might think it's a laughing matter," Anika snarled at him. "But it's not to me. I will make you bleed before I let you hurt her."

Struggling to keep his laughter in check, Tristan waved his

hands, trying to calm Anika. "That's not . . . that's not why . . . I'm sorry."

Catching his breath, Tristan said, "I just never expected to be asked by a Searcher about my romantic intentions toward someone. It's the most bizarre experience I think I've ever had. And considering my history, that's saying something."

Still regarding him warily, Anika sank back onto the chair. "Bizarre or not, I still want to know."

Tristan's irritation with the Searcher was rapidly transforming into respect. Anika's posturing wasn't due to haughtiness or malice. She was protecting Sarah. That was an instinct Tristan not only could relate to, but also admired.

"I love her," he said.

Anika wasn't satisfied. "I don't know what that means to a Keeper."

Taken aback, Tristan hesitated before he spoke again. "It means that my being a Keeper no longer has any bearing on who I am or what I do with my life. Sarah is all that matters."

Anika watched his face closely and then she nodded. "Not bad. We'll see if it sticks."

"It will stick," Tristan felt anger bubbling beneath his skin. He'd never felt anything like what he felt for Sarah and he was finding that being questioned about his love didn't sit well with him.

Anika smiled at Tristan's obvious irritation. "I believe you mean that. But there's something you don't know. Something I've been asked to tell you, and after that . . . Well, let's just say I have reason to doubt you. I don't know how strong you are."

"What are you talking about?" Tristan frowned at her.

"Later today, Micah is going to release you," Anika said calmly, startling Tristan to his feet.

Anika didn't move; she watched him pace beside the bed. "And he's going to send you to Sarah. Everyone assumes that's the first place you'll want to go."

"Of course it is," Tristan snapped.

"I'm sure that Sarah will be over the moon," Anika told him. "You're all she talks about. Well, except for that S&M bitch you had at the castle. She talks about her sometimes too."

Tristan cringed at Anika's sharp look. "It wasn't my idea to have the succubus there."

Anika shook her head. "Look, I'm maybe starting to like you. Just maybe—so don't get too excited, but let's not talk about things that will erode your progress."

"Agreed." Tristan forced himself to sit again.

"Do you know anything about the Scion?" Anika's expression changed, becoming less calculating and more inquisitive.

"I know what the word means," Tristan said. "It refers to an heir."

Anika nodded. "That's the definition, but I'm talking proper noun here. A specific Scion from a particular prophecy."

"What prophecy?" Tristan asked. The hairs on the back of his neck prickled.

"Cian's prophecy."

"Cian," Tristan said slowly. "As in, Eira's sister."

"As in, your great-aunt," Anika answered. "Or so I'm given to understand."

Tristan drew a long breath. "I've never been told about such a prophecy."

"We've kind of figured that out." Anika smiled, but this time Tristan saw genuine kindness in her face. "Let me get you up to speed. Right before Eira killed Cian, Cian invoked old magic. Elemental magic. Her body became a weapon. The only weapon that could banish the Harbinger from this world."

"Banish Bosque?" Tristan stared at her in disbelief. He'd never heard of such a weapon.

"What do you think your sacred sites are for?" Anika said. "Pilgrimages?"

Tristan shrugged lamely. "The sites are the responsibility of other Keepers. Anytime I inquired about them, I was told they aren't important."

"Interesting." Anika pursed her lips. "They really were keeping you in the dark. I suppose that's just further confirmation of what we suspect."

"And you're going to tell me what that is at some point?" Tristan had lost his patience. Not only were Anika's revelations confusing, but Tristan couldn't understand what they had to do with him and Sarah.

"You're the Traitor," Anika said curtly.

Tristan made a low, frustrated sound. "Of course I'm a traitor, and it's fine if you feel the need to point that out, but doesn't it count for anything that I betrayed your enemies?"

"You're not *a* traitor," Anika replied. "You're *the* Traitor. The one named in Cian's prophecy."

"I don't understand," Tristan said, though an icy thread coursed through his veins. *The Traitor.*

"I didn't think you would." Anika nodded. "Or rather, Micah didn't think you would, and asked me to tell you."

"Interesting choice," Tristan murmured.

Anika laughed. "I like you more all the time. Anyway, Micah wanted me to tell you because I'm Sarah's best friend and the fact that you're the Traitor has bearing on her, too."

"How so?" Tristan was suddenly fearful. Did his role in some medieval prophecy put Sarah at risk?

"It has to do with the nature of your relationship." Anika coughed delicately. "Which neither of you has shown qualms about revealing."

"We're in love," Tristan said.

"That's my point." Anika stood up and walked around her chair, resting her hands on its back. "You're in love. And the Traitor is the father of the Scion. The only person who can wield the Elemental Cross and rid the Earth of Bosque Mar and the nefarious influence of his nether realm."

Anika watched Tristan as her words sunk in.

"The father?" he whispered.

She nodded.

Tristan frowned at her. "How can you be sure?"

"Your bloodline," Anika answered. "The Traitor has to be a direct descendant of Eira. That's you."

"It could be Marise Bane," Tristan argued. "She betrayed Bosque by marrying against his will."

"That's pettiness, not treachery," Anika told him.

Tristan wanted to disagree, but found he couldn't. "Does Sarah know?"

"Micah is speaking with her now."

"You didn't think it would be better for us to hear about this together?" Tristan asked, his temper flaring.

"Better for you, maybe," Anika replied. "But not for us. We needed to gauge your reactions individually before you're released."

"So have I passed your test?" Tristan said, more than a little disgusted.

"It's not a test." Anika went to the door. "But you've convinced me we're on the same side."

"Wonderful." Tristan's temples began to throb with the flood of revelations that filled his mind.

"Buck up, kiddo." Anika smiled at him as she left the room. "If all goes well, you'll be reunited with your own true love in a couple of hours."

When she was gone, Tristan lay on his bed and gazed up at the ceiling. He'd known that surrendering himself to the Searchers would be complicated, but he hadn't anticipated prophecy and destiny to come into the mix—not to mention fatherhood. Tristan's mood swung wildly from fearful to exuberant. The Searchers planned to free him. He would be with Sarah again.

But Anika's visit had changed the nature of his reunion with Sarah. Suddenly it meant something different. Something he could never be certain he was ready for and could only hope he proved worthy of.

34

SARAH WATCHED AS a pair of eagles spiraled through the sky outside her window. She shivered, the sight of them reminding her of the Morrígna—it was a memory that would always frighten her, no matter how well the night had ended.

When there was a knock at her door, Sarah turned from the window.

"Come in."

The door opened to reveal Micah. Sarah felt her stomach drop. The Arrow had already visited her once that day, and Sarah didn't feel prepared to hear more about how her life wasn't her own but instead was tied to some prophecy that the first Searcher had died to create. It was all too much. And all Sarah wanted was—

"Tristan!"

Micah had stepped back to let Tristan enter the room.

Sarah ran to him.

He pulled her close, one arm around her back, binding her to him, his other hand buried in her hair.

She heard Micah say, "I'll leave you, then."

Neither she nor Tristan responded.

They held each other for Sarah didn't know how long. It could have been minutes or an hour. All she knew was his warmth, his scent, his touch.

At last Tristan loosened his hold, but only enough so that Sarah could tip her head up and meet his kiss. His taste was so familiar, and at the same time stirred her blood as if it were something utterly new and exhilarating. His hands roamed over Sarah's body, reacquainting himself with the lines and curves of her form.

When their kiss broke, Sarah said, "I've missed you. Oh God, Tristan. I don't have words."

"I know." He kissed her forehead. "I was going crazy without you."

Looking into his eyes, Sarah found love, but something new as well. She didn't have to ask what it was.

"They told you."

He nodded.

"I'm so sorry," Sarah said, pulling her gaze from his.

"Why?" Tristan put his finger under her chin, tilting her face up to look at him. "What do you have to apologize for?"

She reached up to touch his face, tracing the shape of his cheekbones and jaw. "You escaped. You're no longer trapped on that island. I wanted you to see the world the way you said you wanted to. But I've just led you to another prison."

"I don't understand."

"Don't you?" Sarah's throat tightened and she felt her eyes begin to burn with the promise of tears. "The prophecy, Tristan, it means we can't stay here. They want to send us into hiding. We'll always be guarded. We won't be part of the world."

"Sarah." Tristan kissed the single tear that slid along her cheek. "I always knew that I wouldn't be part of the world. Not really. That was never an option. Bosque knows who I am. Prophecy or not, he'll be looking for me."

Unconvinced, Sarah shook her head. "But I wanted to give you choices. To give you freedom. And instead people you've just met are telling you that you're fated to be with me . . . to be the—"

Sarah couldn't finish her thought. It still overwhelmed her as much as she assumed it must intimidate Tristan.

"The father of the Scion?" He smiled at her. "The father of our child?"

She nodded, her pulse roaring in her ears. Simply finding Tristan, falling in love with him, fleeing the island—it had all been so much already. And now this.

"Is that idea so unappealing?" Tristan asked, seeing her furrowed brow.

"It's not that," Sarah told him. "I just don't know how to accept it. This isn't what I meant for us. I feel like I've trapped you."

"I left Castle Tierney to be with you." Tristan kissed her softly. "Not to see the world. It was for you. As long as I'm with you, I am free. It will never feel like a prison."

"But the prophecy, our future," Sarah said. "You're not afraid of what it all means?"

"We won't know what it means until it actually happens." Tristan smiled. "But if there's a prophecy that says our child might someday end this war, I'd like to look at it from the best perspective possible."

"And what's that?" Sarah asked, eyeing his increasingly mischievous smile with suspicion.

"The way I see it, this prophecy means we have our work cut out for us." Tristan took her hand and led her to the bedside. "And I don't think I mind that at all."

Sarah let Tristan push her down onto the bed. He slid her arms around his neck, parting her lips as he kissed her. Letting her eyes close and sensation overwhelm her, Sarah's anxieties were swept aside by a wave of longing.

"I love you, Sarah," Tristan murmured against her skin.

"Whatever happens, whoever we're meant to be, that's all I need you to believe and know. I will always love you. You are my fate."

Tristan's lips moved along her neck and Sarah's blood began to sing.

If this is my fate, I'll take it.

Acknowledgments

The Forbidden Side of Nightshade is a new expedition whose course was charted with skill and enthusiasm by an incredible group of people. I will be forever grateful to Michael Green, who built a bridge from PYRG to Dutton; and for Brian Tart, who was waiting to welcome me on the other side. This series is a work of cooperation, with thanks owed to a roomful of people who were willing to make it happen, particularly Don Weisberg and Jen Loja. Thanks to Richard Pine and Charlie Olsen, who always hammer out the details. And to Lyndsey Blessing, who takes my novels on global excursions.

My editor, Jessica Renheim, has provided keen insights and unflagging encouragement throughout the writing of this novel. The entire Dutton team brought enthusiasm and incredible support to this new project, and I am thrilled to be part of the Dutton family.

Friends and family continue to help me with each new quest. Thanks to Casey Jarrin for always believing in me. Jill Santopolo's care keeps me hopeful and sane. David Levithan brings music and joy that energize my stories. I benefit immensely from the company of writers whom I am honored to call friends: Sandy London, Eliot Schrefer, Beth Revis, Marie Lu, Jessica Spotswood, Michelle Hodkin, Elizabeth Eulberg, Kirsten White, Stephanie Perkins, Brenna Yovanoff, Marie Rutkowski, Ally Condie, and so many others whose talent is a constant inspiration. Thanks to my parents for unconditional love. Thanks to Garth and Sharon Liu Robertson, whose love let me believe again. And finally, thank you to all the feisty women in my life who've led by example and proven that love does not mean surrender.

About the Author

A. D. Robertson is a *New York Times* and internationally bestselling author. Prior to becoming a full-time novelist, Robertson was a professor of early modern history at Macalester College, a background that informs her books' compelling blend of mythology, history, and lore. She grew up in northern Wisconsin and now lives in New York City.